IT WAS ALW

Georgie (

About *It Was Always You*

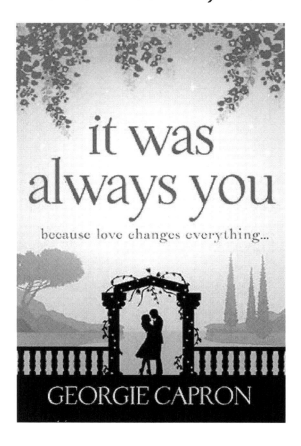

Libby has been drifting through life for too long and, now in her
early 30's, it's time to grow up. She decides to have one last
summer of fun before buckling down, so heads off to beautiful
Positano in Italy.

There, despite all her good intentions, she can't help but fall a little in love with the very handsome, but rather naughty, Luca and, as the summer draws to a close, Libby has some big decisions to make.

Should she head back home and face up to her responsibilities? Is Luca really the right man to start a family with, or has the perfect man been right in front of her eyes all this time?

And, when it comes to affairs of the heart, is it really better to have loved and lost than never to have loved at all?

To my daughter Camilla

Chapter One

A thickset Neapolitan blocked her route out of the station. She could smell the stale tobacco on his breath as he wheezed, '*Ciao bella!* You need taxi?' This was addressed to her cleavage, not her face.

'*Non grazie,*' Libby muttered through gritted teeth. She elbowed her way through the crowds that were lurking around the Stazione Centrale. Her patience with the male half of the Italian population was beginning to wear thin. She had spent the past several hours avoiding the advances of an overweight lothario called Luigi. He had been convinced that she would like nothing more than to tumble straight off the train and into his bed.

Looking ahead with steady determination, she navigated her way through the hustle and bustle in search of a sign for the tram. Libby had studied her *Lonely Planet* carefully to establish the best route from the train station to the ferry port; only now was she beginning to regret her decision to use local transport rather than the comforts of a taxi. Mentally chiding herself for being pathetic (after all, she was here for an authentic Italian experience, wasn't she?) she scanned her surroundings, pausing briefly to rest against her bag. She pulled her brown hair off her back and scrunched it up into a ponytail. God it was hot! She felt beads of sweat forming on her neck; her skin was clammy against her T-shirt.

At last Libby laid eyes on the tram stop. It was just a short walk across the piazza. Remembering that she wouldn't be able to purchase a ticket on board, she found a nearby *tabbacheria*.

'*Posso avere un biglietto per il tram, per favore?*' she asked. The buxom lady behind the counter nodded briskly and gave her a ticket in return for a couple of euros. She made her way out into the blinding morning sun.

After an extremely squashed journey rumbling through the cobbled streets of Naples with her backpack rammed up against her thighs, Libby disembarked at the port. She bought herself a bottle of water and a ticket for the 11 a.m. ferry to Positano. Choosing a suitably shaded spot in which to sit and pass the time, Libby gulped back the ice-cold liquid gratefully as she took in her surroundings. An assortment of tourists of all shapes and sizes were waiting for boats to shuttle them off to the Amalfi coast and the islands of Capri and Ischia. On the opposite side of the port a group of young travellers lounged around, smoking roll-ups and chatting as they listened to the music that was playing from a set of speakers. A small child toddled about haphazardly, picking up discarded bottle tops and chasing an errant pigeon.

Taking a deep breath, Libby stretched out her legs and kicked off her flip-flops, annoyed that the coral Shellac on her toenails had begun to fade. In the last few weeks her skin had gradually tanned to a deep olive brown as she had made her way south through Italy. What a blissful few weeks it had been. She had started her travels in Verona, before winding her way through the major cities, exploring, practising her Italian and enjoying her new-found freedom. She sifted through her favourite memories of the trip so far: visiting the glass-blowing workshops on the island of Murano, eating gelato while wandering over the Ponte Vecchio in Florence, and soaking up the night life in Rome as she walked the streets looking for hidden trattorias to eat in.

At that moment her phone vibrated in her pocket, interrupting her reverie. It was Jules, her best friend. As Libby swiped to unlock the screen she saw a photograph of a computer screen with a complicated spreadsheet flash up on her WhatsApp. 'My view. Kill me NOW!' read the message. Libby chuckled to herself as she snapped a photograph of the sparkling turquoise water lapping against the stone harbour wall to her right and clicked send.

'Poor you. Come and join me!' she added. Seconds later another message pinged on to her screen. 'Lucky cow! I would do anything to be there with you. Can we FaceTime later?'

'Definitely – should be in Positano by this afternoon so will call this eve xx'

As Libby boarded the ferry that had slowly chugged into the harbour, she couldn't help but feel smug at the thought of all her friends and family stuck at work back in London. Here she was on a stunning day in the most beautiful country in the world, with three months of freedom stretching out in front of her. A cautionary voice popped into her head, reminding her to make the most of it. Before she knew it, it would all be over. She vowed once again to appreciate every second of the precious time she had left. She would be signing her life over to the world of law once and for all when her training contract began on 1st October. She knew it was about time she grew up and got a serious job at long last.

Determined not to think about that quite yet, Libby watched as the ferry skimmed over the aquamarine water until they finally began to approach the Amalfi coast. She had dreamed of returning for years, having fallen in love with the place in her early twenties. As part of her degree she had spent a year living in Bologna, and in the summer she had travelled along the Amalfi coast with a group of friends, making a brief stop in

Positano. As she drank in the spectacular views she felt her spirits lift. The emerald coastline soared up from the sea in undulating curves, creating little coves and hidden valleys. In one of these coves lay Positano, the picturesque village to which Libby was coming closer and closer with every passing second. The pastel-coloured houses that cascaded vertiginously towards the sea slowly came into focus. The golden dome of the church in the centre glinted like a beacon in the sunlight. Bright bursts of fuchsia bougainvillea tumbled decadently over the endless sequence of steps that crisscrossed the village. As the boat pulled into the harbour, Libby felt overwhelmed by the sheer beauty of the place. She took a deep breath in, tasting the salty spray from the sea, a huge grin spreading over her face. She knew she had been right to come back here.

Gratefully accepting a proffered hand, Libby stepped on to the jetty. She found her bag amongst the mound of luggage that was piling up to one side of the pontoon and made her way across the beach and up on to the sea front. A selection of restaurants overlooked the beach from which various stone pathways led up in twists and turns to the central piazza. The beach was full of holiday-makers soaking up the sun while jealous waiters looked on, sweating in their aprons and white shirts.

Having made her way to the tiny piazza, Libby turned right, following the pavement to the side of the road for a seemingly endless length of time, reassuring herself that the ordeal was nearly over, she would soon have arrived. On and on she walked, out of breath from the sheer steepness of the incline, stopping occasionally to check the map that she had printed off back in England.

Eventually she saw a sign pointing up a little set of steps to a bright lemon-yellow front door. It read 'Ostello La Casetta' in swirling letters. Elated to have found it at last, she climbed up the steps with a final burst of energy and knocked on the door.

It was opened a few seconds later by a short man with sky-blue eyes and nut-brown skin. '*Buongiorno?*' he said, looking at her with a quizzical expression, one grey eyebrow arching up towards his hairline.

'*Buongiorno!*' said Libby. 'My name is Libby Saunders, I am here to work for the summer,' she explained in her best Italian. 'I spoke to your wife this morning,' she added, slightly perplexed by his blank expression.

'Antonio... *chi è?*' trilled a high-pitched, singsong voice behind him as an equally small lady bustled over to join them.

'*Sono Libby,*' she repeated hopefully. 'I called this morning... I'm here for the summer job? You must be Floriana?'

'Ah, Libby!' cried Floriana, reaching out to embrace her warmly before giving her a kiss on each cheek. 'We are so glad you are here! Excuse my husband Antonio; he never listens to a word I say. I did tell him you were arriving, but never mind! You must be so thirsty... come in! Come in! Bring in her bag, Tonio.'

Libby was swept into the hostel as Antonio shrugged his shoulders and smiled, chuckling to himself with the air of someone who is used to being told off. The hostel was blissfully cool after the scorching heat of the sun, and Libby followed them inside gratefully. 'How was your journey?' asked Floriana, 'It is too hot, no?' she laughed, switching to heavily accented English.

'It is very hot indeed!' replied Libby, determined to practise her Italian as much as possible and therefore starting as she meant to go on. 'The ferry journey was absolutely lovely; it is such a beautiful part of the world.'

'The jewel in the crown of Italy!' said Antonio, gesturing over to the terrace from which you could see breathtaking views right down to the sea.

'Wow! It is stunning!' said Libby. 'I can't believe I am actually here.'

'Let me tell you we are glad to have you!' said Floriana. She showed Libby to her room: tiny, simple and tucked away at the back of the hostel, with a small bed, a chest of drawers and a wardrobe. 'I always try to find extra help in the high season because the hostel gets so full that I can no longer manage with the staff that I have. You will be an extra pair of hands to tide us through.'

'It sounds perfect. When I saw the advert online I knew that this was just what I was looking for. I can imagine why it gets so busy; the whole of Italy must want to come here for their summer holidays!'

Having left her bag in her room she was given a tour of the building. It was higgledy-piggledy and full of charm. Light streamed through the windows, bouncing off the whitewashed walls. The rooms were full of the half-unpacked contents of travellers' backpacks. Little alcoves displayed beautiful patterned blue tiles, and brightly coloured lemon trees in terracotta pots rested on mosaic tables.

'These are the rooms for the guests. We can sleep forty people at any one time and we have a mixture of dormitories and doubles or family rooms,' explained Floriana, tottering along the corridor. 'Here is our little bar,' she said as they entered a spacious room to the side of the building that led out onto the terrace. 'It is run by a man called Luca. It is normally quite busy.'

'Is it just for guests?' Libby asked.

'No, no, it is for anyone who wants to use it – we have a regular crowd of locals who come by. You will get to know everyone soon enough, don't worry!' she laughed. 'In Positano, everyone knows everyone.'

She pointed up. 'At the very top of the building is our little apartment. We tend to spend our evenings there when we can these days, for a bit of peace and quiet. We are not as young as we used to be, you know.'

They made their way back to the terrace, which was decked out with tables and chairs that gleamed in the afternoon sun. 'This is where the guests normally eat breakfast. One of your jobs will be to serve croissants and coffees in the morning, as well as taking bookings, answering the telephones and checking guests in and out. Don't worry, I will explain everything to you later when you have settled in. You'll get the hang of it in no time.'

Antonio, who reminded Libby of a cheerful garden gnome, was busy in the kitchen behind reception. 'Would you like some lunch?' asked Floriana. 'Please join us, we are about to eat.'

'Thank you, I'd love to,' said Libby. 'I'm starving! Can I do anything to help?'

'Don't worry,' said Antonio. 'It's almost ready.'

He brought out a basket of bread and a huge platter of mozzarella, sliced tomatoes and basil. As she ate, Libby could hardly believe how delicious such simple ingredients could taste. The creamy mozzarella melted in her mouth, the sun-ripened tomatoes burst with flavour, and the fragrant basil mingled perfectly with the nutty richness of the olive oil. It was poles apart from the bland tomato and mozzarella salads that she had eaten so many times in England. Her mouth watered at the prospect of three months of such culinary delights. She had always enjoyed cooking and was determined to add more Italian dishes to her repertoire by the time she got home. She looked at her new employers as they ate their lunch. Floriana's greying hair curled softly around her ears and her smile reached the corners of her eyes. Both Antonio and Floriana had wonderfully deep wrinkles etched across their faces, each line a reminder of a memory or experience from what had evidently been rich and long lives. She bet they had a story or two to tell. They told her about their children, who had upped sticks and moved away as soon as they had reached their twenties. Their daughter lived in nearby Sorrento, while one son was in Naples and the other in Rome. Apparently they would be coming home at various stages over the summer.

'You must miss them,' said Libby. 'I can't believe anyone would want to move away from such a beautiful place!'

'Many of the younger generation leave Positano to find work elsewhere,' said Floriana.

'It's a shame but it's not easy for them all to earn a decent living here,' explained Tonio. 'We were lucky because we have this place.'

'I bet the house prices are extortionate,' said Libby. She wondered if the locals had become priced out from buying local properties, unable to compete with rich holiday-makers and foreign investors.

'It's also seasonal here. You can find yourself worked off your feet in the high season and then twiddling your thumbs and struggling to make ends meet when the season comes to an end.' Libby hadn't considered this before. Perhaps, if you put yourself in the shoes of those who were actually born and bred here, life in Positano wasn't as picture-postcard idyllic as it appeared on the surface.

After lunch, Floriana explained in detail what would be expected of her. 'You will have to be up at six a.m. – sorry it is a bit early, I know, but breakfast starts at six thirty, so you will come down and set up beforehand. We have a delivery of fresh croissants from the bakery every day between six and six fifteen. We get plain, almond, chocolate and custard croissants. Each guest has one croissant included and a choice of coffee.' Floriana told her how to operate the coffee machine and froth the milk. After that she showed her how to take bookings and record them on the computer, what to do when new guests arrived and how to check them out. Libby took notes, but it didn't seem anything too complicated. Her many years of temping, darting about different jobs and industries trying to figure out what she wanted to do with her life, had armed her with a flexible and comprehensive skill set, if nothing else.

Libby wasn't officially starting until the next day, so after she had asked all the questions she could possibly think of, she set off to explore. Her hours would be 6 a.m. until 6 p.m., with two days off a week and a two-hour lunch break. In the evenings there was another girl, Giulia, who came to take care of the guests until the reception desk closed at midnight, and someone else called Andrea, who was in charge of the cleaning and laundry. Floriana assured her that both she and Antonio would be around most of the time during the day, and in the evenings there was Luca, who ran the bar with extra help from a young girl called Maria.

'Now, *cara*, you must go out and look around. Have you been to Positano before?'

'Not for many years, but I think I should be able to remember most of it. It's the kind of place you never forget!'

'Yes, and it's hardly very big. But here, take one of these just in case.' Floriana passed her one of the hand-drawn maps on the reception desk. 'Look, we are here, this is the centre and this is the main beach – though my favourite is the little beach here,' she said, pointing to a smaller cove to the west of the Spiaggia Grande. 'You can walk across from here along the sea front.'

Libby went back to her room and changed into her bikini and a light sundress. She was glad to be out of her sweaty shorts and T-shirt. Buzzing with excitement she set off once more down the haphazard steps that led away from the yellow door.

She wove her way down the steep descent to the centre of the village, veering down the famous Via dei Mulini, with its tapestry of entwined wisteria making a natural canopy overhead. Memories came flooding back from her early twenties as she passed a little bar to her right, in which she could remember sitting with her group of friends, drinking carafes of wine and listening to live music. A critical voice flashed into her mind asking her what, exactly, she had achieved in the meantime. Here she was again, spending another summer by herself, abroad, rootless. This was not what she had thought she would be doing in her early thirties. She quietened the voice with reassurances that she was here for a reason, to practise her Italian and help herself get a real job, a serious job; to sort her life out once and for all.

The tiny streets were still lined with shops selling local wares. Pop-up jewellery stalls jostled with jewel-bright clothes that had been draped artistically outside shop fronts. Rows and rows of soft leather sandals in every colour of the rainbow stood next to towering displays of citronella candles, lemon-shaped soaps and colourful pottery. Libby's mouth watered as she passed gelato shops full of enticing flavours like tiramisu, Nutella, and wonderful words that rolled satisfyingly off the tongue like 'stracciatella' and 'frutti di bosco'. It was a joy for Libby to use her Italian again after so many years. She had chosen Italian as a degree subject for two reasons: the beauty of the language and her passion for Italy itself. With its art, opera, architecture, stunning scenery and food, she couldn't think of a culture in which she would prefer to immerse herself for four years of her life. She felt guilty that she had let her Italian slip, and she was determined to regain the fluency she had achieved at university. She regretted her carefree, noncommittal attitude to life in her twenties, drifting aimlessly through the years without sorting out what she actually wanted from life. It felt good to finally have a secure career path planned for when she got home.

Libby's spirits soared as she jumped from the bottom step, landing with a gentle thud on the sandy Spiaggia Maggiore. She decided to take Floriana's advice, so she made her way along the pathway that led to the smaller Spiaggia del Fornillo. She was rewarded with breathtaking views of the dazzling sea that sparkled under the fierce heat of the sun. She was dying to get in the water.

Removing her dress in one fell swoop, she kicked off her flip-flops and padded down to the seashore. The sand felt amazing underneath her feet. She couldn't think of the last time she had been barefoot on the sand under a cloudless sky in such glorious heat. She luxuriated in the sun as it warmed her skin, mesmerised by the gentle ebb and pull of the tide as it lapped the shore. Taking a deep breath, she started to walk forwards into the turquoise water. It was cool and crisp and crystal clear. Her warm skin protested for a moment or two as she immersed herself in the sea. She could see her feet perfectly, even when she reached waist height. Taking the plunge, she dived forwards and dipped her head under the water. It was unbelievably refreshing. After a few minutes' swimming around, she came back to the beach and lay on her towel to dry off, dozing in the sunshine.

Chapter Two

Back at La Casetta, Giulia had started her evening shift. She had curly hair, pouty lips and a husky voice. There was a queue of people waiting to speak to her at the reception desk so, rather than introducing herself, Libby wandered out on to the terrace to watch the sun set over the sea and eat the slices of pizza she had picked up. When the last glowing embers had disappeared beneath the surface, she came back inside. A young couple were talking to Giulia about good local restaurants to eat in that evening. When they left, Libby approached the desk. 'You must be Giulia? It's so nice to meet you. I'm Libby,' she said, holding out her hand.

'Oh yes, Libby. It's a pleasure to meet you, Floriana told me to look out for you.'

'I've just been having a look around,' said Libby. 'I'm already in love!'

'It is very hard to avoid that, I'm afraid – though working here might change your mind,' laughed Giulia.

'Oh really? So far it has seemed pretty wonderful.'

'Maybe I've been here too long. I guess the novelty of dealing with travellers day in and day out wears off after a while.'

'How long have you been here?'

'Five years!' said Giulia, raising her eyebrows towards the sky.

'That is a long time…'

'Sometimes I dream about leaving, doing something else. You're from London, aren't you? I'd love to go there one day…'

'Really? You should,' Libby declared.

'Sadly, I can't – I'll be stuck here in Positano for a while. My mother has dementia, so I need to be around to look after her.'

'Gosh, how terrible,' said Libby. 'That must be so hard…'

'It's not the easiest thing, but it is what it is,' said Giulia. 'And in all seriousness, I do love it here, most of the time. Floriana and Tonio are so good to me; they are like family. The high season is just so busy, that's all. It's great that we have you to help out.'

'I know I'm supposed to be here mostly during the day shifts, but if you are busy in the evenings and I'm around, then maybe I can help?' Libby felt sorry for Giulia; it must be so hard having to care for a parent suffering like that. She thanked her lucky stars that her mother was fit and healthy. She wondered what Giulia would be doing if her circumstances were different. She could see her on stage – a young Monica Bellucci perhaps.

'That's very kind of you to offer!' Giulia said. 'You might regret that!'

At that moment an extremely handsome man – who looked as if he spent a considerable amount of time in the gym – popped his head around the corner from the bar. 'Giu, we're out of one-euro coins. Do you have any?' he asked.

'Sure,' said Giulia, reaching to unlock the drawer under the desk where the petty cash was kept. 'Luca, this is Libby, she's here to help for the rest of the summer.'

'*Piacere,*' said Luca, coming over to shake her hand. He was almost comically good looking, with sun-kissed brown hair and mesmerising brown eyes framed with thick, curly black eyelashes. He had a mischievous grin and a knowing twinkle in his eye, the look of a man who knows he is a hit with the ladies. 'You must come in for a drink later. Sorry I can't chat now but I am in the middle of serving a customer.'

'No problem,' said Libby.

Giulia gave her a knowing look. 'Watch out for that one!' she said, rolling her eyes. 'He's got something of a reputation, if you know what I mean!'

Libby laughed. Yes, she could certainly guess. She wondered whether Giulia was talking from personal experience.

She left Giulia to it as another bustle of tourists came through the door waiting to be checked in. She went up to her room to hang out her damp towel and get out of her bikini. She wrapped a fresh towel around her limbs before going next door to test out the shower. It was simple and old-fashioned, but it pumped out a steady stream of hot water, and that was all Libby needed to scrub away the sand. She would be sharing the bathroom with the residents of a double room on the opposite side of the corridor from her, but she doubted that would be too much of an inconvenience.

Libby towel-dried her long hair as best she could and ran a comb through it. She slapped on a bit of moisturiser and ringed her green eyes with a smudge of eyeliner and a coat of mascara before locking up her room and making her way back downstairs. She wore a pretty coral sundress and gold sandals.

'Nice dress,' said Giulia as she clocked her change of appearance. 'Beautiful!'

'Thanks, it's an old favourite. Giulia, where is the best place to make a phone call using the Wi-Fi? It doesn't seem to be strong enough in my room.'

'If you stand over by the window it tends to be better, but it is a bit hit and miss at the best of times, I'm afraid.'

'OK, thanks, I'll give it a go,' said Libby, pulling out her phone.

The first person she called was her mum; she didn't have anything as hi-tech as a smart phone, so Libby couldn't FaceTime her. It went straight to answerphone just as Libby realised that it was probably her book-club night, so she left her a voicemail saying that she had settled in well and would call her tomorrow. Next she FaceTimed Jules.

'Oh my god I can't even look at that tan, turn off the video! Turn it *off!*' shrieked Jules, laughing, as Libby came into focus on her screen.

'Hi Jules! Nice to see you too,' she chuckled.

'How are you my love? We miss you so much.'

'I miss you guys too.'

'Are you there? Did you make it in one piece?'

'Yup, I arrived at around midday, found the hostel OK. It is so cute, just like the photos on TripAdvisor.'

'What about Positano? Is it as amazing as you remembered?'

'Better!' said Libby. 'There are no words to describe it, seriously. It's the most beautiful place I've ever been to, and I cannot *believe* I'm going to spend three months here. What a joke!'

'Total bliss. How's the Italian? Are you fluent again yet?'

'It's not bad – some of the accents down here are quite tricky to understand. Some of the older generation slip into local dialect at times, so there's no way I will be able to understand that, but on the whole I'm doing pretty well. It's amazing how it comes back to you so quickly.'

'Like riding a bike,' said Jules.

'Exactly! I've been trying to avoid speaking English where possible, though obviously with the guests being mostly foreign, I expect my English is probably one of the main reasons why Floriana hired me.'

'That's OK, I reckon you'll be fine so long as you always speak Italian to the locals. Have you got any mates yet?'

'Hardly! I've only been here five minutes.' Lowering her voice so as not to be overheard she added, 'There are some people around my age working here too, so that should be fun. So far I've met a girl called Giulia who works on reception, and a guy called Luca who is the barman.'

'Hot?'

'*Very*. But I think he knows it a little too well, if you get what I mean!'

'Typical Italian stallion, hey?' laughed Jules.

'Exactly. Anyway, how are things with you?' asked Libby. Jules had recently been promoted within her firm.

'Not bad. Busy at work at the moment, which isn't great. I'm still struggling to cope with the new workload.'

'Poor you. Hopefully it will ease up as time goes on.'

'I doubt it…' Jules said mournfully.

'How's Angus?' Libby was slightly hesitant to ask. They hadn't been in touch these past few weeks, which was very unusual for them. The last time they had seen each other before she left, Angus had given her a tough talking-to. He had challenged her to get a grip on her life. He thought she was pretty useless and self-indulgent, and that it was high time she grew up and took control of herself, to use his words, 'to start acting like an adult.' He couldn't believe she was setting off on yet another solo trip abroad and clearly thought her justification of learning Italian was just an excuse to avoid 'real life' for as long as possible.

'He is very well; do you want to speak? He's right here,' said Jules.

'I'd love to, pass him over.'

'*Mi amore!*' laughed Angus as he appeared on her screen. 'It's good to see you.' She was relieved that he seemed to be acting normally. Perhaps he had missed her and was going to be nice.

'You too! How are you? Hopefully you're not missing me too much.'

'Oh it's all we talk about Lib,' he chuckled. 'So tell me about your travels so far. How's it all going? Are you fluent in Italian once again? Ready for your new job?' She knew it wouldn't take him long to bring up the real world.

'I am working on it, don't worry. I don't need another lecture, thank you very much.'

'Look, Lib,' Angus said, 'I'm sorry if I upset you before you left. It's only because I care.'

'I know.'

'I just want to see you settled, with your ducks all in a row.'

'So do I... I think this time it'll be different, though. This is my last adventure before serious life begins.'

'It's about time.'

'I've worked hard to get here, Angus. I'm not going to let all that work on my law conversion go to waste.'

'I hope not. It's just not the first time I've heard you say that.'

'I know, I know. But I'm determined this time. I am going to prove all you doubters wrong. In three months' time, I'll be a high-powered lawyer, working full time. You won't recognise me!'

'That'll be the day!' laughed Angus. 'Little Libby all grown up in a power suit... I've been waiting for this for thirty years!'

They chatted for a while longer before Angus had to go and check on their dinner. 'Right, I'd better go, I'm in the middle of cooking spag bol and it needs a bit of attention.'

'Ooh yum, lucky Jules,' said Libby. 'Let's speak soon?'

'Definitely. Keep us updated and have the most wonderful time.'

'Will do,' said Libby, waving and blowing a kiss as she ended the call. There was nothing like speaking to your oldest friends to put a smile on your face. She felt so fond of them both.

Libby, Angus and Jules had all grown up together in a small town in Kent and had been the best of friends for as long as Libby could remember. Angus was a bit like a brother to her. He had always been extremely protective of her, and she knew she drove him mad with her spontaneity and her lack of stability as she jumped from one interest to another at the drop of a hat.

As she thought of them both sitting down for dinner, Libby wondered momentarily how her life might have turned out differently. What if she had been the one to marry Angus, not Jules. It had actually been Libby who had first kissed him, back in their mid-teens. He had taken her to one side one evening and told her how beautiful she was, how much he liked her. Then they had kissed on the beach. Libby had been far too shy to do anything about it, a characteristic that she had long since grown out of, and had pretended it had never happened the next time she saw him. Angus had been embarrassed about the whole incident, clearly, because he had never brought it up again either. They had never spoken about it, and before long Jules had decided she fancied him and that was that. She had made it very clear that he was hers, and Angus had never looked back. There had been several occasions where Libby had allowed herself to wonder what might have happened had she and Angus been the ones to start dating instead; how their lives might have worked out…

Both Angus and Jules had been a fantastic support throughout the stress of her law conversion. Angus in particular had seemed so proud of the hard work she had put in, despite the fact it had nearly killed her. She really felt as though she needed this break before starting the daily grind in the autumn. Having ended the call, Libby felt the pull of a nice cold beer enticing her.

Libby took a seat at the bar and waited for Luca to finish pouring a pint of Peroni for a customer. Music played softly from a sound system behind him. There were a few guests at the tables inside using the Wi-Fi on their phones and relaxing. Some people had taken their drinks outside to sit on the terrace under the canopy of stars that speckled the inky-black sky. The lights of several boats out at sea blinked dozily in the distance.

A couple of minutes later Luca came over. 'What can I get you?' he asked in heavily accented English accompanied by a winning smile.

'A beer please,' said Libby, answering in Italian.

'Peroni? It's the only one we have on tap.'

'That would be great.'

'So, you arrived this morning?' asked Luca as he tilted a pint glass under the nozzle and pulled down on the lever.

'Yes that's right,' said Libby. 'Tomorrow is my first day. Have you worked here for long?'

'A few years now, yes,' explained Luca as he handed over her drink. 'I moved away to Naples for a while but I missed the sea too much. I am Positanese born and bred; there is nowhere else for me but here. Maybe I am like a mermaid – I will shrivel up if I am out of the water too long!'

'Perhaps a merman?' laughed Libby. Luca nodded, realising his mistake. 'Do you work here full time?'

'Pretty much, especially during the summer months. I also design websites and do a bit of freelance graphic design during the day. But I like La Casetta, meeting lots of people, having lots of fun, you know?' This last sentence was said with a very cheeky wink. Libby was fairly sure that she did know exactly what type of fun he was referring to.

Luca was exactly the kind of guy she had gone for in her twenties. The kind of guy she had completely sworn to avoid after one too many heartbreaks. They were great fun, these players, but in her experience it nearly always ended badly. Giulia's warning rang in her ears. This time, she was determined to listen to her instincts. She would not flirt back. An Italian romance, though tempting, was not a sensible idea at this point in her life. Though the thought did cross her mind that it might help with practising her Italian…

'Floriana told me that there was another girl who worked in the bar – Maria, was it?'

'Yes Maria has a day off today, but she will be in tomorrow. We tag team so that the bar is always staffed and we are usually both here when it is busy at the weekends. So, Libby, what brings you here to Positano? Travelling?'

'Kind of, I suppose. I'm here to practise my Italian, though your English is so good that I feel bad trying to use it on you!'

Luca immediately switched to Italian, 'In that case from now on I shall speak only Italian to you.'

'Thank you, that'll be a great help,' replied Libby in her best attempt to do the same. 'In October I am starting a new job in a law firm, where I will be required to deal with Italian clients and colleagues from our Italian offices, hence the need for me to get in lots of practice. As you can probably tell, my Italian is a bit rusty!'

'Nonsense. It's fantastic! How do you speak such good Italian in the first place? It's very unusual to find British people who can…'

'I've always loved Italy. I did a degree in Italian and spent a year living in Bologna,' explained Libby. 'But I never use it in London and so I've forgotten quite a lot.'

'So you have the summer off before serious life begins?' asked Luca, his eyes sparkling mischievously.

'Exactly! I have to make the most of it!' laughed Libby.

'I will do my *very* best to help you,' grinned Luca, with more than just a hint of suggestion in his eyes.

Oh dear, thought Libby. *This could be dangerous...*

As the evening passed by, Libby had another beer and tried her best to read an abandoned copy of *La Corriere della Sera* newspaper that had been left on the bar. She finally got around to checking her emails, reading one from her sister Helen who had recently arrived in Hong Kong. She chatted a bit more to Luca between serving customers, and Floriana came to talk to her before going up to her apartment. Giulia also popped in every now and again. Libby remembered Giulia's warning. She must know Luca pretty well, having worked with him for so long. She would be wise to listen to her advice.

At about ten o'clock, Libby said her goodnights and headed up to bed, keen to get an early night before her 5.30 a.m. alarm call. She felt exhausted after her day of travelling and the influx of new information that she had received. She brushed her teeth and washed her face in the bathroom next door, then went into her room to change into the oversized shirt that served as her pyjamas. She imagined she was back down on the beach at Spiaggia del Fornillo, the sun beating down on her as the sound of the sea lapped the shore. Before she knew it she had drifted off.

Chapter Three

Libby had a deep and dreamless sleep, waking just before her alarm feeling full of energy and *joie de vivre*. She jumped out of bed and opened her curtains, stretching in the morning sunlight. It was a wonderful novelty rising each morning to a clear blue sky. She had a quick shower and brushed her teeth before pulling on a pair of denim shorts and a T-shirt. As she made her way downstairs, she listened for signs of life in the rooms and dormitories that she passed by. Apart from the sound of someone using the shower, it was all pretty quiet. Downstairs, she opened up the blinds that covered the windows and unlocked the front door. She opened the door that led out on to the terrace and stepped out into the dry heat. She wandered over to the railing, spending several minutes soaking up the view. The sea gleamed softly under the rose-tinged dawn. She could smell the sweet scent of the sprawling honeysuckle that covered one whitewashed wall of the terrace.

Floriana appeared moments later. She was going to join Libby on her morning shift. As the guests trickled down, Floriana and Libby made them breakfast, answered their questions, cleared the plates and manned the phone. The first set of new arrivals came at around eight o'clock, and Libby watched carefully as Floriana checked them in, chatting happily to her guests as she scanned their passports and showed them to their room. Nothing too tricky, she was relieved to see. This kind of work was right up her street.

Libby enjoyed chatting to all the guests of so many different nationalities. She took careful note of the recommendations

Floriana gave out, writing them in her note pad so that she would have them at hand to pass on if Floriana wasn't around. A group of Belgians, dressed head to toe in suitable hiking gear, asked for a recommended walking route. Floriana gave them a map and explained that her favourite was called 'Il Sentiero degli Dei' or 'The Walk of the Gods'. It was a long and winding footpath that connected the two hilltop towns of Agerola and Nocelle, just above Positano, offering jaw-dropping views of the coastline and spectacular scenery.

It all sounded so beautiful that Libby couldn't wait to start exploring on her days off. There was just so much to do: incredible walks, day trips to the picturesque towns of Amalfi and Ravello, boat trips to the islands of Capri and Ischia; even Pompeii wasn't far away. She wanted to find out more about the ancient Roman city. She was ashamed of her lack of knowledge about Pompeii, despite having done a degree in Italian, and was determined to ensure she finally made it there this time around.

'Which is your favourite, Capri or Ischia?' Libby asked Floriana that afternoon. She had spent her lunch break sitting on the terrace, sunbathing and reading about the islands in her *Lonely Planet* guide.

'Ooh, that's quite a tough question. Let me see… I think I prefer Ischia, in a way. Capri is stunning but it can be a little overcrowded. The Grotta Azzurra is beautiful, you should definitely visit it, but personally I prefer Ischia.'

'I definitely want to visit them both at some point,' said Libby. 'I'm so excited about all the exploring I can do.'

'You should get Luca to take you. His best friend has a boat and they are always going on excursions. Luca?' she shouted in the vague direction of the bar. He had arrived several minutes before and was setting up for the day.

'At your service, Floriana,' he appeared, giving an over-the-top bow, a tea towel draped over one bulging bicep.

'I was just telling Libby here that you must take her to visit the islands next time you go out with Gian Matteo.'

'Certainly! We would love to have you on board,' he winked, smiling broadly.

'That's very kind of you,' Libby smiled back at him; it was hard to resist his infectious enthusiasm.

Just then a fresh-faced girl let herself in through the front door.

'*Buongiorno tutti*,' she smiled at the room.

'*Ciao* Maria,' said Floriana.

'*Buongiorno bella! Come stai?*' asked Luca.

'*Bene, bene, grazie*,' said Maria. 'It's so hot out there today, though; I'm drenched! Thank god for the air conditioning in here.'

'Maria, this is Libby, she's here for the summer,' explained Floriana.

'Pleased to meet you,' said Maria with a broad smile.

'*Piacere*,' replied Libby, shaking her hand. Maria and Luca went through to the bar to continue setting up.

The bar opened at around four o'clock, and soon all around was the sound of chatter and laughter as a large group of American backpackers gathered there, chinking bottles of beer and reliving their recent escapades in Rome. Libby laughed along with them as she listened to their conversation through the open door. Travelling was such a carefree time in anyone's life, it did wonders for the spirit to be around so many people just living in the moment; not bogged down by doom and gloom and the daily grind. She loved being surrounded by people who were taking so much pleasure from their surroundings, just as she was. Not for the first time she wished that she could apply the same mentality to her 'normal' life in London as she did to her travels. Whenever she arrived back home and established a routine for herself, she began to feel claustrophobic and trapped. She knew she had to learn to take pleasure in the small things; to make herself happy no matter where she was or what she was doing. Her habit of throwing in the towel when boredom struck to take herself on holiday wasn't sustainable, and she couldn't keep chopping and changing jobs forever.

The clock ticked closer to six o'clock, and soon enough Giulia came sauntering in through the door. Her lips were stained a deep berry red today, her hair pinned back at the nape of her neck. She really was very beautiful. Libby was embarrassed at herself for feeling a pang of jealousy. She reminded herself about Giulia's difficult circumstances, caring for her mother; it was amazing how Giulia managed to remain so upbeat and positive.

'Evening,' said Giulia brightly. 'I'm here to relieve you. How was your first day?'

'I loved it, thanks,' said Libby. 'Though I have no doubt messed something up one way or another.'

'Don't worry – if you have, we'll fix it. Luckily Tonio and Flori are pretty relaxed. And, this is Italy… balancing the books is important, but not so important that they can't turn a blind eye to the odd slip-up.'

'Well, let me know if you notice any glaring mistakes,' said Libby.

'Will do.'

Free to spend the evening how she wished, Libby made her way down into the village for a walk. This time she turned left at the piazza, and wound her way along a set of crisscross steps that twisted and turned back and forth, eventually coming out on a tiny ledge overlooking the sea. She found a deeper set of steps that cut through the rock and curved back around to the right, bringing her out on to the far side of the main beach. A group of bars lay further to the east and she could hear the gentle thudding of rhythmic music playing out over the sea. The sun was like a drop of molten lava finding cool relief as it eased its way, inch by inch, into the sea. Libby sat on the bottom step and watched the sunset, admiring the effect of the changing light on the clouds, tinged first orange, then gold and eventually pink. The sea reflected each changing shade like a mirror. She could never grow bored of watching the sun rise and set. It was a luxury that was denied to her in London. In the city you were either at work or asleep, and if you did happen to be outside at the right moment, or near a window, you would undoubtedly have a towering block of concrete or brick blocking your view.

It was this slight sense of claustrophobia that had stopped her from settling down like all her friends had done. Whenever she felt close to having a stable relationship, or a steady job, she seemed to panic, and before she knew it she had run away, taking refuge in the transient life of the traveller. It was what drove Angus crazy. He was constantly telling her she needed to figure out her priorities and stop jumping ship the moment things got tough. She wished she could be more like everyone else, but she couldn't seem to help it. She had periods of self-doubt and panic that she was missing out, but it didn't make it easier for her to change. She had promised herself at the beginning of her law conversion that this time things would be different. She was going to sort her life out once and for all – get a proper job, forge a successful career, have a relationship, maybe even get married and have children one day. She wanted to prove to Angus that she could do it, and to herself, of course.

Later, having enjoyed a delicious bowl of pasta at a trattoria on the sea front, Libby walked back up to La Casetta. She made her way to the bar. Luca poured her a Peroni as soon as he saw her come in and offered it to her as she sat down.

'Thanks Luca.'

'*Piacere*,' he said. 'Where have you been?'

'I just went down to the beach to watch the sunset.'

'Beautiful, eh?'

'Stunning. I ate at Luigi's on the sea front and went for a little walk around town.'

'Good choice,' laughed Luca. 'Luigi's was set up by my great-uncle!'

'Really?' Libby smiled. She supposed there were a lot of family connections within Positano.

'I'll take you there some time and introduce you. He's a real character; he has so many stories about this place.'

'I'd love that,' said Libby. 'You are going to be my tour guide by the sounds of it.'

'Well, I don't do that for just anyone, I can tell you,' laughed Luca. 'Only the most beautiful women.'

Libby couldn't help laughing at his outrageous flirting. 'I bet you say that to all the girls.'

'No, no! Only the genuinely deserving. And you, Libby, are extremely beautiful.'

'So… I take it you don't have a girlfriend?' Libby cut to the chase.

'No, no, no. What do you take me for?' asked Luca. 'Who would want monogamy?'

'Lots of people,' Libby retorted. 'Most people, in fact, I'd say.'

'Monogamy is an unnatural state of affairs, if you ask me. Sooner or later, someone gets bored, they see someone they like and… *ecco!* They have cheated. Heartbreak follows, everyone is upset – a recipe for disaster.' She thought of Angus's reaction if he were to hear this and could imagine him rolling his eyes in despair.

'Well, when you put it like that, it does sound fairly depressing I admit.' Perhaps there was still time for her to have some fun before reality kicked in…

'Exactly.'

'But don't some women refuse to be with you unless they are in a relationship?'

'True. So in my eyes, honesty is the best policy. I always say from the start to any women I like that I can't promise anything. Though, I must say, when I fall in love, I want to spend all my time with that one person, it's just… sooner or later I fall out of love and then…' He tailed off, looking rueful.

'Sounds as if you know yourself pretty well,' Libby said. She knew this should put her off him but, on the plus side, could Luca be the perfect holiday fling? There would clearly be absolutely no strings attached; just a bit of fun during the summer.

At that moment Maria came in from the back with a box full of bottles that looked twice her weight. 'Maria, give that to me! It's far too heavy for you to be carrying!' Luca scolded her.

'Thanks Luca,' said Maria, panting slightly from the exertion. 'We need to change the barrel on the beer, too – it's about to run out.'

'I'll go and do that now. Are you OK here?' he asked.

'Sure,' said Maria. She poured herself a glass of water. The Americans had all gone out on the town, suitably fuelled with beer, and the customers in the bar were disappearing in dribs and drabs into the cool evening. Maria and Libby chatted for a while.

'So Maria, what do you do?' asked Libby. 'Apart from working here.'

'I'm a student,' said Maria. 'This is my holiday job – I work here during my vacations from uni.'

'What do you study?'

'Hospitality.'

'Cool, which university?'

'Naples.'

'Do you like it?'

'Yeah, it's okay. I'm only halfway through my degree, but so far so good.'

'And what do you hope to do afterwards?'

'I want to come to the UK actually. I'm going to try and get a job in a hotel or restaurant in London, or maybe Edinburgh.'

'I'm amazed that everyone wants to leave this place,' Libby told her. 'It's such a dream here. I was saying the same thing to Tonio and Floriana the other day.'

'It's all right in the summer, that's for sure,' Maria told her. 'But in the winter, it's completely dead. It's hard to earn a living without the tourists in town. You are so lucky in London; there are so many opportunities.' It was beginning to occur to Libby that perhaps she had been quite naïve in her assumptions about what life was like in Positano. She wondered if there was ever such a thing as a perfectly balanced life. Did sacrifice and enjoyment always lie side by side?

Libby spent the rest of the evening chatting to Luca and Maria, on and off between serving customers and clearing up the bar. They were a funny pair. Luca obviously looked on Maria as he would a little sister, and she clearly adored him, though perhaps in less of a fraternal way on her part. At about ten thirty, Libby said goodnight to them both and went to find out how Giulia was getting on. She hadn't come across any mistakes from the information Libby had entered on to the system that afternoon, which was a relief to hear.

Libby made her way up to bed and fell on to her mattress in a heavy slump, her head spinning with Italian phrases, a roll call of all the faces she had seen that day flashing through her mind, lingering finally on Luca's hazel eyes, his dark curly lashes and that cheeky, knowing grin as she drifted off to sleep.

The next day she finally spoke to her mother. Libby had legged it down to the beach as soon as her two-hour lunch break had begun, leaving the hostel in Floriana's capable hands. She had raced straight into the sea on the Spiaggia Maggiore, plunging in and swimming out as far as she could, lolling in the water and gazing up at the towering hills overhead. She imagined all the hikers up on the secret, hidden pathways near the skyline: the Walk of the Gods. She splashed back to shore and dried off, taking a seat on one of the loungers that were dotted about the beach. She dialled her mother's landline.

'Hello?' Her mother's voice came down the line.

'Mum, it's me, Libby!'

'Libby darling! Finally! How are you?'

'I'm great thanks. I'm on the beach!'

'How's it all going? I'm dying to hear all about it.' Libby could always rely on her mother for support. She knew that she doted on her as the youngest daughter and felt guilty that her older sister Helen had suffered the high expectations of the first-born child, saving Libby from a similar burden. Unlike Angus, Miriam didn't seem too judgemental over her lack of direction in life. She was more concerned with Helen, and seemed to allow Libby's shortcomings to flit underneath her radar.

'I'm learning the ropes pretty quickly,' said Libby. 'There's nothing too challenging to do. Everyone is charming and the hostel is so cute, you must come and visit.'

Libby filled her mother in on her first couple of days in Positano, on Floriana and Tonio, Luca, Maria and Giulia and some of the guests she had met.

'It all sounds incredible… Actually, I'm glad you called, darling. I'm a bit worried about your sister. Have you heard from her recently?'

'Not much since she arrived in Hong Kong. I had an email a few days ago. Why? Do you have reason to be concerned?'

'It's just that she was in such a bad state when she left. I do hope she hasn't bitten off more than she can chew.'

'But the whole point of this change of scenery is a fresh start for her, Mum. That's why she has gone in the first place.'

'I know, I know. And we all know Helen needed something different, a change. But I just wonder if we should have let her go… a new place, a new culture, no friends. It's hardly going to make it easy for her. Her confidence is already so low and she hasn't got much resilience these days.'

'I'll try calling her later. Have you managed to get through?'

'No I just keep getting her voicemail. What did she say in your email?'

'Nothing much, to be honest; that she had arrived, that the flight was long but OK. I think it's good for her though, Mum, I really do. She's got her TEFL qualification so she might as well use it. When she actually starts teaching she'll meet people through that, and there'll be more of a structure, more of a timetable, which is just what she needs.'

'I just feel so helpless. It's so hard to understand depression if one is not depressed oneself.'

'I know, Mum, it is really hard. If it helps, I spoke to Angus about it a while back; you know his dad has suffered badly from it. He said that he sees it a bit like being stuck in the mud. Every time you try to pull yourself out, you end up sinking deeper, so after a while you just give up trying.'

'Yes I can see that. But that's why I worry so much. I think she really needs antidepressants to help her deal with her emotions.'

'I know, but she's not interested in taking drugs.'

'Well I wish she would at least give them a try. Or go and see a therapist again. She never admitted it, but I'm sure her sessions with Cynthia helped.'

Miriam struggled to understand Helen's depression. She tried her best not to show it, but Libby could tell she thought depression was a form of self-indulgence. Libby was constantly sticking up for her sister when her mother became exasperated by her lack of motivation, thankful that it never seemed to be directed at her.

'I'll talk to her, Mum. Don't worry. Or at least try not to. This fresh start could be just what she needs, a change of scenery. And at least she's not going to bump into Alan in Hong Kong.'

'Yes, well I suppose that has to be a blessing.'

'Exactly. All right Mum, I'll give her a call now and I'll speak to you very soon. Let me know if you hear anything in the meantime?'

'I will darling, take care now. And have fun!'

As Libby hung up the phone she sighed. She felt terrible for her sister. She had always struggled somewhat with her confidence, as had Libby herself at times. Helen had suffered from depression and anxiety throughout her twenties and early thirties, having better years and worse years, never really committing to a career and moving from one disastrous relationship to another. Though Libby had not fared much better in either of these respects, she wasn't cursed with a tendency towards depression, for which she was extremely grateful. To make matters worse, Helen was also desperate to have a baby, and at thirty-seven she was only too aware that time was running out. She had thrown her heart and soul into her last relationship with a slightly dweeby-looking musician called Alan, whom Libby had found bemusingly arrogant. Four years later, with no proposal on the horizon, Helen had confronted him with questions about their future. He had dumped her callously on the spot and claimed that he wasn't interested in settling down, leaving Helen heartbroken and plunging her into her worst depression yet. She had spent months at her mum's house in Kent before announcing that she was moving to Hong Kong to teach English as a foreign language. She had upped sticks and gone a couple of weeks ago, whilst Libby had been in the north of Italy, and neither her mum nor Libby had heard much from her since. She sincerely hoped this would be the making and not the breaking of her.

She scrolled down to Helen's name in her phone and pressed call. A foreign dial tone sounded in her ear. After several rings the mechanical voice of her voicemail kicked in. Libby left a message asking her to call her, saying how much she missed her and how she hoped she was settling in OK. She lay back down on her sun lounger, sending up prayers that her sister would be all right. She loved her dearly and knew just how fragile her state of mind was. She hoped her luck would change and that Hong Kong would help her turn over a new leaf and find her feet once again.

Chapter Four

Having arrived on the Wednesday and worked steadily through the weekend, Libby was given Monday and Tuesday off. She was longing to get out and about, no longer restricted to her two-hour lunch break, and was planning on tackling the famous Walk of the Gods. She set off bright and early on Monday morning with a small daypack. She followed Floriana's advice on which bus to catch to get to the start of the Sentiero degli Dei. The bus wound its way along the perilously curving roads, depositing her in a small village, from which she followed the hand-drawn map she'd got from La Casetta. She climbed up a series of winding steps to the start of the path. It was an old mule track which had once been the only path connecting the hilltop villages. As Libby walked she could see why the path had received its name. There was a low mist hovering at the top of the mountainous hills, waiting to be burned away by the heat of the sun as it rose. At times she felt as if she could reach out her fingers and touch the cloud of vapour. When it cleared about half an hour into her walk, she could barely believe her eyes as the staggering views of the Amalfi coast were revealed in their full splendour. The endless curves of the coastline plunged thousands of metres down to the emerald sea. The path was so well worn; even the natural stone steps that she came across at times seemed somehow softened and moulded underfoot. She was glad that she had brought a large bottle of water with her as the sun rose higher and higher in the sky.

Hours later, exhausted and sweaty from her endeavours and having finally made her way back to the main road, she decided to hitch a lift back into Positano. A kindly bespectacled man pulled over and let her into the passenger seat of his car, dropping her up the hill from the church. Libby was desperate to get into the sea, so she made her way straight down to the beach, opting for Spiaggia del Fornillo to settle in for the rest of the day. After a well-deserved swim, she ordered a panini from one of the beach restaurants and another bottle of water. Sipping the cooling water and munching on the slightly salty bread with its filling of soft mortadella ham and cheese, she wiggled her toes in the sand and watched her fellow beach-goers amble along the shoreline. Just then her phone beeped in her pocket.

'Libby?'

'Luca, hi! How are you?'

'You made it in one piece?'

'Yes, I didn't get lost. It was so stunning, I couldn't believe it. Hard work but worth every second.'

'I'm sorry I couldn't come with you—'

'No worries. Did you get everything sorted with your graphic design stuff?'

'Yes all sorted, thanks. Now, this afternoon we are going out on Gian Matt's boat. Do you want to come?'

'Oooh, how exciting! Where are you going?'

'Just around the coast. We can show you the Sirenusas, a bunch of islands between here and Capri.'

'Wow, that sounds amazing. Are you sure Gian Matteo won't mind me coming too?'

'Absolutely. He's right here with me. Where are you now?'

'I'm on Fornillo.'

'OK, we'll pick you up from the jetty there in half an hour.'

'Thanks, Luca.'

Libby was excited about getting out on the open water. She adored travelling on speedboats. In Kent she had often gone down to Chatham where Jules's family had a boat. Some of her favourite memories were of sunny days in her childhood whizzing out over the bumps looking for dolphins, eating picnics, and swimming off the boat in secluded bays with Angus, Jules and their friends.

Soon enough she spotted Luca and Gian Matteo approaching the jetty. She was looking forward to spending some more time with Luca. They had grown close quickly since she had started working at La Casetta, and she could see them becoming very good friends.

'This is Libby,' Luca held her hand as she stepped aboard the boat. 'My beautiful new colleague.'

'Nice to meet you Libby. I've heard quite a lot about you from your greatest fan here,' said Gian Matteo.

Luca gave Gian Matteo a shove, ignoring him. 'And this is my sister, Nicola,' said Luca, introducing Libby to a very pretty brunette who was sitting at the back of the boat.

'Hi!'

'Hi Libby, come and sit next to me. It gets quite bumpy out there, the back is much more comfy.'

As Libby took her seat Gian Matteo pushed down the throttle and they eased their way out to sea, accelerating faster as soon as they rounded the first crop of rocks and hit the open water. Libby chatted to Nicola, a charming and friendly twenty-nine year old, only three years younger than Libby and the spitting image of her brother. Libby could tell that they would get on well as they fell into an easy rapport, laughing about Luca and teasing him about his salmon-pink T-shirt, which was just a touch too tight.

After a good blast of sea air had cleared the cobwebs from their lungs and added a pinch of colour to their cheeks, Gian Matteo set his course for the Sirenusas.

'How did they get their name?' asked Libby.

'Legend has it that three enchanted sirens, half women and half birds, lived on the islands,' explained Gian Matteo.

'They were said to lure sailors closer and closer towards them with enchanting music and singing, causing boats to shipwreck on the rocks and the sailors to drown,' continued Luca.

'Oh! A lovely story!' laughed Libby. 'Very morbid!'

The boat slowed down as they slowly circled the jagged rocks. The sea was such a vivid turquoise, it seemed almost impossibly clear and bright. Gian Matteo found a secluded spot and dropped the anchor. He didn't want to swim himself. Libby wasn't surprised, he didn't look the type to enjoy getting wet, but he sat with a beer from the cool box while Nicola, Luca and Libby stripped down to their swimwear and dived in. Luca gave Libby an admiring wolf whistle as she surfaced next to him. 'You certainly look incredible in a bikini,' he said.

She laughed, splashing him and diving back under the surface, chiding herself for being secretly pleased with the compliment. She was meant to be immune to those easy tactics from the opposite sex – she was not a teenager, after all. They swam around to the rocks and clambered up on to the island, taking care not to cut their feet on any sharp stones. After a bit of exploring, they swam over to the boat and climbed back on board, drying off in the sun as they sipped cool beers. Nicola told Libby stories about Gian Matteo and Luca growing up, causing indignation on Luca's part if ever he were portrayed in a less than perfect light.

'You don't want to give Libby the wrong impression of me, sis,' he scolded.

'I already have an accurate enough impression of you, thanks Luca,' laughed Libby.

'She's not stupid, Lu… she can see straight through you,' chuckled Nicola.

'Finally, a woman immune to Luca's charms.' Gian Matteo chinked his bottle against Libby's. 'I've been waiting thirty-seven years for this!' Libby laughed, though just how immune she was turning out to be, she wasn't so sure…

That evening, having got back to Positano and disembarked from the boat, and following a couple more beers at a beachfront bar, Luca suggested they all go up to Luigi's for dinner. Libby was enjoying herself enormously; she loved flirting with Luca and was aware just how much she was beginning to fancy him. Nicola and Luca were given a rapturous greeting by their great-uncle, whom Libby recognised immediately as the bearded man who had been walking around the tables chatting to all the guests the night she had been for dinner there.

After mouth-watering bowls of spaghetti vongole and huge mounds of fluffy tiramisu, not to mention several vats of wine, they were all stuffed to the brim. Luigi came to sit with them, proffering a bottle of Limoncello, which was passed around with tiny shot glasses as a *digestivo*.

'So Luigi, what was Positano like when you were a child?' asked Libby. 'Has it changed enormously?'

'Ahhhh… well! It was so tiny when I was young – peaceful, idyllic. No tourists, nothing. I remember when there was only one telephone line in the village. It was at the post office in the centre. If anyone got a telephone call, one of the local boys would have to race as fast as they could up to the far end of the village, sometimes up thousands of steps, to tell the recipient. Then you had to run all the way back to the post office and hope that the person trying to contact you hadn't got bored of waiting and hung up the phone.'

'Oh my goodness, how amazing!' said Libby.

They reminisced further about Positano's development from a tiny fishing village into the tourist hub that it is today. Luigi was full of interesting and funny anecdotes. He had welcomed his fair share of famous faces into his restaurant over the years and he marched Libby over to his wall of fame by the bar. It was covered in framed photographs of Luigi posing with his famous clientele. Libby spotted Elizabeth Taylor, Goldie Hawn and Tom Hanks among the gallery of stars.

After dinner, Luca and Nicola walked up with her to La Casetta, depositing her at the door before making their way on to their own flat. Luca had three sisters altogether. Nicola was the second youngest, and he and Nicola lived together about a hundred metres further up the hill from the hostel.

'Thanks so much for such a fun day!' Libby said, suddenly reluctant to part company with Luca.

'It was great to meet you,' said Nicola.

'And you,' Libby grinned. She liked Nicola.

'Let's do it again soon.'

'I'll try and persuade Floriana to give you days off when I am not working,' said Luca.

'That'd be great,' said Libby. 'You certainly make an excellent tour guide.'

'All she wants me for is my tour guiding,' said Luca to his sister, looking morose. 'She has no idea how it hurts—'

'Shut up.' Nicola gave him a shove. 'Ignore my brother!'

'Oh don't worry, I do,' laughed Libby, as she skipped up the steps and opened the yellow front door. 'Night,' she called, closing it behind her.

'Night, *bella!*' shouted Luca. Despite herself, Libby grinned the whole way through her bedtime routine; her heart was dancing the tango and she knew there was only one person to blame.

The following day was spent in a slump on a sun lounger, dozing in the sun. Her calf muscles were aching terribly after her walk and she felt quite exhausted.

She called Jules, who was always willing to pick up while at work; any excuse for a brief respite from her spreadsheets. Jules was not a natural number-cruncher. She was desperately plotting her escape from the world of accountancy to do something more creative. Libby was incredibly sympathetic. There was nothing worse than doing a job that you just didn't feel cut out for, as she knew only too well. She just wished that Jules would have the strength of mind to do something about it. She had almost got to the point of handing in her notice when they had given her another promotion, which had had the desired effect of enticing her to stay put once more. Thankfully Angus was an extremely sympathetic husband. She was sure that his support was the secret to Jules keeping it all together despite her frustration.

'Libs! Perfect timing, I've just gone out for lunch.'

'How's it going?' Libby asked.

'Deathly. The usual. You?' Libby caught her up with all the details of her first week in Positano, in particular the wonderful time she had had the day before with Luca and the others.

'Sounds heavenly. It's great that you've got Luca, and his sister sounds nice. I thought you might get quite bored without any mates, but it sounds like you're making friends no problem.'

'They're all just so friendly. I'm really lucky, though I think it's also something to do with the Italian character; they're such open people and very generous with their hospitality. I'm having dinner this evening in Floriana and Tonio's apartment. Their son Ugo is down from Rome for a couple of days, and Tonio is cooking his speciality gnocchi. I can't wait!'

'I hope you've at least put on about a stone in weight. That will be my one compensation for losing you to Italy for four months. You have to promise me you'll come back fat.'

'I'll certainly try my best! Though I'm sure I'm burning rather a lot of calories simply going up and down the stairs – there is not one flat path in the whole village. It's like living on a StairMaster!'

Satisfied that they were both fully up to date with each other's lives, they hung up the phone, leaving Libby to immerse herself in her novel for the rest of the afternoon. She had tried her sister again but still had no luck getting through.

Before Libby could catch her breath, her working week was over once again. Her two days off stretched out luxuriously in front of her. She was delighted that Luca had once again negotiated the same day off as her, secretly thrilled that he wanted to spend as much time with her as possible. Today they were planning on driving to Ravello. They set off mid-morning and wound their way up the perilous roads once more, veering across to Amalfi and then further up the Via del Dragone high into the hills.

'I'm impressed with your driving skills,' Libby told Luca as he negotiated his way past an enormous bus packed full of tourists that had broken down on a hairpin turn. She found his coordination and confidence on these difficult-to-navigate roads very attractive.

'I've grown up driving on these roads. It's not the easiest place to learn, but once you've mastered driving here, you can drive anywhere!'

Luca was wearing khaki shorts and a blue T-shirt and Libby's heart had skipped a beat when she had seen him that morning. He wouldn't have looked out of place on the big screen, he was so perfectly chiselled. Libby felt a wave of attraction for him, and for a moment regretted the huge quantities of pasta, pizza and ice cream she had been enjoying. She sucked her stomach in, hoping Luca wouldn't notice her expanding waistline.

She drank in the breathtaking views as they drove. 'Luca, what's the deal with you and Giulia?' she asked, her curiosity finally getting the better of her.

'Deal? What do you mean?'

'Is there any history between the two of you?'

'Why do you ask?'

'Just a feeling!'

'Well now you mention it, we may have hooked up a couple of times.'

'I knew it!'

'How?'

'Something about the way she is around you…'

'It's my fault. I should never have gone there. As soon as I did it, I realised that it was a bad idea – don't mix work with pleasure and all that…'

'Well, I can see why that's a good philosophy. Not great if things go wrong.' Libby wondered what had happened, but she didn't want to pursue the conversation further. Not for the first time she considered whether Giulia had warned her off out of jealousy or out of compassion? It was hard to tell.

Luca parked his car on the outskirts of the town and they wandered through the cobbled streets, drinking in the divine panoramic views that had made the town so famous. Libby thought of Wagner, D. H. Lawrence and Virginia Woolf, who had all fallen in love with Ravello. She was amazed at just how much she remembered about Italy from her studies. It was as if the wealth of information she had accumulated over the years had lain dormant and was now welling up inside her, fuelling her love for this magical place more and more.

'Let's head to the piazza,' said Luca. 'There's a market on every Tuesday morning, selling local produce.'

'Ooh yum!' said Libby, rubbing her hands with glee. 'Great idea!'

They pottered around the market tasting the local delicacies, laughing at some of the more interesting designer clothes on sale. They had lunch in a small café in the shade of a canopy of bougainvillea, eating risotto and drinking white wine. Luca was a truly entertaining guy and she found herself laughing out loud at the stories he had accumulated from years of working at La Casetta.

'There was this one German guy who, after too many drinks, decided that he would try and balance on the railings out on the terrace like a tightrope walker.'

'No!' gasped Libby. 'That's so dangerous – he must have been crazy.'

'Tell me about it. Maria screamed and as soon as I realised what was happening I ran out to grab him, pulling him towards me to get him down to safety. He landed right on top of me, knocking me over in the process. Thankfully he was safe… The only problem was that he had decided to strip naked beforehand. I ended up with my face wedged into his crotch.'

Libby cupped her hand over her mouth, laughing as she imagined the scene.

'Let's just say it was the first and hopefully the last time that I will ever be getting quite so up close and personal with a male customer!'

'If it had been a female customer you wouldn't have minded so much, right?' she teased him.

'That depends,' laughed Luca.

After lunch, Luca had to get back in time to start his shift. Libby left him at La Casetta and made her way down to the beach. If she were being honest with herself she felt a bit disappointed that – despite his flirting – he still hadn't made a move. It had to be all talk and no action, she reasoned. He clearly didn't fancy her. She told herself off for caring. She found herself thinking about what she should be looking for in a partner. She wished she knew. Chemistry was vital, definitely, but she knew how important it was to have someone kind, dependable, someone who would be good with her family, a great father... It was a lot to ask. Did people really just know when they met the one?

Later that afternoon she tried calling her sister. Still no luck. She decided to phone her mum instead.

'Hello?'

'Hi Mum, it's Lib.'

'Oh hi, darling. Hang on, let me just come inside. I'm knee-deep in the rose garden doing the dead-heading and the line is terrible on this portable phone.'

Libby waited for her mother to get inside to the kitchen phone. Ever since her father had passed away, ten years ago now, her mum had taken over the care of the rose garden in his memory. It had been his pride and joy. She took it very seriously, and to her credit it was just as splendid as it had ever been under his notoriously green fingers. As ever when Libby thought of her dad she felt the familiar ache of pain deep inside her, just as raw as it had been the day that he died.

'OK, here I am!' Her mum's voice sounded much clearer on the landline.

'Hi Mum, how are the roses getting on?'

'Jolly hard work, especially in this heat!'

'Haven't you still got Gavin helping with the garden?'

'Normally I would, but he's in Tenerife with his girlfriend this week, so I'm trying to keep on top of things myself. It's good exercise for me anyway – good to get out in the fresh air.'

'Absolutely.'

At the thought of her beloved dad, Libby blurted out the question that had been running round her mind. 'This might sound a bit weird, but I've been doing some thinking about relationships, wondering what it will be like to finally meet someone and settle down…'

'Right, darling…' her mum said curiously.

'When you met Dad, did you have any doubts in your mind at all that he was the one? How did you know for certain?'

There was a pause as Miriam dragged her mind back to those bittersweet memories. She and Ronald had met at school, but they hadn't started courting, as she called it, until their twenties.

'I must say, darling, I don't think I had a single doubt in my mind. He was the one and that was that. I knew I couldn't be with anyone else.'

'I think that's what I'm going to need, Mum. That certainty. I have never met anyone that has made me feel that way.' Libby wondered whether she ever would.

'Well I hope that you meet this elusive Mr Right soon, darling. You are thirty-two! And with Helen in the state she is in, you might be my only chance of being a mother of the bride, or a granny.' Libby knew that under the jovial tone her mother was deadly serious.

'Yes I know that, thank you Mother! Only too well! When I have a spare moment from working around the clock in the law firm, I will make sure I squeeze in a few dates, all right?'

'I'll do some investigating myself… maybe I can do a little matchmaking with some of my friends. Maureen was telling me just the other day about her lovely son Dominic—'

'Right, Mum, knock yourself out. No promises though!' Libby laughed as she hung up the phone. She thought about Helen and her desire to have a baby. She knew she wanted a family of her own one day as well, but there seemed an infinite number of hurdles to get through first. She knew she needed to work on herself, to make sure she was happy and independent and sorted, before she embarked on that kind of journey. For now she just had to focus on sorting out her career. Perhaps when that was in hand a relationship would follow, and then, who knew, maybe she would have a baby of her own. She fell asleep in the shade, daydreaming about Luca.

A while later her dreams were interrupted by the buzzing of her phone. 'Libby? It's Helen.'

'Good to hear from you at long last, stranger.' Libby smiled at the sound of her sister's voice. 'I've missed you!'

'I've missed you too. Sorry it's taken me so long to call,' Helen said.

'Don't worry. I bet you've been manic settling in to your new life. How are you? Mum has been worrying – she says she hasn't spoken to you for ages. How's it all going?'

'I feel bad for not calling her, but you know how she drives me nuts with her worrying. I just needed to have a break for a few weeks while I tried to settle in.'

'I understand. Maybe just send her the odd email, though, just so she knows you are OK.'

'I will, you're right…'

'Where are you staying?'

'I'm in an apartment provided by the school. It's tiny and pretty central so it's easy to get around. It's perfectly fine.'

'And have you started work yet?'

'Yup, I've done my first week. It's OK. Colleagues are all right, kids seem fine.' Helen was hardly an expert at description.

'That all sounds great!' Libby tried to sound as enthusiastic as possible as they chatted. She was determined to encourage her sister and felt proud of her for being so brave. In return she told Helen all about life in Positano so far, realising just how lucky she was to be there – it all sounded pretty idyllic, she had to admit. As she ended the call, with Helen promising to get in touch soon, a beach-seller came along selling cups of ice-cold lemon sorbet. Libby bought one and relished the refreshing spoonfuls of crushed syrupy ice as she looked out on the sea. It reminded her of the Slush Puppies her dad used to buy them after trips to the local swimming pool: blueberry and cherry. He would laugh as the dye slowly turned Helen and Libby's lips bright blue and neon pink. She felt overcome with emotion at the memory.

Later that afternoon she wound her way back through the shops, buying a pair of blue espadrilles and some ingredients to cook pasta arrabbiata back in the hostel kitchen. Tonio offered cooking lessons to interested guests, teaching small groups how to cook local specialities. Libby was determined to watch and learn as much as she could; she would sneak into the kitchen during these sessions, keeping an eye on the desk and listening out for the phone whilst scribbling notes. This evening's meal would be an exact replica of his recipe, and she hoped it tasted as good.

She was remarkably pleased with the results of her culinary efforts. The heat of the chilli was complemented perfectly by shavings of Parmesan cheese. She knew she would never get bored of Italian food.

After dinner she decided to call Jules and Angus on their landline.

'Hello?' It was Angus. As soon as she heard his voice, Libby realised that it was Angus she had been hoping to get through to.

'Angus, it's Libby.'

'Libby! What a lovely surprise. Jules is out this evening so you're stuck with me, I'm afraid.'

'I was actually hoping to speak to you.'

'Well I'm flattered. Not that Jules and I compete over the affections of our oldest friend... much!'

'Ha! I love you both, equally, you know that.'

'You damn well better. So, what's up? *La dolce vita* still going well?'

'*La dolce vita* is truly incredible. I'm still determined you must come and see me – the Amalfi coast would be your idea of heaven; so much inspiration for your painting. No it's not Italy, it's Helen. I'm worried about her.'

'Have you spoken to her?' Angus asked.

'I spoke to her today. She seemed OK actually. I guess I just feel so sorry for her, and the thought of her all by herself in a foreign country, trying to sort out a life for herself, it makes me anxious.'

'She's quite tough you know, Libby. I am sure she will be all right. She just needs time.'

'But what if she takes a turn for the worse?'

'It can happen... You just need to be there for her, keep checking in on her.' Angus's father had suffered from depression on and off all his life, taking a lot of his frustrations out on his son; as a result they had had a very difficult relationship. As the eldest child, Angus had been the voice of reason, trying to calm any explosions of temper, attempting to mediate between his parents and his siblings. He had spent a long time in his teens and early twenties studying depression, and had always been Libby's sounding board for any problems that had arisen with Helen.

They talked about her for a while, Libby feeling reassured – as always – by his words of wisdom. 'I think she just really needs to meet a decent guy…'

'There'll be someone out there – for both of you, Libs. Maybe you just need to stop trotting the globe to give them a chance to find you!'

'I hope so. One day…' said Libby. 'When the time comes, I just want what you and Jules have – to marry a best friend who I adore. Something natural and uncomplicated.'

'You mean me and Jules minus the arguments, I hope!'

'You and Jules have always argued – you don't know any other way.'

'She's certainly feisty,' Angus said ruefully.

'Tell me about it… I honestly don't know how you cope sometimes.' Libby laughed as she thought fondly of Jules.

'Me neither.'

'Angus!' He might say that, but Libby knew he loved her best friend just as she did.

Sadly they had been having some of their very worst rows over the last couple of years about having children. Angus was desperate to start a family, whereas Jules seemed to be becoming less and less convinced. It really worried Libby. Such a fundamental disagreement couldn't be resolved without one or the other of them making an enormous compromise.

'Have you had any more talks about kids recently?' Libby dared to ask the question. She could feel Angus tense at the topic. He drew in a long breath and let out a deep sigh.

'Not since the last one.'

'Do you think she'll come round in the end?'

'I don't know. She's just so determined not to disrupt her life. I know she would love it as soon as she actually had a baby; it's just the thought of it that freaks her out. But there must be loads of women who couldn't imagine what it would be like to become a mother, but now wouldn't change a thing.'

'You're right. I'm sure she'd be a great mum.'

'It's really hard. We got married so young that we didn't even really talk about it. I just assumed it would happen, and now I really am not so sure.'

'She'll come round.'

'Are you sure?'

'Yes, she will.' Libby crossed her fingers and hoped she was right. If there was one characteristic Jules certainly wasn't lacking, it was stubbornness. And this was such a delicate area that it was hard for Libby to get involved. She so wanted Angus to be happy. To make matters worse, she knew that he would be the most incredible dad.

They chatted for another half an hour or so; it was so great to catch up properly with him. He was working on a new series of oil paintings following a recent trip to the Lake District. Angus was a successful landscape artist and Libby loved his expressive, colourful style, as did the majority of the art world. The value of his work was going up and up year by year. She was so proud of him. What a long way he had come since that first exhibition she had been to of his art GSCE work at school – abstract geometrical prints had been his preferred subject matter at the time. Just as well that had only been a phase, she smiled to herself.

Chapter Five

That Friday night Libby finally had a taste of the local nightlife. A huge group of guests from the hostel decided to hit the local club, Music on the Rocks, after a boozy session in Luca's bar. Libby spent the night dancing with an American surfer named Bret who had been staying in the hostel that week. It felt so good to let her hair down and lose herself in the music. Luca watched from the side, having joined them after the bar shut for the night, and it felt great to feel the jealousy radiating from him as she moved closer and closer to Bret. She knew it was a bit childish but she couldn't help it. She wanted Luca to want her. She could tell Bret was seriously into her, but she was enjoying the power-play too much to give in and kiss him. Instead she headed to the bar to order more shots with some Aussie girls who were gathered there. They had danced all night, ending up swimming in various states of undress in the sea.

The next day was spent in a hung-over haze down on the beach, sleeping and swimming, eating and hanging out, while Diego, a Spanish guy who had been at La Casetta for a few days, brought out his guitar and strummed away. Libby sipped on cold beer, her chosen hair of the dog, and listened to the music. It was all so far removed from her normal life; she couldn't imagine it ever coming to an end. She didn't want it to.

That evening, Maria was covering Luca in the bar. He had the evening off. Libby saw him heading out through the door and called down to him from the balcony to wait up. She met him on the steps leading down from the hostel.

'Hey!'

'Hi.'

'Are you getting food? Can I join you? What do you fancy? Pizza?'

'I'm not sure. Yeah probably,' Luca shrugged.

'I'm in the mood for a pizza. Let's go to Marco's and get one to take away?'

'OK.' Luca hardly seemed thrilled at the prospect. He had been off with her all day. She wondered if it was due to her flirtation with Bret – perhaps her tactics had worked? She chattered away to him as they walked down to Marco's. Placing their orders, they watched as the guy behind the counter loaded up the dough with tomato, mozzarella and pepperoni before shovelling it into the pizza oven. Libby's mouth watered as the dough rose and the cheese began to bubble, golden brown. Clutching their boxes, they went to sit on the wall overlooking the beach, with an excellent view of what promised to be a glorious sunset.

They sat quietly, eating their pizzas and soaking up the view as the sun sank into the sea. Libby kept up a stream of chatter, but Luca's responses were fairly monosyllabic. When they had finished eating and the sun had set, they made their way back up towards La Casetta. Luca lagged behind.

Just before they turned the final bend that would lead to the steps and the yellow front door, Libby stopped and turned to face him. Unable to bear the tension any longer she said, 'So are you going to tell me what's up?'

Luca stopped. 'What do you mean?' His brow was furrowed, his dark eyes looked troubled.

'Oh come on, Luca! It's obvious that you are annoyed with me and I want you to tell me why.'

Luca was silent for a few minutes. He gave out a deep sigh. 'I saw you flirting with Bret last night—'

'Oh come on. What's wrong with a bit of harmless flirting?'

'I know it's crazy but I can't help it... It really upset me.'

'What do you mean?'

'Look Libby, if you are going to make me spell it out for you, then I will. I like you. Not just as a friend, I mean I like you. I really like you.' He ran his hands through his hair and rubbed his temples. He looked so upset, she realised he must be serious.

Libby's heart pounded as she realised the implication of what he had just said, feeling overwhelmed at the strength of her reaction to this news. She was ridiculously happy that the crush she had been trying so hard to stifle was in fact reciprocated. But at the same time she realised it was an utterly hopeless case.

'Oh,' she said. She couldn't think of anything else to say.

'When I saw you dancing with him, I felt so jealous. I had to walk away before I chased after him and punched him in the face.'

Libby looked at him and smiled sheepishly. 'I had no idea. I'm sorry. It was harmless flirting. It didn't really mean anything.'

'It's not your fault. You don't like me in the same way, I know that.' He sighed, looking extremely sorry for himself.

'That's not strictly speaking true, Luca.' She took a deep breath as he looked up at her, a glimmer of curiosity on his face. 'I thought you weren't interested in me. Part of the reason I was flirting with Bret was to stop myself from thinking about you. I do like you. Really, I do. My feelings have been getting stronger each day since I arrived. But... I know we would be an absolute disaster. You don't want a relationship. I don't think I could move from a friend to a friend with benefits and just be OK with that. I know you don't believe in monogamy. I'm leaving in a couple of months – it could never end well.'

Luca smiled at her, a dazzling smile that wrenched her heart. He took her hand in his. 'Libby, I know we haven't known each other that long, but the truth is I am absolutely crazy about you. I have been thinking about you nonstop every second of every day. First thing in the morning when I wake up I see you, last thing before I go to sleep I see you. I am not interested in any other women.'

'But you said it yourself; you fall in love and then out of love again just as easily. You are besotted until you are not. I can't handle that, Luca. I'm either in or I'm out. I can't set myself up to get hurt.'

'Look, Libby, what if I changed?' Luca said. 'My sisters are always telling me sooner or later I'll meet someone special and that'll be it. That I'll change and she will be the one for me, just like that.'

'No one ever changes that much,' Libby sighed. She suddenly felt seriously emotional. She could feel tears welling up in her eyes.

'I think I can. I will.' Luca took a step closer to her. 'Give me a chance?'

'I don't know…'

'Please?'

'I'm sorry, Luca, I just don't think it's a good idea. I don't want to get hurt.' He ignored her and took another step towards her. It was so quiet; she was suddenly aware of the sound of her heart hammering against her rib cage. Her head spun with this turn of events.

Time slowed down as Luca inched closer and closer towards her. Electricity thrummed through her body, pulse after pulse. She felt as though a magnetic force was pulling them together. She forgot to breathe. The balmy warm air and the sheer beauty of her surroundings added to the heady sense of longing she was experiencing. She felt absorbed in the magic of the place, of the moment. She tried to force the thought of all the other hundreds of women he had kissed before out of her mind. He took hold of the back of her arms. His mouth was millimetres from hers, hovering irresistibly close to her lips. She could feel his breath on her cheeks. She felt dizzy with lust, dizzy with the musky smell of his aftershave. He stroked the back of her arms with his thumbs, sending thrills down her spine. She thought she might pass out from longing.

'*Sei bellissima*, Libby,' he whispered. Slowly, he grazed his lips against hers. At the touch of their lips a pulse of electricity kicked through her pelvis with incredible force. Tantalisingly slowly, he brushed his lips with hers once again, so softly it was barely a kiss. Her whole body started to tremble. She was desperate for him to kiss her properly but he refused. He stroked her hair and he moved his kisses to her cheekbone, her temple, her eyelids and then back to her lips. Her body was tingling with longing. After what felt like a thousand torturous kisses he stopped and pulled away. She opened her eyes in confusion, willing him to kiss her again.

'I think I had better go home,' Luca said. 'I'm serious, *bellissima*, about my feelings for you. I think this could be different for me, I really do. Will you at least think about it?' Libby was rooted to the spot, speechless. She nodded.

'*A domani, bellissima, la mia piccola inglesina*,' he said. He lifted her hand and kissed it, before turning on his heel and walking away, leaving her senses reeling.

Chapter Six

Libby spent a sleepless night tossing and turning in her bed, tormented by thoughts of Luca. Everything had changed for her since that first kiss. By chance she had a day off the next day, and so did Luca. He texted her first thing asking her if she wanted to meet up. She was torn between playing safe with her emotions – protecting herself from potential upset, and living in the moment, following her instincts. Her heart wanted to run into Luca's arms and see where the journey took her, but her head was urging her to proceed with caution. She leant out the window to get signal on her phone and called Jules. There was no way she was going to risk someone overhearing this conversation.

'Jules? It's me.'

'Hi Libs. To what do I owe the pleasure of a phone call at this early hour of the morning?'

'I need to talk.'

'What's going on?

'It's Luca.'

'The hot barman?'

'Yes… despite my determination not to, I have really started to like him—'

'Ooh Libby, I *knew* it!'

'He saw me flirting with this American guy called Bret, and yesterday I could tell he was in a mood with me.'

'Right…'

'I confronted him and forced him to tell me why he was acting so strangely.'

'What did he say?'

'He told me that he had feelings for me, that he'd seen me with Bret and had been really jealous, that he wanted me to give him a chance.'

'*Whaat?* This is *huge!*'

'I know!'

'What are you going to do?'

'I don't know. This is the guy who told me when I first met him that he doesn't "do" monogamy. That he falls in love easily, but just as easily out of love…'

'Well, he hadn't fallen for you then, Libs. You might be the one to change everything!'

'Unlikely. I always thought it sounded romantic being the woman to tame a serial ladies' man, but now I'm not so sure. It just sounds like a recipe for heartbreak.'

'Anything is possible Lib—'

'And I'm also going to be leaving in a couple of months.'

'So what? See how it goes… You can't plan your whole life out. Just live each day as it comes.'

'So you think I should go for it?'

'Absolutely. What have you got to lose? Sure, it could all go wrong and you might end up with a broken heart, but at least you will have given it a shot. Hearts always mend…'

'You're right,' Libby said thoughtfully. 'Nothing lasts forever. Look at Mum…'

'Exactly. She'll never stop loving Ronald but time has definitely healed her. And that was losing the love of her life *and* her husband.'

'Yes, that's true… God, I'm suddenly terrified.'

'Well I'm excited for you. What are you going to do? Run downstairs and jump over the bar?'

'He wants to meet up. We both have a day off.'

'Ah, perfect! But whatever you do, don't jump straight into bed with him.'

'Jules, I'm hardly going to shag him immediately.'

'And to *think* I've only ever slept with Angus – it kills me!'

'You've had way less drama that way, Jules. It's better, trust me.'

'Yeah, yeah. Now don't be a slut.'

'I won't,' Libby laughed.

'And good luck. Text me later.'

'OK.'

Libby hung up the phone. She felt a lot better having spoken to Jules. There was a reason why she had chosen to call Jules and not Angus; she knew exactly what he would say. He would be furious with her for pursuing yet another pointless romance that could lead nowhere. Anyway, Jules was right, you only lived once. What was the worst that could happen? She only had two months left – she might as well enjoy a summer of fun with Luca. It was unlikely that it would last much longer than that. Libby was not sold on the idea of a long-distance relationship, and she could hardly imagine either of them changing their plans and relocating for one another. No, it would probably just be a summer romance, that was all. If she ended up moving back home with a broken heart, then so be it. The old cliché 'better to have loved and lost than never to have loved at all' popped into her mind.

A shot of adrenaline rushed through her as she grabbed her phone and replied to Luca's message. They agreed that he would pick her up and drive her to a small beach that he had told her about a while ago. Ten minutes later she was standing on the road with her small rucksack full of beach gear, her heart pounding nervously as Luca's red Fiat pulled over. She jumped in.

'*Ciao bella*,' Luca bent over and kissed her on the cheek. Her heart flipped at the sight of him. He grinned at her with raised eyebrows and she laughed.

'So?' he asked.

'So?' she replied.

'Do you accept my proposition?'

She shrugged her shoulders nonchalantly, saying, 'Why not?' She laughed as Luca tooted the horn enthusiastically, startling a pair of old grannies crossing the road outside the butcher's as he revved his engine.

'*Mi amore*, that makes me so happy. I promise, no funny business. You have my heart's complete devotion.'

'Let's just see how it goes, Luca.' Libby wanted to keep him on his toes. 'I'm only here for two more months anyway. So you might get your way… you'll probably be sick of the sight of me by then.'

'Don't talk about leaving. I can't bear it. I will be heartbroken.'

'We'll see!'

'But until then, we are together?'

'We can see how it goes,' she repeated.

'*Bellissima*, you have made me a very happy man.' Luca sang cheerfully along to the radio as he drove, turning his head regularly to beam at Libby, his hand resting on her knee.

As they neared their destination, Luca took a hairpin turn to the right then manoeuvred the car into a tiny parking space between a three-wheeler and a small van. He opened the door for Libby, pulling her close to him and kissing her briefly on the lips. She couldn't wait for him to kiss her properly, and tingled at the thought with nervous anticipation.

Luca led the way down a hidden set of steps to a deserted beach. The small wooden sign saying '*spiaggia*' was hanging from one nail, so faded it was hard to read. 'Only locals know about this beach,' explained Luca. 'We all try very hard to keep it a secret.' He was carrying a freezer bag that he had packed with cool drinks and lunch, because there was no beach bar or restaurant down below.

'Once you have climbed down all these steps, you certainly don't want to have to come back up until it is time to leave,' he said. Libby could see why. Steep stone steps had been carved into the cliff. There must have been close to fifty of them, zigzagging down a sheer drop to the sea. The sight of the beach below was an enormous incentive to make it down in one piece. The golden arc of sand was framed by a riot of greenery and brightly coloured bougainvillaea. Large boulders appeared to have been thrown at various intervals across the beach and into the sea. As always the water was so crystal clear it almost seemed to magnify the detail of the seabed below.

Soon they were setting up camp on the beach: towels side by side, umbrella firmly embedded into the sand between the two of them. The sun was beating down and they were both desperate to get in the water. Libby ripped off her dress and ran into the sea, with Luca chasing close behind. They fell into the cool water, laughing as they splashed each other and shrieking as their skin adjusted to the plunging temperature. They swam out into the deep water and dived under. They were the only ones there, apart from one other sun-seeker at the far end. It was amazing, like having their own private beach. They swam closer to the shore so that they could stand. Luca pulled Libby closer to him and kissed her, properly this time. She could smell his aftershave again and taste the salty water on his lips. She could feel him pressing against her hips and could tell how much he wanted her. It felt so good to kiss him, to finally allow herself to cave in to all the desire she had been suppressing. She could have kissed him forever. He was certainly an expert; all the practice had definitely paid off.

'Wow!' she said as he pulled away several minutes later. His brown eyes sparkled in the sunlight and beads of water glistened on his mahogany skin. He looked devastatingly handsome.

'Yes, wow!' laughed Luca. She dived under the water and swept the hair away from her face before swimming back to shore. They lay on their towels and chatted, Luca frequently interrupting their conversation with kisses. 'I've been wanting to kiss you for so long,' he said as he kissed the tip of her nose. 'You are so beautiful.'

When she had dried off he rubbed sun cream on her then they dozed in the sun. She lay her head on his lap, resting against the damp fabric of his swimming trunks.

At lunchtime they tore into Luca's picnic. He had brought cold prosecco, water, sandwiches, crisps and strawberries. After they had eaten they fell asleep, their stomachs full, feeling relaxed and rather light-headed from the prosecco they had shared. Later, as the sun began to drop lower in the sky and the temperature gradually fell, Luca retrieved a bat and ball from his bag and they played beach tennis. They cooled off in the sea before eventually calling it a day, packing up and heading back into Positano. Libby accompanied Luca to his flat, greeting Nicola with a kiss as she came through the door. She was busy preparing some delicious-looking lamb chops in a thick marinade.

'Are you staying for dinner?' she asked.

'Yes please,' replied Libby. 'That looks incredible. What's in the marinade?' she asked, always keen to pick up cooking tips.

Nicola talked her through it. 'Giovanna is coming around too, by the way,' she added.

'Ah, the sister I haven't yet met,' laughed Libby. 'Great!' She had met Antonia, the oldest sister, and her husband Matteo one evening in the bar. Giovanna, the youngest of Luca's three sisters, had been away on business for the past month and had only recently arrived back in Positano. Luca drove Libby back to the hostel to run in and get a change of clothes.

'*Ciao Giulia*,' said Libby. Giulia was sitting behind the reception desk doodling on a pad.

'Where are you off to in such a hurry?' she asked as Libby rushed past her.

'Luca's waiting in the car. I'm just grabbing a change of clothes before dinner.'

'Really?' asked Giulia, one eyebrow arching towards her hairline and her mouth settling into a pout. Libby hoped Giulia wouldn't disapprove of her now that she and Luca were seeing each other. As Luca had said, wasn't it all water under the bridge between them? If she took against the idea, it could make for a rather frosty working environment. She wondered once again whether Giulia was jealous, or just trying to protect Libby from getting hurt.

Libby grabbed her coral dress, a fresh set of underwear and a pair of earrings, then turned and ran back downstairs. 'See you later,' she called, waving cheerily at Giulia.

Luca was waiting with the engine running, having turned the car back around. He drove her back to his apartment. She showered in his huge power shower, rinsed out her wet bikini and got dressed, hanging her bikini on Luca's balcony to dry off. She had already decided that she would walk home later; it would be a while until she felt ready to spend the night with him and she knew sleeping in the same bed would prove too much temptation for her to resist. For now she just wanted to enjoy the early stages of a new romance.

Giovanna arrived half an hour later. She had a mass of bouncing curls that seemed desperate to break free from her hair tie. 'Libby it's lovely to meet you. My brother has mentioned you quite a few times,' laughed Giovanna.

'It's a pleasure to meet you too. Now, apart from the parents, I've met the whole family.'

'Oh you must meet our parents,' said Nicola. 'They would absolutely love you.'

'And she will, soon,' added Luca, kissing her on the cheek. Libby blushed as she noticed both Giovanna and Nicola exchange a grin at this display of affection from their brother.

They had a happy dinner, chatting and teasing Luca, as always, at any opportunity. Libby relaxed into their company, feeling part of the family. They were all so easy-going, such warm people. Luca was very tactile with her now, resting his hand on her knee or putting his arm around her shoulder, dropping kisses on her head when he walked past to get another bottle of wine. It was amazing how simply getting your feelings out in the open and being honest with one another changed the dynamic of a relationship so completely.

Later that night, Luca walked her home. She was grateful that he didn't try to persuade her to stay, that he respected her and clearly wasn't only interested in getting her into bed. As they stood outside the hostel she found it hard to tear herself away from his increasingly passionate kisses. Eventually she found the strength to turn and walk up the steps, letting herself in through the yellow door before turning to blow him a final kiss. Beaming from ear to ear, she came through into the reception.

'Have fun?' asked Giulia as Libby hastily wiped the grin from her face.

'Lovely thanks,' said Libby. 'Giovanna and Nicola were there; they're both so nice.'

'Mmm,' said Giulia. Again, she hardly seemed thrilled that Luca and Libby were growing so close.

Libby went up to her room and closed the door, allowing the smirk to come back on to her face. She really, really liked him! And he really seemed to like her. Despite their different nationalities and the complete implausibility that they would work out as a couple, she couldn't shake the feeling that this could be the beginning of something amazing. She fell asleep with the shadow of a smile tracing her lips.

On her days off, now always coinciding, thanks to Floriana, Luca took her to incredible local restaurants, well off the tourist trail. They went out on the boat with Gian Matteo and they drove all over the Amalfi coast, finding hidden coves and hiking along hilltop paths. Libby felt heady with happiness; she felt herself falling hook, line and sinker for Luca. Likewise, Luca seemed absolutely smitten, utterly devoted to her, the perfect gentleman, constantly spoiling her. He introduced her with pride to his parents, choosing his father's birthday as the perfect opportunity.

Things were going so well that during a phone call with her mother she decided to tell her about Luca.

'So, Mum, I've actually been dating someone out here for the past few weeks,' confessed Libby.

'Really darling, how fabulous.' Her mother sounded delighted. 'Is he Italian?'

'Yes, he is.'

'How exciting! So… who is he? Tell me all about him.' Libby proceeded to tell her mum all about Luca and his family; her mum seemed impressed that she had already met his parents. When Libby had finished answering all Miriam's questions, they moved on to discussing Helen.

'Have you heard from her recently?'

'No, not for a couple of weeks. I've been meaning to call her,' Libby said, guiltily. She'd been so occupied with Luca recently, all other thoughts seemed to have gone out of the window.

'I'm going to send her an email this afternoon. I've taken to writing a weekly update of any news I can think of, though it has to be said it is quite boring – not much goes on in Kent these days. But I feel it's important not to let her feel too cut off.'

'I know. I don't feel as though I've got a good enough idea of what her life out there is like yet.'

'Well I'm glad it's not just me,' said Miriam.

'No, it certainly isn't anything personal. I hope she's all right.'

'Me too.'

'I'll call her at the weekend. I usually have a better chance of catching her when she isn't at work.'

'OK, well let me know if you manage to get through... And good for you, darling, getting back out there on the dating scene. I'm proud of you.' It had been about six months since she had broken up with her last boyfriend, once again not feeling that he was quite right for her.

'Thanks Mum!' said Libby. 'Speak soon.'

'Love you.'

'Love you too, bye!'

The next day Libby got a surprising phone call from her sister. Miriam had obviously mentioned the fact that Libby was dating someone in her email, which had clearly piqued Helen's interest.

'Mum tells me you're seeing someone!' said Helen. 'An Italian stallion, I hear!'

'Ah, Mum's good old weekly update... yes, I thought she might mention it. I was going to call you this weekend actually, but you beat me to it!'

'So... who is he? I'm intrigued.'

65

'He's actually a colleague of sorts. He runs the bar in the hostel here and he's also a freelance graphic designer.'

'What's his name?'

'Luca Morelli.'

'Luca… and you're quite keen on him?'

'Yes I am actually. He is kind of amazing.'

'How so?'

'He just looks after me pretty well, treats me all the time – and we have fun.'

'Lucky you!' said Helen. 'Though goodness knows how you find these eligible men – I'm clearly doing something wrong. It's only six months since you ended things with Nick, isn't it?'

'Don't worry, Hels, it will happen for you soon. I guess it's mainly just chance…'

'Mmm, I'm not so sure.'

'And taking a risk on someone once in a while…' Libby trailed off. She tried to think of something helpful to say.

'Well, I try to be open to possibilities,' said Helen. 'There just don't seem to be many decent men around.'

'I know you do, and it will happen, I know it will. Just keep on getting out and about and – sooner or later – someone great will come along.'

'We'll see. It's just quite tough trying to meet new people. Well, for me, anyway – you don't seem to have had much of a problem in Positano.'

'It just so happens that Luca worked in the same place as me, that's all. Pure coincidence… You need someone who can act as your wingman,' Libby told her sister.

'I thought I had that. A German girl called Rosanna, but she's seeing someone now so she isn't really around much.'

'Oh dear! That's annoying. Is there anyone else you can go out with?'

'I'm fine,' her sister told her firmly, changing the subject. 'Anyway, I'm busy with work, so that's good.'

Relieved that Helen had moved off the subject of their respective love lives, Libby quizzed her sister about the school she was working in and listened to her describing her new job in more detail. By the time she ended the call she felt a little better about Helen's mental state. She was still fragile, there was no doubt about that, but her job seemed to be going well and she seemed to have a nice group of colleagues. Libby phoned her mum to let her know Helen's news. She was glad they had had a good catch-up at long last, though she did wish her sister would meet someone. She couldn't help feeling that a new man was just what Helen needed.

Chapter Seven

By the end of August, Libby and Luca had been seeing each other for over six weeks. They had finally slept together, and Libby had been overwhelmed at the strength of her feelings for him when it happened. Making him wait had certainly paid off; he had driven her wild with lust. She had felt like a goddess being worshipped, and since then barely a night had gone past when they hadn't made love. They had also established a great friendship. He had helped her discover more and more hidden treasures in the local area, and they never seemed to run out of conversation, both enjoying finding out more and more about each other and their very different lives to date.

On one of their double days off Luca told her that he had planned a surprise. 'You need to pack a small bag with enough clothes for two nights,' he said.

'Where are we going?' Libby asked. 'How exciting!'

'I'm not telling you!' he laughed. He clearly enjoyed keeping her in suspense and refused to say a word.

They drove along the coast towards Ravello, turning up into the hills and following a winding road that led away from the sea. She couldn't imagine what he had planned.

'No one has ever taken me away on a surprise like this before,' said Libby. 'It's so fun not knowing where we are going.'

After about twenty-five minutes, they pulled into the driveway of a luxury five-star hotel.

'No!' gasped Libby. 'We aren't staying here?' She looked at Luca, who was grinning at her and nodding his head.

'We are. I've booked us into a suite for two nights!'

'Oh my god, this place is ridiculous!' Libby squealed with delight as she leapt out of the car and ran over to the side of the car park to look at the view. It was even more magnificent than the view from Ravello.

'It is run by my cousin. They had a last-minute cancellation, so he's given it to me as a very special favour. Just wait till you see the pool!' laughed Luca. He took her hand and led her down a series of steps, past the reception and out to the swimming pool. It was an infinity pool that seemed to topple off the edge of the cliff, with a truly breathtaking panorama of the Amalfi coastline down below.

'Wow.' Libby was lost for words. She grabbed Luca and pulled him towards her, kissing him and muttering, 'Thank you, thank you, thank you! I don't know how I can thank you enough – this place is *incredible*.'

'Don't worry,' said Luca, leaning to whisper in her ear. 'I'll show you exactly how you can thank me as soon as we get into our room.' She felt shivers of anticipation run down her spine at the thought.

The rooms were just as you would expect from a five-star hotel. There were only twelve of them and each one was decorated differently. Theirs was named 'Bali' and was decked out in Balinese wooden furniture and brightly coloured cushions. Libby had never felt so spoilt. The hotel was full of couples on honeymoon, and Libby felt just as deliriously happy as any one of them. They spent the two nights entwined in each other's arms, tearing themselves from bed to spend blissful sun-drenched hours by the pool, eating the delicious food provided by the restaurant under a canopy of stars, and taking walks around the surrounding countryside. Libby felt herself falling head over heels for Luca; he was surpassing her expectations in every way and, though she knew they were living in a fantasy bubble, that this hedonistic holiday romance was far removed from the reality of a real, day-to-day existence back in the real world, a proper relationship, she was so glad she had given him a chance.

On their subsequent days off they had visited Amalfi and many other beautiful towns and villages. They had also spent a day walking around the ruins of Pompeii, the fulfilment of a long-held ambition for Libby. She had been reading about the ancient city in a book from the hostel's library, and had been astonished to learn all about the ancient civilisation that had inhabited the ghostly town. Her imagination was carried away by the stories. She couldn't believe that the people who lived there hadn't even known that Vesuvius was a volcano, that it had been dormant for nearly two thousand years until that fateful day. It was amazing to think that the city and all its secrets had lain buried until the late eighteenth century. It felt strange to be walking the streets where so many people had lost their lives. She was intrigued by the plaster casts on display. During the excavation, archaeologists had poured plaster into the cavities left by human remains, creating exact moulds of the people of Pompeii as they had met their sorrowful end: mid-flight, covering their mouths with their hands and hugging their children close to them, trying to protect them from the falling ash. It was a truly sobering sight and she was glad that she had finally visited the ruins for herself.

Luca and Libby had also explored the islands of Capri and Ischia, taking day trips with Gian Matteo and various other friends; swimming in the Grotta Azzurra and visiting Ischia's hot springs. Her summer of love had certainly been epic, and her eyes filled with tears whenever she thought of it all coming to an end. There were only a few weeks left before her flight home on 23rd September. This left her just about a week to get settled back into her flat and mentally prepared to start her training contract on 1st October. It seemed another world away.

One morning Floriana came bustling down to the reception desk in a fluster. 'Cara, Andrea just phoned, she has got a vomiting bug. *Dio mio!* Do you think you can be an angel and do some cleaning today while I man the desk? My back just isn't good enough to be bending over and doing that sort of work. Gabi is coming in to cover her from tomorrow, but she isn't around today.' Gabriella was a young girl who cleaned on Andrea's days off.

'Poor Andrea. Of course I can! I'm more than happy to do the cleaning. Just tell me what you want me to do.'

Floriana thanked her and set her off with various tasks. She had to gather the laundry and bundle it up ready for collection, unpack the fresh delivery when it arrived, sweep and mop and dust the hostel and finally clean the bathrooms. It was tiring yet satisfying work.

Libby had left the toilets, her least favourite job, till last. Eventually she reached the last one. She dumped her bucket of cleaning products on the floor and began scrubbing away. 'Damn!' she said, accidentally knocking a box of tampons off the back of the loo. They rolled all over the floor, scattering this way and that. Libby chased after them, scooping them up in her gloved hand and shoving them back into the box. Suddenly a thought occurred to her. It seemed an awfully long time since she had had to buy any tampons. As she finished cleaning the bathroom, she tried to calculate when her last period had been. She knew it had been during the first week that she and Luca had been dating. This meant that her period should have arrived over a week ago… she was at least a week late.

She raced back to her room, dumping the cleaning products, mop and broom in the cleaning cupboard en route. She grabbed

71

her diary to check her dates. Her heart was beating so fast she could feel it pulsing against her chest. She skimmed through the pages of her diary. She was right. She felt a sheen of sweat break out across her brow. She was never, ever late. She and Luca had slept together so many times; maybe one of those times the condom had slipped off, or broken, and they hadn't noticed? She felt her blood run cold. She had to get her hands on a pregnancy test, but in this small village, how the hell would she get away with it without anyone seeing? Thinking quickly, she decided to get a taxi to Amalfi in her lunch break. She would go for a walk and book it to meet her up the road; then she would jump in and keep it on the meter as she ran into the pharmacy.

Her plan came off unhindered and, by the end of her lunch break, she was back in the hostel, the paper bag with enclosed pregnancy tests concealed safely in her room. Her mind was completely unfocused as she took to the reception desk, relieving Floriana.

'Are you all right, *cara*?' Floriana asked. 'You look rather pale.'

'Oh, I'm fine thanks! Probably just got a little head rush from bending over so much this morning.' Libby laughed it off. She took refuge behind the desk, going about her duties with one eye firmly fixed on the clock, sipping water and counting down the hours until Giulia arrived to take over.

Eventually she came through the door. As soon as they had done the usual cursory handover, Libby legged it back upstairs. She took the twin-pack of pregnancy tests into the bathroom and read the instructions several times, making sure she had translated them correctly. It was pretty clear: pee on the stick for five seconds, replace the cap and wait three minutes.

She followed the instructions and within moments was waiting nervously for the results. She couldn't bear to look at the window which would soon reveal her fate, so she covered it with the box. Her heart was still thumping like crazy as she prayed fervently for it to show a single line rather than a cross. Surely the fates wouldn't be so cruel. She didn't want a baby now; it was the last thing on earth she needed. She crossed her fingers and stared at her watch as the three minutes came to an end. Terrified, she kicked the box out of the way to reveal the test.

There was a big blue cross in the results window. Frantically she grabbed the paper, surely it couldn't be… The instructions said '+ = pregnant'. It was there as clear as day. She unwrapped the second test and peed on it once again, grateful for all the water she had drunk that afternoon. It must be a false alarm. She stared at the results window this time, willing it to have a single line. But sure enough, a second cross appeared, faint at first but getting darker and darker. She wanted to scream in horror. The result was clear: she was pregnant. What the hell was she going to do?

Chapter Eight

She stayed on the bathroom floor for about forty-five minutes, feeling faint with panic and anxiety. Eventually coming to her senses, she stumbled back to her room and slammed the door. Her heart was pounding loudly in her ears. She felt as though all the blood had drained from her head to her feet, making her feel dizzy. She lay on her bed and took a deep breath. Her eyes filled with tears.

How could she have been so stupid? she thought. *How on earth had she got herself into this mess?* This was by far the worst situation she had ever found herself in. She knew she had messed up in the past, but this was far beyond anything that had happened before. A baby… This wasn't something she could brush off, or run away from. This was real and growing inside her: an inescapable, unavoidable reality to face.

She suddenly felt feverishly hot. She flung the window open and gulped in some fresh air. Her head was spinning so fast she was struggling to make sense of her thoughts. She needed to get out of La Casetta. She needed to avoid seeing Luca, or anyone, until she had had some time to think. As luck would have it, her rota was free for the following two days. Making quick decisions, she stuffed some clothes into a bag, packed a few valuables and slipped out through the door. Giulia was in the bar talking to Maria. Hardly daring to breathe, Libby sneaked out of the hostel, closing the door behind her. Breathing a sigh of relief she walked quickly up the hill, her pulse racing, nervously checking over her shoulder to see if she had been spotted. She knew where she was aiming for; on the edge of the village there was a rickety car-hire shop that was open twenty-four hours a day. As the dusk settled she pounded the pavement, cutting through the back streets until she reached her destination. Without asking any questions, the elderly man behind the desk took a copy of her licence and showed her out to a small hire car. Thanking him, she flung her bag into the boot and turned on the ignition. She remembered how perilously steep the roads were and crossed her fingers that there wouldn't be too much traffic around, given the time of day.

Putting her foot on the accelerator she set off, turning inland and away from the dangerous coastal roads at the first opportunity. She drove for a couple of hours, finally finding herself in a sleepy village with a small bed and breakfast. Parking outside she grabbed her bag and rang the bell. To her relief they had a room available. A middle-aged lady showed her upstairs. As soon as she left, Libby shut the door, grateful to have found refuge somewhere far away from prying eyes. The tears that she had been holding back spilt freely down her cheeks. She collapsed on to her bed and cried. She reached into her bag and found her phone, sending Luca a text to explain that she had gone to meet a friend from the UK who had suddenly called to tell her she was passing through on a cycling holiday. She told him she would be back either the following day or the day after. He seemed satisfied with her excuse. She lay back on the pillows once again, her mind spinning. She kept staring at her stomach, still as flat as a pancake, trying to imagine what was going on in there. Eventually she drifted off to sleep.

The next morning she woke up in confusion as she assessed her new surroundings. It took her several minutes to figure out where she was. All too quickly the memories of the day before came flooding back. The familiar tide of panic rose once more up her throat. She wanted nothing more than to run away from the situation, but this time she couldn't. She was stuck. She had behaved irresponsibly one too many times and now here she was, with no choice but to face up to the fact that she was pregnant by her Italian lover, her summer romance. It had been a while since she had had any food, so she made herself go down and get some breakfast and a cup of coffee, even though the last thing she felt like doing was eating.

Back in her room, she sat and stared out of the window, looking down at the little garden, lost in her thoughts. She wasn't sure whether her relationship with Luca was strong enough to cope with a bombshell like this. It was all very well being swept up in a bubble of new love when you knew you only had the summer together, but in her heart of hearts she didn't think the relationship would survive when she moved back to London. Even with the best intentions, being physically separated from your partner was never easy. Luca would be working at the hostel, while Libby would be starting the most intense eighteen months of her life with her training contract. This brought another wave of utter panic crashing down over Libby. Her training contract... what would she do about that? She had worked so hard and for so long to finally, *finally* get her act together and sort her life out... she would have no choice but to tell her employers. She could hardly disguise a pregnancy, not to mention the fact that in less than nine months' time she would have to leave to have the baby. She rocked back and forth on her chair, the tears spilling down her cheeks once again. This really was a disaster. She felt utterly helpless and completely trapped.

Pulling herself together, she knew she had to face some facts. She had no choice but to deal with this in the best way she could. She needed to make sure she was properly informed. She got out her phone and typed in the B & B's Wi-Fi code. She opened her browser and navigated her way to the NHS webpage about pregnancy. When it downloaded, she read through the advice offered to her. She found out that she would need to contact her GP as soon as possible. The NHS's due date calculator told her that she was five weeks pregnant, according to the date of the first day of her last period. She would need to see a midwife in about three weeks, in the same hospital in which she would have the baby. Her head spun. Her eyes were drawn to the section which said, 'Pregnant and don't know what to do.' Taking a deep breath, she scrolled down and read the options available to her. She could have an abortion. That would be one way of getting herself out of this situation once and for all. She was sure she would be able to find somewhere to do it in Italy; she could probably even find somewhere that very same day if she drove into Naples. She could take a pill and be rid of the baby then and there. She knew that it was the right choice for some, but it had never been something she had felt she would be able to do. At the thought she felt a surge of protectiveness for the fledgling life growing inside her.

Besides, she knew of enough friends who had been trying to have a baby, only to suffer from miscarriage after miscarriage, to know that perhaps the pregnancy might not last anyway. The NHS page said that one in six pregnancies ended in miscarriage. So maybe this would all disappear naturally. Perhaps she should just sit tight and hope for the best? Maybe the problem would sort itself out.

She lay on her bed and felt tears running down her face once again. This was not her plan. If the baby didn't miscarry she would be giving birth the following April. How was she meant to start her training contract pregnant? What would they say? What would her mum say? What would Luca say? What would Angus say? She dreaded to think. He already thought she was irresponsible enough; the thought of the look on his face when he found out made her stomach churn. Her mind whirled with a cyclone of tormented thoughts. She drew her knees up to her chest and shut her eyes, trying to calm herself down.

Later that day she went for a walk through the village and into the surrounding countryside. She was feeling pretty under the weather and she thought some fresh air might help her feel better. She couldn't work out whether it was morning sickness or the fact she hadn't slept a wink the night before. She suspected it was the latter. She felt sick at the thought of food but knew she had to eat, so she bought a panini and a bottle of water en route. She decided to call Jules. She couldn't tell her mother, and her sister was the last person she wanted to talk to right now, but she just had to speak to someone before she went completely insane. She would have to make Jules swear not to tell Angus. She just couldn't bear the thought of him knowing, how disappointed he would be.

'Jules?'

'Hi Libs, how's tricks?'

'I have serious news. I'm completely freaking out. I don't know what to do...' Libby burst into tears.

'Woah, woah, woah. Tell me what's happened. Are you OK?'

Libby wiped her eyes and tried to steady her breathing; it was coming out in great ragged gasps.

'Take a deep breath, it's OK, Libs. Whatever it is, it will be OK.'

Libby took another deep breath and breathed out a long and shaky exhale. In a barely audible whisper she said, 'I'm pregnant.'

'What? I couldn't hear that...'

'I'm *pregnant*.'

'You're pregnant?' Jules's voice had gone strangely high pitched.

'Yes.'

'What? How?'

'I don't bloody know,' Libby wailed. 'I realised I was a week late and so I did a test yesterday and it said I was—'

'Have you done another one just in case?'

'Yes, I did two.'

'Is it Luca's?'

'Of course. Whose else's would it be?'

'Oh my god.' She could hear how shocked Jules was. 'This is *massive*.'

'Tell me about it.'

'What are you going to do?'

'I have absolutely no idea. My head is spinning. I didn't sleep a wink last night.'

'Are you going to keep it?'

'I'm not sure I can face the alternative.'

'I suppose it might not work out… naturally…'

'I'm hoping that. But what if it does? What the hell will I do then? What do I do now?'

'Have you told Luca?'

'No. I needed time to think, so I pretended I was visiting a friend who was passing through the area. I hired a car and drove out to some random village. That's where I am now. I can't tell him; he will completely freak out. And I'm leaving in three weeks, so the timing couldn't be worse. I'm starting my new job – what will they think if I turn up pregnant?!'

'Don't worry about any of that, Libby. It's not ideal, I admit, but it's their problem, not yours, if they don't like it. You'll have it covered by your contract and they'll have to comply. The only thing you need to worry about right now is yourself. You need to concentrate on looking after yourself and you need to tell Luca.'

'Do you think? Shouldn't I just wait and see—?'

'Libby, he's going to know something is up. You can hardly hide a secret like that from your boyfriend… Anyway, it's not fair on you that you should try and handle this by yourself. Just because you're the woman doesn't mean you need to deal with it alone. Tell him.'

'You're right, you're right. I know I have to tell him. I just cannot even begin to imagine what his reaction will be.'

'There's only one way to find out. He has a right to know.'

'I'm terrified!' Libby rubbed her forehead with her hand. 'This is the kind of thing you always hear about and think thank god it's not happening to me. But it *is* happening to me. I am *that* girl. The girl who got pregnant out of wedlock, in a new relationship, in another bloody country…'

'Libby, everything happens for a reason. You know that. If this is meant to be it will somehow work out. Maybe Luca will move to London; maybe you will end up getting married. Life doesn't always have to happen in the order you would expect.'

'God, I can't even think that far ahead.'

'Don't. Just take each day as it comes, that's all you can do. Look, Libs, I'm so sorry but I've got to go into a meeting…'

'OK. But Jules, you have to swear to me one thing…'

'Anything.'

'Swear you won't tell Angus.'

'Really?'

'I mean it, Jules. Promise me. This is just between you and me… I don't want *anyone* else to know. What if it all disappears by itself anyway? There is no point upsetting anyone and I know how Angus will react—'

'But—'

80

'No buts, Jules, I mean it. Do you swear?'

'OK, I swear, don't worry…'

'Promise?'

'I promise… now I've really got to go…'

'OK, don't worry, off you go.'

'You'll be fine. Good luck. You are doing the right thing.'

'Thanks.'

'You know whatever happens you will have me by your side, no matter what, right?'

'I know. Thank god for you. Even though you don't even like babies.'

'Angus bloody loves them; he will be at your beck and call. And I'll love yours, of course. It won't be just anyone's baby.' The thought that this pregnancy could end up with a real baby still made her head spin. It was one thing getting her head around the fact she was pregnant – the thought that there would be an actual child at the end of it was too much.

'Thanks Jules. God, this is so surreal.'

'I know.'

Jules went off to her meeting leaving Libby to work out how she was going to drop the bomb on Luca. She decided to stay a second night in the B & B before driving back to Positano in the morning. Luca was working on a new graphic design commission for a company called Prospero, and she knew he would be driving to Sorrento for a meeting. Maria had swapped a shift with him and would be working in the bar. Libby and Luca were supposed to be going out for dinner together tomorrow evening, so she would have the perfect opportunity to talk to him alone.

She forced herself to eat the sandwich and drink the water; her mouth felt peculiarly dry and she found it difficult to swallow. How could life change so dramatically in an instant?

One moment you were cruising along, everything working out beautifully, as happy as could be, and the next you had stepped off a precipice without realising and found yourself on a completely different plain, in a parallel reality. She stared blankly ahead of her. Even the beauty of her surroundings couldn't lift her spirits. She felt utterly numb and confused.

The following day back at La Casetta passed in a blur. Nervous butterflies jangled in her stomach, making her feel nauseous. Before she knew it Luca was there, kissing her on the lips and saying *'Buonasera, bellissima,'* as he hugged her. Taking her hand he led her out of the hostel and they began to walk into town.

'Can we go to the beach to watch the sunset before dinner?' asked Libby. She wanted to get him by herself, away from prying ears, to tell him her news.

'Of course we can,' said Luca. She was trying to act as normal as possible, but even so she was amazed he couldn't see the secret emblazoned across her face.

'How was the meeting?' she asked.

'It went pretty well, thanks. They are offering me a big commission which would start in the autumn, working on their new website, and on all of the graphics for a new business they are launching next year.'

'That could be perfect for when the high season finishes,' said Libby, already wondering how transportable his freelance work might be.

'Yes, it might work out rather well. It'll be a lot of work, though, combined with my shifts at La Casetta. The good thing is that it'll keep me busy when I am missing you...' The fact that in less than three weeks Libby and Luca would be separated, in different countries, was the elephant in the room that neither of them had wanted to think about. They had both known it was approaching rapidly, despite their best efforts to pretend it wasn't.

They walked along the beach and found a suitable spot to sit. Libby looked out at the golden sea and watched as the waves rolled in. The relentless ebb and flow of the tide comforted her; there was something peaceful and reassuring about it. No matter what happened, life always went on.

'So how was your friend? It was very mysterious of you, disappearing off like that for a couple of days. I thought maybe you were disappearing with a lover!' he chuckled. 'What have you been up to, eh?' he asked.

She took a deep breath and turned to face him. 'Luca, there's something I have to tell you.' Her heart wrenched as she saw the immediate concern shadow his beautiful face.

'OK,' he said, looking quizzically at her.

She bit her lip, unsure how to say it. In the end she just blurted it out. 'I'm pregnant.'

'Pregnant?'

'Yes.'

'Are you sure?'

'I've done two tests. I'm sure.'

Luca let out a slow whistle. 'You are pregnant?' he asked again.

'Yes,' she repeated softly. 'I found out the day before yesterday.'

'*Dio mio*,' he whispered. She could tell his head was reeling in the same way that hers had been, and still was.

'I don't know what to say,' she said. 'I didn't know how to tell you.'

'How did you know?'

'My period was a week late, I suddenly realised. I went to Amalfi to buy tests in case anyone saw me and I did them after work… I was too shocked to talk to anyone. I didn't know what to do. I made up the excuse of seeing my friend but really I just had to get away from here to have some time to think.'

'What do you want to do?'

'I want to keep the baby,' she said, watching him to see his reaction. He nodded slowly. 'Would you want me to get rid of it?' she asked.

He paused then shook his head. 'I'm Catholic, Libby. I am opposed to abortion. Any child is a gift from God. Plus my family would never forgive me.'

She was relieved that he felt the same way.

'This changes everything,' he said. She could tell he was in a deep state of shock. She felt responsible somehow, and kept telling herself it wasn't her fault. 'How did this happen?' he asked. 'We were careful…'

'I don't know. I keep asking myself the same question. We used condoms, every time we've had sex we've used one – the only explanation is that one must have broken or come off without us realising. I feel so irresponsible.'

Luca nodded. 'What will you do about going home?' he asked.

'I can't change my plans,' Libby said. 'I need the money, for starters, and will need the money more than ever if the baby arrives. I can't throw away all my training, all that hard work, and give up my ambitions when this might not even work out.'

'What do you mean?'

'One in six pregnancies miscarry.'

'Really? That's a lot.'

'Exactly. So we have to accept that might happen. Which I am sure would be a relief to us both.'

'But if not, then what?'

'I don't know.'

'I can't leave my job, my flat, my family… I can't just give everything up, my whole life—'

'I know. I wouldn't ask you to.'

'Oh my god, this is impossible,' Luca rested his head on his hands and sighed.

'I'm so sorry,' she whispered, rubbing his shoulders.

'I'm sorry too, Libby,' he said. 'This is a lot for you too.'

They sat side by side and talked through their options, all appetite lost. They decided to wait and see what happened in the next three weeks. Libby would go back to London as planned, and they would let nature take its course. If the pregnancy got as far as twelve weeks when the rate of miscarriage dropped considerably, then they would reconsider.

'So you want to continue being with me?' asked Libby. 'Despite all of this?'

'Libby, I adore you. I am not going to abandon you because you are pregnant – who do you take me for?'

Libby's eyes filled with tears as she realised that she had been anticipating exactly that outcome. 'I think I am falling in love with you,' he said softly, taking her hand.

'Oh Luca, I think I am falling in love with you too.' She smiled through her tears and he took her face in his hands and kissed her. Even as she said the words, she couldn't help but wonder whether it would be enough. It was still so early in their relationship. She knew she had a responsibility towards her unborn child to make a life for them both. She couldn't rely on Luca to make it all OK; she needed to take responsibility herself, to make sure they would be provided for, that they would have everything they needed without being dependent on someone else.

'We will figure this out,' he said. 'I have no idea how, but we will figure this out somehow.'

'Thank you,' she said. 'Thank you for being so supportive.'

Eventually they made their way home, grabbing a pizza margarita to share back at Luca's flat. Libby was grateful to discover that Nicola was out, so they had the flat to themselves. They decided to keep the pregnancy a secret. There was no point in opening that particular can of worms, in fuelling the local gossip, until they knew that the pregnancy would last.

Libby carried on working, Luca carried on running the bar. He was incredibly sweet with her, checking on her frequently, giving her secret smiles and compassionate winks if she looked as if she was struggling. Her morning sickness kicked in during her last week in the form of tiredness. Thankfully there was no sign of nausea or vomiting as yet, so she was able to put on a brave face and hide her symptoms well from Floriana, Tonio and the rest of the team at La Casetta.

On her last night, Tonio cooked a huge meal for her, taking over the terrace with an open invitation to all the friends she had made in her three months in Positano to come and share the feast. Luca and his family were there, Luca firmly by her side. He barely let her out of his sight, unable to bear the thought of her leaving the next day. It was horrible knowing that they were about to be parted. Leaving Positano would have been hard enough, without having to leave her new boyfriend too. She never could have imagined that she would have met someone as wonderful as Luca. God, what a lot had happened in the past few months.

That night as they lay in bed, making love and wiping away each other's tears, they promised that they would make the long-distance relationship work, that they would speak every day and that they would visit each other for the weekend whenever possible. 'I love you, Libby.' Luca kissed her for the hundredth time. 'I am so glad you came into my life. I can't imagine what it's going to be like being here without you. Everywhere I go I will be reminded of you.'

'I love you too,' Libby said. She held him close and dared to hope that everything would somehow work out for them. She had never really considered continuing their relationship once she returned to London, but now the thought of leaving and breaking up with him was impossible. She tried to imagine him fitting in with her life back in the UK. It was so hard to even picture him there. He would be so out of context; he seemed so inextricably linked with the sun and sea, with Positano. The thought of him leaving this life was impossible to imagine, but she knew she couldn't leave everything she had worked so hard to achieve back home. A suspicion of doubt pulsed through her – how could this work? They were bound to each other for a lifetime but, without the baby, would that ever have been the case? Libby tried to force these negative thoughts from her mind.

'We are lucky that we have FaceTime, cheap flights and WhatsApp, you know,' Luca told her. 'In the olden days we would just have had to write each other letters.'

'Exactly, long distance is much easier now. We just have to make it work.'

'So what's the next step for you in terms of the baby?' Luca asked.

'My GP is booked for the day after I get back, then I'll have to go and see a midwife fairly shortly after that. I'll let you know when they schedule me in for my twelve-week scan. It would be great if you can be there for that. Work will have to let me off; I'll probably say I've just got a medical appointment and leave it at that. Oh my god, I dread to think how I will tell them.'

'Don't worry about that yet. So, the twelve-week scan: that will be in about six weeks' time, you think?'

'Yes, I think so.'

'OK well, I will do my best to be there.'

'Thank you.'

'I'll be longing to see you by then anyway.'

'Me too.'

They fell asleep in each other's arms. The next morning Luca drove Libby to the airport after tearful goodbyes to Floriana and Tonio, Maria and Andrea. She had said her farewells to everyone else the night before. Tearing herself away from Luca, whose eyes were shining with tears, she took herself through security, turning to wave one last time. He was so handsome in his white shirt and chinos, her heart dropped somewhere near her boots as she left him behind her and walked away. It felt so strange to be leaving. As she sat on the flight back to London, she let the memories of her time in Italy wash over her, one by one.

Chapter Nine

The clipped tones of the British Airways pilot welcomed her. It felt remarkably good to be back in the familiar surroundings of Heathrow Airport, with its Marks & Spencer, Boots and Pret. She had missed all the usual home comforts while she had been away, and was looking forward to seeing her flat, having all her clothes back and settling back into normal life. Though just how normal her life could possibly be now that she was pregnant was a question she was finding it difficult to answer. She felt a thrill of excitement, while a sickening sense of dread rose through her simultaneously.

'Libby!' A familiar voice called out unexpectedly across the busy Arrivals lounge.

'Angus! What the hell are you doing here?' Libby's heart soared at the sight of her dearest friend. With his tousled auburn hair and deep laughter lines crinkling at the corner of his dazzling blue eyes, he was a welcome sight.

'I've come to pick you up! The pros of being freelance, I'm available for chauffeuring any time.' He kissed her on both cheeks and gave her a big bear-hug.

'How are you feeling?' he asked. Libby panicked momentarily that Jules had broken her promise and told Angus about the baby. 'Does it feel weird to be back?'

She breathed a sigh of relief as she realised he was none the wiser. She knew she had to tell him soon and she was dreading it.

'It always feels a bit strange but it's a good feeling too, and all the better for seeing you! You are an absolute legend, Angus.

Thank you so much for coming to get me.' She suddenly felt rather emotional.

'You couldn't have stopped me even if you'd tried.' He reached down and grabbed her backpack, slinging it over his shoulder as though it weighed as much as a feather. He was so tall and broad he made the enormous backpack look tiny. He tried to carry her handbag too but she refused. Angus had the most impeccable manners; he was old-fashioned and chivalrous. Not for the first time, Libby thought how lucky Jules was; she just hoped she appreciated him as much as she should.

'So how's the painting going?' she asked as they drove along the M4 back into London.

'The latest series is almost complete – do you want to come and look?' he asked.

'I'd love to. Can I come over tomorrow? Give myself a night to sort myself out?'

'Absolutely, I'll cook if you like.'

'Awesome. When's the exhibition going to be again?' Libby asked.

'It's on the twenty-fifth of November; enough time for them to dry out thoroughly and be ready to hang.'

'You're doing so well; I'm so proud of you!'

'Ah, thanks Libs. I must say it feels good finally to be making decent money from my work. I feel like I've been dependent on Jules for far too long.'

'These things take time. You can't become an established artist without putting in the legwork.'

'True.' He glanced at her curiously. 'How are you feeling about next week?'

'Terrified. I need to get ready this week so that I can remember what the hell I'm talking about. Law has been the last thing on my mind these past few months.'

'I bet. Will you bring your laptop tomorrow so we can have a slideshow?'

'Sure. I've got a million photos, I'm sure it will bore you senseless.'

'I am desperate to see what you've been up to. And to see pictures of Luca, the Italian who has finally stolen your heart!'

'There are plenty of him, don't you worry,' Libby laughed.

Angus dropped her back home and helped her open all the windows to let in the air and freshen the place up. The short-term tenants had moved out a few days before and she was relieved to see they had left it in pretty good condition. The fridge and freezer were empty and clean and they'd clearly given the whole flat a thorough scrubbing before moving out.

'Right, I'd better be off then,' said Angus. 'I'll see you tomorrow for dinner?'

'Great. What time?'

'Come for seven?'

'OK, perfect, see you then,' Libby said.

She spent a couple of hours unpacking and loading the machine with her dirty washing. Luca was already WhatsApping her like crazy, wanting to know if she had arrived safely and asking for photos of her flat so he could picture exactly where she was. She went outside and scanned the road for her car, an old green Polo, and was pleased to see that it was still where she had left it all those months before. She drove to her local Sainsbury's and did a big shop, restocking her fridge and cupboards with the basics, dropping some prenatal vitamins into her trolley – she knew it was high time she started taking them.

The next evening she swung by Jules and Angus's house at around seven. Jules answered the door and squealed.

'You're home early!' Libby said. The hours of an accountant weren't great, and Jules was rarely home before eight thirty.

'I was so excited about seeing you that I left early in your honour!' Jules gave her a massive hug, immediately lifting up her top to scrutinise her stomach. 'How are you feeling?'

'Tired. I had to have a nap this afternoon to make sure I didn't fall asleep in the middle of dinner.'

'Poor you.' She took the bottle of wine Libby had brought and led her down the corridor. They walked through into the kitchen where Angus was stirring a huge casserole on the hob. He was an incredible cook, and what was more he really enjoyed it. He was always experimenting with new recipes, and loved nothing more than being in the kitchen rustling up meals to share with friends.

'Hi Angus, that smells amazing. What is it?' Libby hugged him and peered into the stew. Antonio's cooking lessons had really boosted her confidence in the kitchen and she was determined to keep it up now she was home.

'Chicken, chilli, chickpea, peanut butter and tomato casserole.'

'Yum!' Libby's stomach rumbled. 'You'll have to give me the recipe, that sounds delicious.' They chatted for a while as Angus added the last few ingredients. 'Do we have time to have a look at your artwork before we eat?' asked Libby.

'Definitely,' said Angus. They went up to the top floor of the house. The loft had been converted into a huge, spacious studio. The north-facing windows had been enlarged to allow streams of light to flood the room. Paintings from his latest series depicting the Lake District rested on shelves all around the walls, and a huge canvas stood proudly on the easel in the centre of the room.

'Oh my god, they're incredible!' Libby couldn't believe her eyes. The colours were vivid and bright, yet muted by the softening effect of light that seemed to permeate each piece, as though lit by the sun itself. The effect was breathtaking. 'You are unbelievably talented.' Angus glowed at the compliment.

'They're not bad, not bad at all,' agreed Jules.

'Thanks Libs. I am very pleased with them, it has to be said. They've turned out better than I had hoped. Let's hope they sell well.'

Jules took her phone out of her pocket and said, 'Damn, I've got to make a call before we eat. Sorry… there's no rush is there?' she asked Angus.

'No it's fine bubbling away,' said Angus. 'Don't worry.'

Jules gave Libby an extremely knowing look. She had phoned her earlier in the day and told her in no uncertain terms that she was not keeping her secret any longer, and that Libby had no choice but to tell Angus about her pregnancy that evening. This was clearly Jules's tactic to give her a chance to do so in private.

Libby took a deep breath as Jules went down the stairs. She paused at a particularly striking painting of a lake illuminated by the soft light of twilight, trying to work out how to start the conversation.

'Angus, I have something to tell you,' she said, finally working up the courage.

'Oh yes?' he replied. He seemed lost in contemplation as he studied one of his larger canvases.

She turned to face him. 'I told Jules a couple of weeks ago. Don't be mad at her for keeping it from you, I made her swear. I needed to tell you face to face…'

This had caught Angus's attention. He was scrutinising her face with a quizzical expression, clearly trying to work out what she could be talking about.

'Right,' he said. 'What's happened?'

'I'm… I'm pregnant,' she mumbled, suddenly unable to make eye contact, her eyes staring blindly at the floor.

She was greeted by silence. Looking up she could see that Angus's eyebrows were hovering somewhere near his hairline; his forehead was creased with surprise and shock. He clearly hadn't been expecting that.

'You're *pregnant?*' he repeated, aghast.

'Yes.' She felt as though she was standing in her headmaster's office at school, that sickly feeling she remembered so well churned at the pit of her stomach.

'What the hell, Libby?' he shook his head. His eyes flashed with disappointment, even anger.

'I know… I know…' she trailed off. Her eyes welled with tears. 'It was an accident.'

'Well I'm not surprised to hear that…' Angus said.

'We used protection, always. I don't know how it happened.' She could see that Angus didn't believe her. He thought she had taken her reckless approach to life to a new level. She felt annoyed with him on his immediate judgement. 'There's no point looking at me like that,' she said. 'It could happen to anyone.'

'But it doesn't, does it Libby? It happened to you. For god's sake, a baby? Are you even nearly ready for that? You barely even know this guy – how long has it been? A couple of months? What about your training contract, everything you have worked so hard for. Are you just going to throw all that away?' He rubbed his temples. 'How could you have been so careless?'

'Angus, I've told you, we used protection. It wasn't carelessness, it just happened. There's no point talking like that. That's hardly what I need to hear right now. It's not just going to go away, I need to face up to the reality of the situation, whether I like it or not.'

'I'm sorry. I'm just so disappointed for you. The timing couldn't be worse… Do you think Luca will stay with you? What did he say?'

'He was very shocked but supportive.'

'Is he coming to be with you? You can hardly bring up a child together in different countries.'

'I don't know what is going to happen, Angus. He is coming for the twelve-week scan, hopefully.'

'Hopefully?' asked Angus. This was clearly not a satisfactory response.

'I'm pretty sure.'

Angus sighed heavily, then shook his head again. 'Bloody hell, Libby. This is unbelievable, even for you.'

She longed for him to react differently, to show her support rather than judgement. She had known he would be disappointed in her, but she hadn't predicted that he would react quite like this. She felt sick and ashamed that she had got herself into this situation. All she wanted was for him to give her a hug and tell her that it would all be OK.

They went back downstairs and found Jules waiting at the kitchen table. She looked nervously from Libby to Angus.

'Don't worry, he knows,' Libby said.

'Mmmm, I can see that,' said Jules.

'Right, let's eat shall we?' said Angus.

They sat down and ate their dinner. It was so awkward and uncomfortable. Jules tried to alleviate the tension, talking to Libby about how she was feeling and what her next steps would be now that she had seen her GP. She knew it must be particularly hard for Angus when he so desperately wanted a baby of his own, to know that she hadn't even asked for it and was pregnant. She tried to put herself in his shoes and see it from his perspective but, try as she might, she just felt hurt by his response.

As requested, Libby had brought her laptop. Jules insisted on a slideshow of her holiday photographs. Libby bit her bottom lip to stop it from trembling as she clicked through the images, trying her best to put a brave face on and talk normally as she described some of the places she had seen. She noticed a nerve pulsing in Angus's jaw-line whenever Luca appeared on the screen. Jules, on the other hand, was incredibly enthusiastic in her praise of Luca's good looks.

'I just wish he was here too; I think you guys would get along so well with him.' Libby crossed her fingers that Angus would warm to him when they finally met. It would be so important to her that he liked him.

'When is he coming over?' Jules asked.

'In time for the twelve-week scan, hopefully.'

'Well, we should have dinner together then,' said Jules. 'We have to meet him.' Angus nodded his head in agreement.

'OK, let's do that, great idea.' Libby said. 'I'll let you know dates as soon as I have them.' After dinner she said her goodbyes and walked home, trying to keep her eyes open as the tiredness set in. They smarted with tears as she replayed Angus's reaction over and over in her mind. She felt flat and miserable, and she wasn't entirely sure why.

Chapter Ten

Libby spent the rest of the week preparing to start her training contract the following Monday. She would be working at Digby and Edwards, a fiercely competitive law firm in the city of London. She would begin an eighteen-month training contract with three six-month rotations in different seats around the firm. She would be fighting with twelve other trainees to win a position with the firm.

She scoured her contract to find out about her maternity leave rights. Thankfully it was an extremely secure one which, once signed, meant they couldn't get rid of her during the eighteen-month period her contract set out. Obviously they would be unhappy about the situation, but being a legal firm they would have to honour the terms of their own contract. She would be entitled to take maternity leave and then to resume her training when the period of leave ended. Angus was right, though: she would certainly have her work cut out to secure a place in the firm after that.

She couldn't stop thinking about Angus's reaction to her pregnancy news. He was plaguing her thoughts and it made her feel so uncomfortable. She hadn't heard from him since. Besides, she knew there was no point thinking about what would happen after she had the baby quite yet. She kept thinking that the pregnancy might not progress that far, running through all the sad stories she had heard; sometimes it seemed impossible that anyone actually managed to have a child at all. She wanted to try and protect herself somehow from the disappointment that would come with a miscarriage. Despite the fact that this pregnancy was unplanned and unwanted, it was hard to remain emotionally disengaged with what was happening inside her body. Occasionally her imagination conjured the image of a beautiful, gurgling baby, of Luca carrying a tiny bundle in his arms. A flicker of excitement would pulse through her, which she would immediately try her best to suppress. Often her mind swirled with doubt. What if he left them and she had to struggle though this all alone? Without Angus's support, the thought seemed too much to bear.

Luca phoned her around lunchtime every day before starting work in the bar. It worked well while she wasn't working, though she knew it would be harder to talk when she was working all day, and he would be working all evening after she got home.

'I miss you, *amore*,' he said.

'I miss you too. Hurry up and come over.'

'I am already looking up flights. I can't wait to come and see you, to check out your flat. It looks so nice!'

'It is actually really lovely to be home. Though I do miss Positano terribly.' Libby looked around her flat, her eclectic mix of furniture and brightly coloured furnishings were so familiar to her. Her flat was full of bags of personality and quirky finds that she had collected over the years. She tried to visualise Luca there with her, but found it almost impossible to imagine. If he ever came to live here, she wondered how he would cope.

'How's the bar? How's La Casetta?'

'It's not bad, you know. Somehow we are surviving without you. How are you feeling? Has the morning sickness kicked in properly yet?'

'It's not great but I guess I've been quite lucky so far. I haven't actually vomited. I just feel incredibly tired and a bit nauseous. I've downloaded this app which gives me an update every day. It said that the sickness tends to kick in around now, so I'm worried it's just going to get worse and worse. Perfect timing for starting a new job, right?'

'Oh, *poverina*. Are you sure you want to go ahead with it?'

'I've got a signed contract; I can't just leave. And I don't want to anyway. I've worked so hard for this.'

'So what does this app say about the baby so far?'

'Today it says that its teeth are beginning to form. It's the size of a strawberry now it's eight weeks.'

'That is so tiny…'

'I know!'

'I can't believe it can be developing teeth if it's that small.'

'The whole thing is so mind-boggling.'

They talked for a good hour each day and, though she missed him physically, seeing him on FaceTime and being in such regular contact via WhatsApp took away some of the hardship of separation. She couldn't wait for four more weeks to pass so she could hold him in her arms once again. He had offered to come sooner, but she wanted to keep her head down and focus all her effort on work. She didn't know how hard it was going to be, and she wanted to make sure she wasn't distracted. The initial phase would be so important, the first impressions so crucial, she didn't want to mess them up. It was vital she did well, especially if she was going to make herself unpopular at some point in the not too distant future when she announced her news.

Monday arrived quicker than expected. She dressed with great care in a smart navy suit with a silk shirt and low heels. She felt ill with a toxic combination of nerves, adrenaline and morning sickness as she walked to Shepherd's Bush to jump on the Tube.

It felt strange to be back in the slog of commuters. She longed for the peace and quiet of Positano as she crammed herself into a packed carriage of smartly dressed workers, skimming their copies of the *Metro* and checking their smartphones to make a start on the day ahead.

The first week at Digby and Edwards passed by in a flash. There was so much to take in. The facilities they offered were unbelievable. You could go to the doctor, the beautician, the gym all on site… they certainly did their best to ensure you never left the building. She met her supervisor, a senior associate called Jane with a very frosty demeanour, and was shown around the commercial litigation department which would be her seat for the first six months of her contract. She met the other eleven trainees, bonding immediately with a chatty, confident northerner called Samantha and a beautiful Nigerian called Tammy, who were sharing her seat in litigation. She knew she would need some allies to keep her mentally sane through the whirlwind induction process. They were given details about the firm and the work it did, as well as training on key skills such as time recording, work management and drafting, and information on how to get the support and advice they might need. They were also given the opportunity to meet some of the second-year trainees to discuss key pointers to help them through their first year.

By the weekend Libby just wanted to lie in a darkened room. She hadn't actually been sick still, but it would almost feel a welcome relief if she was, the nausea was so constant and debilitating. She made sure she had a steady supply of ginger biscuits and mints in her bag to try and keep the nausea at bay and her sugar levels high. It would have been tough enough to cope with the first week at Digby and Edwards, without being pregnant to boot. She felt so guilty that she might not even make it through the first year of her training contract. She knew it wasn't her fault, but she was also aware of how competitive it was to even get this far into the firm. They had chosen her from a number of potentially suitable candidates, essentially taking a place from someone else who desperately wanted one, only to announce her pregnancy.

During the weekend, Libby slept as much as she could. She was amazed at her capacity to sleep, getting a full ten hours at night and then an hour mid-morning and several hours in the afternoon on top of that.

'It's been so hard to get hold of you,' Luca complained. 'Every time I call, you are asleep.'

'I am just so tired; I can't keep my eyes open for longer than half an hour after I get home from work. I am literally just eating a bowl of cereal and going to bed.'

'It's hard when we can't talk…'

'I know it is, but trust me it's worse trying to start a new job when you feel this terrible. So you should be feeling sorry for me, not complaining that I'm not available to chat.'

'I know, I know. I'm sorry. I just miss you, that's all.' They had finally managed to agree to phone each other on Saturday morning before Luca started work. There wasn't time to speak in the weekday mornings; she just got up and went straight to the Tube, and the evenings had been a complete write-off.

'How was your first week? Tell me everything.' She talked him through it day by day. It felt good to be able to share it all with him, even though he couldn't possibly understand exactly what it was like. He was so interested, and asked so many questions, she could tell he was trying his best to get an accurate idea of what she was going through. On Sunday her mum called to find out how it was all going. Luckily she called in the early evening when Libby was still awake.

'Hi Mum, how are you?'

'All is well with me, my darling; I had a lovely day with Uncle Tony and Aunty Sue yesterday. We went around a National Trust house and walked through the gardens. How was your first week at work?' Libby ran her through the details, excluding anything to do with morning sickness.

'My goodness it does sound awfully complicated! I don't know how you manage!'

'I've honestly got no idea what I'm doing half the time. I feel like a fish out of water. It's so confusing, there is just so much to learn.'

'Have you had to use much Italian yet?'

'Yes I've been reading through Italian documents, speaking to the Italian office and sitting in meetings with Italian clients. It's just as well my Italian has improved so much. It wouldn't have been anywhere near good enough before.'

'Hopefully it'll give you an advantage over the other trainees.'

'It does give me priority to work on the Italian cases.'

'That's great! I suppose it's all about making yourself indispensable to the firm.'

'Exactly. Anyway, enough of all that, what other news is there?' asked Libby. 'Any exciting village gossip to fill me in on?'

'Well, I don't know about that darling. Oh! Guess who telephoned me yesterday...'

'Helen?'

'Yes!'

'Wow, that is a turn-up for the books.'

'I know. The third phone call in at least as many months.'

'So how is she?'

'She seems OK, I think. Not much news, but she seems to be plodding along well at work. I don't think she has much of a social life to speak of. I didn't really question her too heavily, just chattered away about trivia really.'

'Well, I think it's definitely a good sign that she called.'

'Fingers crossed things are starting to look up for her.'

Libby hoped so too. She needed her to be in the best possible frame of mind when she told her about the baby.

By week nine the morning sickness began to fade just the tiniest bit. For the first time she agreed to go out for drinks with Tammy and Sam on the Friday after work. She pretended she had dinner plans so that she wouldn't have to stay too late.

'What'll you have?' asked Tammy, leaning over the bar to get the barman's attention.

'Rosé please,' said Sam.

'I'll just have a lime and soda please,' said Libby.

'Are you not much of a drinker?' asked Sam.

'No, not really,' lied Libby. 'Never really have been…' she trailed off. The good thing about meeting new people now was that they wouldn't know she was not being entirely honest in this respect.

Tammy passed them their drinks and they went and sat down at a round table near the window. The bar was jostling with city slickers, all desperate to down several pints or a few glasses of wine as a reward for making it through another busy week. It was chaotic and noisy. Normally Libby would have loved the buzzing atmosphere, but today she plastered on a brave face and sipped her lime and soda, taking the opportunity to get to know her colleagues outside work.

'So how are you both finding it?' Libby asked. 'I'm so glad we've got a chance to talk away from prying ears.'

'It's bloody hard work,' said Sam. 'I'll tell you that much.'

'It's not really what I expected,' said Tammy. 'I mean, I've spoken to people, I watched all the vlogs and read blogs online, you know, "A Day in the Life of a Trainee", and all that, but it can never really prepare you for the real thing.' Tammy had come to law late, like Libby, after working in finance for several years. Sam, on the other hand, was fresh out of a law conversion following university. She was quite a few years younger, but you wouldn't know it from talking to her, or from outward appearance.

'There's a lot to learn in a very short space of time,' agreed Libby.

'I'm sure the next few weeks will get easier now we've got the first three under our belts,' said Sam. 'I'm so used to being a student, I can't quite believe I'm actually employed!'

Libby laughed, 'Oh to be young and in your first job! You're so much more sorted than I was at your age. I think I was temping at a magazine right about now.'

'So girls,' Tammy leant forwards. 'Jane, what do you reckon? Total bitch? Or actually nice underneath that ice-queen exterior?'

'Total bitch, definitely,' voted Sam.

'I'm not sure,' said Libby. 'I didn't warm to her instantly. She is so inexpressive, it's hard to figure out what she's thinking. When I give her something to read over it could be the best thing or the worst thing that she has ever read – you'd never know by looking at her. She gives absolutely nothing away.'

'She could try smiling every once in a while; it might lift the mood of the office somewhat!' Tammy had definitely taken against their supervisor. She certainly was the polar opposite of Tammy's warm, sunny disposition.

'We've got to keep her on side, though. She'll be the one to evaluate our performance over the next six months. And she'll have a say in which seat we get next.'

'Exactly. We need to win her over, somehow.'

The conversation soon moved away from work and on to their personal lives.

'So I see you have a stonking great ring on your finger,' said Sam. 'When's the big day?'

Tammy laughed. 'I am engaged, yes, but we haven't set a date for the wedding yet. We aren't in any particular rush and I think I'm going to be too busy to start planning a wedding any time soon!'

'Who is the lucky guy?' asked Libby.

'He's called Jake. We met at my last job in the City. He's pretty great!'

'What about you Sam?' Libby asked. 'Do you have a partner?'

'No... not right now. I broke up with my ex-girlfriend last year.'

'Oh, I'm sorry to hear that,' said Tammy.

'No, it was the right thing. It had run its course and the feelings were pretty mutual.'

'Are you looking to meet someone new?' asked Libby, always looking for an opportunity to matchmake.

'No, not really. I just want to focus on my career for a while. Do you have a partner, Libby?' she asked. Libby told them how she and Luca had met that summer in Italy.

'What a romantic story!' said Tammy. 'A real Italian romance!'

'I suppose it is rather,' laughed Libby. If only they knew the whole story!

Tammy and Sam decided to stay and order food; they had both had several drinks by this stage and were getting rather merry. Libby made her excuses and left, unwilling to risk the smell of cooked food setting her off on another bout of retching.

By week ten the nausea had begun to settle down, leaving only the residual tiredness and a new side-effect of extreme bloating. She had to wear baggy tops and loose-fitting dresses to stop anyone from noticing her stomach at work; her boobs had already gone up by an entire cup size. By now the baby was apparently the size of a kumquat. Libby had had to use Google to find out exactly what a kumquat was.

That weekend her mum was up in London. She was going to the theatre with a group of friends on Saturday evening. As always when Miriam came to London, she stayed the night with Libby. Having been delayed on the train coming in from Kent, she had arrived at around tea-time and gone out fairly swiftly. She had her own set of spare keys, so Libby had gone to bed and left her to let herself in after the show. The next day they had breakfast together. Having warned Luca not to mention the 'p' word the previous day, she and Miriam had talked to him after breakfast. Miriam was fascinated by the 'modern technology' that allowed them to talk face to face, and was delighted to be able to meet her daughter's boyfriend, albeit virtually.

There were only two weeks left until her scan, until she would see Luca. Now that she had reached ten weeks, the chances of miscarriage had dropped quite considerably. Having been utterly convinced the pregnancy wouldn't work out, it seemed she was perhaps going to be proven wrong. Libby had decided that she had better confess the truth of her predicament to her mother.

'Mum, I've got something to tell you and you aren't going to like it,' she said. She was arm in arm with her mother as they walked around the common, soaking up the morning sun.

'Oh dear,' Miriam replied. 'That sounds rather ominous.'

'I didn't really know how to tell you…' Libby looked at her mother and took a deep breath. 'I'm pregnant.'

Miriam stood still in shock.

'What?' she asked.

'I know. It's a massive shock. I'm pregnant, ten weeks in fact. The baby is Luca's.'

Miriam made her way over to a nearby bench and sat down. 'Oh my!' she said. Libby joined her on the bench.

'I'm sorry to tell you like this, out of the blue, but there hasn't really been an opportunity and I didn't want to tell you over the phone.'

'No… I can see that.' Miriam shook her head. 'But… you and Luca have only been together such a short time. How do you know he's the right man to be having a baby with?'

'I suppose I don't really. It wasn't planned, Mum. Luca and I love each other and we are serious about each other, but we wouldn't have chosen this to happen now.'

'Certainly not,' said Miriam.

'I feel so foolish, so cross with myself that I've got myself into this situation. But the fact is, somehow, despite the fact we were very careful to use protection, this has happened. A baby is coming and there's not much either of us can do to change it.'

'Does Helen know?' asked Miriam.

'No, I haven't told anyone except Luca, Angus and Jules. I can't bear the thought of telling Helen. Telling Angus was bad enough… he thinks I've really messed up. At least Jules has been supportive. Knowing that Angus thinks I'm making a terrible mistake has been really hard to take.'

'You'll have to tell her.'

'I know. She's not going to take it well.'

'All she wants is a baby.'

'I know. I feel guilty, really I do, but as I said, this was an accident…' She tried to repress a surge of panic that suddenly swelled within her. This situation was so completely out of her control. She had no choice but to forge a path through it, but it was so hard.

'Oh my goodness. I'm going to have a grandchild! I just can't believe it's going to happen quite like this. Out of wedlock. I mean, your father would turn over in his grave. What will everyone say?'

'Do you really think Dad would be that shocked? Things are quite different these days; people decide to have children without getting married all the time. There are lots of single-parent families – and at least Luca and I are still together...' For now, she added quietly to herself, unable to shake the doubt that things might not work out between them.

'Well, I suppose it's a blessing he didn't leave the second he found out.'

'He's not like that, Mum.'

'I wouldn't know. I've never even met him!'

'You will. He's coming over in two weeks for the scan. It's going to be on the Friday afternoon. Why don't you have lunch with us on the Sunday so you can meet him properly? We will have a picture of the baby by then, all being well, so you can have a look...'

This seemed to cheer Miriam up slightly. Libby knew she needed to keep her mind focused on the positives. Her mother would be desperately worried about what other people would think. She had always played by society's rules and hated the thought of any kind of scandal. The trouble was that Libby's pregnancy probably would count as a disgrace amid Miriam's small-minded circle of friends in Kent, and Libby would probably be the talk of the village when word got out. But Miriam had always said how desperate she was for a grandchild, so Libby was sure the fact that she would be a granny in just over six months' time would be a major comfort to her.

'What was your morning sickness like when you had me and Helen?' asked Libby. She wanted to compare notes.

'I don't think I really had much. To be honest, I can't really remember. One of you was worse than the other but I'm not sure which.'

'I'm so worried about the scan,' said Libby. 'What if there's nothing in there?'

'Darling, that is extremely unlikely if you've been feeling sick!'

'What if the baby has Down's Syndrome?'

'The chances of that are very slim. But there are plenty of Down's children who go on to live perfectly happy lives, so it doesn't have to be the end of the world. They will do further testing if it looks as if it might be a possibility.'

'Yes, I suppose we would try and find out everything we could.'

'You'll have to decide that together.'

'Thank god Luca is coming over for it.'

'I'm sure he'll be just as curious as you are to see the baby,' Miriam told her.

After they had walked back home, Libby helped her mother gather her belongings and then drove her to the Tube so that she could make her way back to Kent.

'Bye darling,' said Miriam. 'Look after yourself.'

'I will, and thanks for being so understanding.'

'It is what it is, darling.'

'Call me when you get home?'

'I will.'

Libby watched her mother disappear into the underground system. She felt a big weight lift off her shoulders now that she had told her the truth. She realised she had been dreading her reaction. Whilst it had hardly been overjoyed, she hadn't been completely furious either, so Libby couldn't complain. There would be plenty of time for Miriam to get her head around the idea. On a roll, Libby decided to bite the bullet and call her sister. Unsurprisingly she didn't pick up. Libby left a message asking her to call back, but she didn't receive any calls until the following Saturday.

'You took your time getting back to me!' said Libby. She was sitting on the sofa with her feet up and a cold glass of iced water by her side. At week eleven her baby was the size of a Brussels sprout, though the bloating she was suffering from made it look more like the size of a small pumpkin at this precise moment.

'Sorry, sorry! I know, I'm useless on the phone.'

'And on email…'

'Yup. I'll admit it. I'm a terrible sister.'

'How's it going?' asked Libby. As always it was good to hear her voice.

'Same old, same old. Nothing much to report. You?'

'Well as it turns out, I do have something to tell you…' Libby bit her lip and winced as she envisaged the reaction she would get from her sister. This was going to be awful. She felt crippled with guilt as she imagined how this news would impact Helen. 'Hels, I'm… I'm pregnant.'

There was silence down the other end of the line. Then, 'You're *what?*'

'Pregnant. I know. It's absolutely crazy—'

'You are pregnant?? What on earth…? Oh my god! Are you going to keep it? How many weeks are you?' Helen was never one to beat around the bush, and Libby appreciated her directness.

'Eleven weeks… It happened by accident. Luca and I had only been together six weeks or so when I found out. We used condoms, but somehow one of them must have broken or something. And yes, I am going to keep it.'

'I'm sorry, I cannot quite get my head around this. You've only just got together with Luca and now you are *pregnant?*' Each word was exaggerated with disbelief.

Libby winced as she realised how this would sound to Helen, single for a year and about to turn thirty-eight. If anyone should be getting accidentally pregnant, it should have been Helen.

'Are you happy about it?' Helen asked.

'Well, initially I was just unbelievably shocked. I was so upset that I had got myself into a situation like this, but I knew we had been careful. It's not like I had unprotected sex or anything like that. It was just coming up to the end of my time in Italy, and the timing couldn't be worse with starting my training contract. It's hardly ideal and there have been moments when I have felt as if I'm going out of my mind worrying about the future. But Luca and I are determined to at least try and give it our best shot, and I suppose I'm coming around to the idea, slowly.'

'Well, I guess you are lucky, in a way. So many people never get the chance. Even if it is in completely the wrong order, and you would never have chosen for it to happen this way, at least you will have a baby. I'm actually a little bit jealous,' Helen managed a small laugh. Libby's heart broke for her sister; she knew how hard this would be for her.

'Look, I'm sorry, Hels. I know this must be really weird for you and that it'll have taken you massively by surprise. I still can't get my head around it. Of course I'd rather have had a more traditional route to having a family, like we both always wanted, but it just hasn't worked like that for me by the looks of things…'

'I suppose sometimes the traditional route isn't so great after all. You have avoided all the years waiting for the perfect man to show up. You're pregnant and you'll deal with whatever happens next, I know you will. You could have waited around and never met anyone you wanted to father a child with… I may never… And I really do want a baby…' She trailed off, sounding wistful and sad. Libby felt awful.

'Perhaps you could adopt as a single mother, or use a sperm donor?' suggested Libby. 'There are lots of options out there for women these days.'

'Yes, I suppose you're right,' said Helen.

'Maybe when you get back?'

'We'll see,' replied Helen. They talked for a while longer. It felt good to know that Helen would be by her side, and her mother. She knew just how much she would need the support of her whole family on this uncharted path.

Chapter Eleven

Libby's heart thumped nervously as she waited in the Arrivals lounge at Heathrow. Luca's flight had landed forty minutes ago. He would be walking through the door any minute now. Her palms were sweaty and her throat felt dry. It was the evening before her twelve-week scan and, as promised, Luca had flown over to support her. Libby had come straight to the airport from work to meet his flight. She was suddenly terrified that it would be awkward between them; that she wouldn't know what to say, that she would be self-conscious. She looked down at her stomach, skimmed over by a loose grey top. Would he notice that it had grown? She drummed her fingers on the railing. Suddenly she saw a familiar face pushing a trolley laden with suitcases through the crowds. Her heart skipped several beats and she broke into an enormous grin, pushing her way around to the opening in the barrier and calling out his name.

'Libby!' he shouted, rushing towards her. He abandoned his trolley and wrapped her in a huge hug, covering her neck, her cheeks, and finally her lips in kisses before pushing her away to look at her, then hugging her once more.

'I've missed you so much,' he said, gazing adoringly into her eyes. He was even more handsome than she remembered; his eyes shone and his beautiful smile stretched across his face from ear to ear.

'I've missed you too,' she said. 'I can't believe you are actually here.'

He put his hand on her belly and said, 'I'm here for both of you, Libby. And I'm not going anywhere. I promise you.' It took her a few seconds to realise what he was saying. She looked at the trolley and realised that, rather than a weekend's carry-on, he had two enormous suitcases with him.

'Do you mean you are staying? For longer than the weekend!' She could barely believe it might be true.

'Exactly. I've told Floriana – it's nearly the end of the season and she is happy to let me finish a bit early. My work for Prospero can mostly be done from home and I can always fly over if I have any meetings that can't be done via Skype. I will look for more work in London. If that's what you want?' He suddenly looked worried, as if perhaps he had presumed too much.

'Luca, are you crazy? Of *course* that's what I want! I can't believe you would do that for me… What about your family, have you told them?'

'I told them last night. They were more than a little shocked, I must say, but they definitely approve of my being here by your side.'

'Oh my goodness. I just can't believe it. Thank you! God, I hope you like it here. I hope you like the flat! I have a spare set of keys so that's going to be fine.' Libby wittered on nervously, thinking aloud as she adjusted her train of thought to this change of events. They got a taxi back into London with all Luca's stuff, and she let him into her flat.

Picking up a letter that was lying on her doorstep as he came in he read, 'Forty-four Lansdown Road. My new address, I'd better get used to it!'

'Yes, you are now an official resident of Shepherd's Bush.'

She showed Luca around. There wasn't much to see: bedroom, bathroom, kitchen and separate sitting room with a small dining table. There was also a tiny spare room which her mum used when she came to stay.

'So this would be the nursery, I guess?' Luca asked.

'I think so. Though we might have to get rid of the bed or there won't be any room for a cot and stuff. But we've got plenty of time to figure all that out.' Luca hung his coat on the back of the door. Libby felt so nervous she didn't know what to do with herself. If she could have drunk, she would have necked a glass of wine to still her nerves, but she couldn't even do that. Luca, on the other hand, appeared not to have a care in the world. He seemed completely at ease in his new surroundings and in her company. He turned around, listening to her nervous chatter. Smiling, he crossed the room towards her and silenced her mid-sentence with a kiss. Her heart was beating so loudly that each beat echoed in her ears like a rhythmic drum. She thanked god that her morning sickness was over. A week ago she would not have been in the mood for this, but Luca's kisses were having a forceful impact on her libido.

Slowly, Luca undressed her, one item of clothing at a time. She had put the radio on after arriving home and the room was filled with music. He took his time, caressing her softly and kissing her over and over again. Every touch sent a thrill though her body, small electric shocks that drove her into a frenzy of longing. He pressed himself against her and pulled her towards him. He muttered endearments into her ear. He picked her up as though she weighed next to nothing and carried her into the bedroom, closing the door behind them, determined to remind her just what she had been missing since they had been apart.

Libby was relieved that he had come to London; it felt good to have him with her. She realised a part of her had been unsure whether he would turn up. Now, they sat at the table in candlelight and talked and talked late into the night. She was suddenly excited beyond recognition that he was here to stay. This meant that they had a real shot, a real chance to be a family when the baby arrived. It was more than she could have dared hope. This amazing guy, this handsome, kind and sensitive man wasn't going to leave her to cope alone. He was there by her side and he would be there every step of the way. It made her realise just how much she had been dreading facing it all by herself. Even if their relationship had worked out long-distance, what would have happened when the baby arrived? You could hardly have a family straddled across the continent. They fell asleep, as they had done on their last night together in Positano, wrapped in each other's arms.

The next day was the day of the scan. Libby had to go into work in the morning. The scan was at four o'clock and she gave Luca instructions, choosing to meet at the closest Tube and walk to the hospital together rather than leaving him to his own devices. The Tube would be confusing enough for him. He had barely left Italy before, except for the odd family holiday when he was young. He was the opposite of Libby in terms of how much he had travelled, and again she wondered just how well he would cope with life in London. Reluctantly she tore herself away from bed and got dressed.

'My god you look sexy in your work clothes,' he said. 'I loved beach Libby too, of course, but this is a whole new you.'

'Well I'm not sure how much longer I'm going to be fitting into my old outfits, so enjoy them while you can,' she laughed. She blew him a kiss as she shut the bedroom door behind her. It was so nice having someone in her apartment again. It had felt so empty without a man around since she had broken up with her ex. She wasn't used to living completely alone and was glad to have someone to share her home with once again.

After a busy day in the office, she made her excuses, explaining that she had an unavoidable medical appointment. She was relieved to see Luca at the exact location she had written down for him when she emerged from the underground, looking very cool as he lounged against the wall, staring down at his mobile phone. His good looks were rewarded by several admiring glances from women passing by. Luckily he seemed oblivious as he scanned the crowd for Libby. Catching a glimpse of her, he smiled. Her heart melted at the sight of his dimples.

'*Ciao bella.*' They had slipped into an easy mix of Italian and English. He would have to be using English a lot now that he was to be based in London, and her Italian had improved so much over the summer she felt confident about sliding between the two now she was home.

'I'm so nervous,' Libby said, clutching on to his hand.

He leant across and kissed her on the cheek. 'Me too. I'm sure it'll be fine, though. Think of all the millions of babies that are born each year, perfectly healthy.'

'Yes, that's true. For every horror story there are hundreds of happy endings.'

'Exactly.'

After a short wait in the waiting room they were collected by the sonographer and led to a small room. She invited Libby to lie down on the bed. Luca sat on the chair by her side.

'Is this your first pregnancy?' the sonographer asked. She was a smiley lady with rosy, round cheeks.

'Yes it is. I'm terrified,' Libby told her frankly.

'Every mother-to-be feels exactly the same, don't worry. Now let's see what we have here.' She squirted some cold jelly on to Libby's belly and turned on the monitor. 'Any history of twins in either of your families?' asked the sonographer.

'No neither of us have any twins,' replied Libby.

Luca cleared his throat. 'Actually, my father is a twin,' he said. 'You haven't met him…'

Libby was mortified that she didn't know about this. What would the sonographer think? She flushed with embarrassment.

The ultrasound was projected on to a small screen on the wall in front of them. The sonographer pressed quite firmly on Libby's stomach and a grainy black-and-white image emerged on the screen. Libby found it impossible to make head or tail of what she saw, until the sonographer talked them through it. She confirmed – to Libby's relief – that there was only one baby, and that it looked perfectly healthy. The relief Libby felt was immense. She held Luca's hand and squeezed it, her eyes welling up with tears as she looked at the little baby on the screen. It was hard to believe that it was really inside her. It was like a miracle. She knew in that moment that she had been right to keep it. It was meant to be, this baby, and she vowed to the baby that she would do everything in her power to love and protect it for as long as she lived.

Having got the all-clear, they were given a small photograph of the scan and allowed to go home. Luca immediately phoned his family, passing on the good news, and Libby phoned her mum and Helen, and Jules and Angus, to tell them all was well. She was seeing Jules and Angus the following evening to introduce them to Luca, and the same with her mother on Sunday. Miriam was delighted to hear that Luca was intending to stay. That normalised the situation just enough for it to be socially acceptable among her friends, just in time for her to be able to spread the happy news that she was to become a grandmother. Jules seemed equally excited, declaring it even more important that they should meet, seeing as they were going to be part of each other's lives from now on.

Libby decided not to go back to work, knowing full well that the rest of the team were working late that evening but refusing to care. As soon as they found out she was pregnant, she would be compromised anyway. She wouldn't be able to hide it for much longer, and there was no point trying to impress everyone with her commitment when she was going to be off work for nine months in six months' time. Instead she took Luca into central London, deciding to have a glass of champagne (she would allow herself one) at the Ritz. He had always wanted to go to the iconic hotel, and what better way to celebrate?

They stayed for a couple of drinks and then found a nearby French restaurant for dinner. For the first time Libby allowed herself to accept the fact that she was becoming a mother. They talked about arrangements for the baby, Luca's own experience as an uncle to Antonia's little girl, and what they would need to do to the house to prepare for a baby's arrival. They also decided that they wouldn't find out the sex at the next scan, preferring the idea of a surprise. It was both surreal and exciting.

Libby marvelled at how life could turn on its head in mere moments, uprooting every plan you had made and throwing you completely off course with no notice. It was amazing to her how well everything seemed to be working out. An unexpected bonus of the pregnancy was the refreshing sense of perspective that it gave her about work. She realised undoubtedly that there were more important things in life than a career in law. If her training contract didn't work out, she would cross that bridge when she came to it. From her limited experience thus far, she had a sneaking suspicion that she was not a natural lawyer in the making. She had chosen law because it had seemed like a sensible, grown-up job to have, something respectable and with good earning potential that would set her on a steady career path once and for all. But she found the work rather repetitive and dull, and the levels of stress within the firm were extremely off-putting. It was hard to avoid being sucked into negativity and complaining, although Tammy and Sam were both remarkably upbeat. They genuinely seemed to enjoy it. Maybe that was why Libby was so drawn to them.

The next day was spent mostly in bed. Libby cooked them some lunch and they went for a walk in the afternoon. By the time they got to Jules and Angus's house for dinner, they were as close as they had ever been, the last month and a half of separation forgotten. Libby felt extremely nervous at the thought of Angus and Luca's imminent first encounter.

'Welcome,' said Angus, throwing open the door and shaking Luca by the hand. 'It's good to meet you!' Angus had a grubby apron on over his shirt and jeans and, judging from the smells that were emanating from the kitchen, he had clearly been hard at work. His underlying good manners stopped him from showing it, but Libby could tell that he was masking his true feelings about their situation as best he could, for her sake, and for that she was really grateful.

'It's great to meet you too,' said Luca. It was endearing listening to his Italian accent when he spoke English. Every consonant was exaggerated and every vowel elongated. Moments later, Jules came pounding down the stairs, her hair wet from the shower.

'Sorry, sorry!' she cried. 'I was running so late I only just jumped in the shower.'

'Luca, this is Jules,' Libby introduced them.

'Meeting in person is much better than on FaceTime,' laughed Jules as she kissed him on both cheeks. 'It's so amazing to have you here.'

When everyone had a drink they raised their glasses and made a toast. 'To Libby and Luca,' said Jules, 'and their little baby!'

Jules pored over the photo from the scan, trying to figure out which way around the head was. Even Angus couldn't resist the temptation, quietly studying the image, that vein pulsing in his jaw once again. Libby explained what the sonographer had showed them. She felt so sorry for Angus as she watched him, knowing how much he would like Jules to be in the same boat. She hoped fervently that seeing Libby go through all of this might inspire Jules to follow suit, though she wasn't convinced that was ever going to be an option.

Jules asked Luca hundreds of questions over the course of dinner, determined to get to know him as quickly as possible. Angus was much more detached, uncharacteristically quiet as he topped Jules and Luca up with fine wine and produced three courses of delicious food. They finished with perfectly risen raspberry soufflés dusted with icing sugar and decorated with fresh raspberries.

'How on earth did you make those?' gasped Libby. 'They look so professional. Mastering the art of soufflés is next on my list.'

'You certainly are a great cook,' said Luca. 'This food has been amazing.'

After pudding and coffee, decaf for Libby, they left Angus and Jules to tackle the washing up and walked home. 'They seem like a lovely couple,' Luca said.

'They are the best,' agreed Libby.

'I can see myself becoming friends with them both.'

'I certainly hope so! You'll be spending a lot of time with them.' Libby crossed her fingers that Angus would come around and accept them as a genuine couple. Surely now that Luca had committed to make a go of things with her in London, he could be happy for her? It felt so wrong having this slight distance between them. She was so used to him being there for her, it was very disconcerting.

'Jules is wonderful, so chatty! So full of life and inquisitive.'

'Yup. She just needs to figure out a way to harness all that energy. She hates her job so much – she is definitely not cut out to be an accountant.'

'No, I can see that.'

'I wonder when she'll finally pluck up the courage to quit,' Libby mused, letting them into the flat. She suddenly felt exhausted. Two evenings out in a row had definitely taken their toll. She fell asleep as soon as her head touched the pillow.

Miriam also seemed charmed by Luca over lunch the next day. He certainly knew how to work his magic on the ladies, and his girlfriend's mother was no exception. He was the perfect mixture of self-deprecating humour and courteous good manners, throwing a little flattery into the mix too. He complimented Miriam on her brooch, an antique favourite that she had inherited from her mother, and his obvious affection for Libby was enough to persuade her that he genuinely adored her daughter. Miriam began to feel rather pleased with the whole situation. If only he would propose, then she could relax even more. Watching Luca and her daughter together, she allowed herself to imagine that this might not be too absurd a possibility. Libby was clearly on cloud nine. She was delighted that things seemed to be working out, for one of her daughters at least.

Chapter Twelve

The idyllic bubble of Luca and Libby's reunion burst several weeks later. Libby had been assigned a massive case at work without either Tammy or Sam to act as her wingmen. The hours she was working suddenly seemed to double. Endless nights were spent poring over documents and case notes; she found herself getting taxis home at midnight or one in the morning, grabbing a few hours' sleep and then starting all over again the next day. Luca hated the lack of attention he was getting. He was starting to look for work but not having much luck and he was worried that the website commission he was working on was not going as well as he had hoped. Libby knew this was the first test of their relationship, that it was inevitable that there would be rough patches and that her pregnancy hormones were not helping her handle things as well as she might. She found herself snapping at Luca when he was short with her.

'I never see you,' he moaned.

'I know. There is nothing I would like more than to be axed from this case so that I could have some semblance of a life back, but I can't.'

'I don't know anyone… it's so boring for me here when you are not around.'

'Look, Luca, I can't babysit you. You need to start making some friends of your own. Join a local sports team or something.'

'It's not that easy to just click your fingers and make friends you know, Libby.'

'I know it's going to take time. Maybe you can give Jules a call… I know Angus is busy every waking moment with the exhibition, but she might be able to entertain you, at least this weekend.'

'OK, maybe…'

Libby left him to sulk while she focused on getting the task in hand done as efficiently and quickly as possible. She was irritated by his lack of independence and it concerned her that he was finding it so hard to settle. As someone who was used to fitting in – and making an effort to fit in – wherever she travelled, Libby found it exasperating. But hadn't she known it wasn't going to be that easy all along? Maybe she had been kidding herself. Perhaps Luca was never going to be happy living this life with her.

She pushed her doubts to one side, unwilling to explore them in too much detail for fear of the conclusions she might come to. Jules kindly agreed to take Luca on a tour of some of London's hotspots that weekend, for which Libby was extremely grateful. He seemed much perkier after that. Maybe he really was just lonely. He had seen so little of her, thanks to her unsociable hours of late.

Things quietened down when the case was adjourned and Libby finally got some regularity back into her working life. She was once again able to get home in time for dinner. Luca had started cooking most week-nights, and Libby was getting used to coming home to the aromas of freshly cooked meals. It was such a treat. They both knew that Luca still needed to make some friends of his own, but she wasn't going to force him into anything. She didn't love the fact that he was so dependent on her, but she knew it wasn't really his fault. He didn't know anyone in London and he was only there at all because of her. She had to remind herself that he had plenty of friends back home. He was naturally a very sociable guy and he probably found his lack of mates and dependence on her just as frustrating as she did.

In December it was Libby's thirty-third birthday. They had invited Jules and Angus over for a drink and a bite to eat before her birthday party kicked off in a pub down the road. She had invited a group of friends to come and celebrate with her. It was high time she introduced Luca to everyone, and this was the perfect opportunity to do so in one go. As the four of them toasted the birthday girl, Jules made an announcement.

'Guess what? I have quit my job.'

'What?' Libby almost spilt her elderflower. 'Oh my god. *Finally*. That's amazing!'

'Thanks. I can't believe I have finally done it either.'

'Neither can I,' said Angus. 'I still can't.' He had seemed distracted since arriving at their house. Libby assumed it was down to this announcement. She could imagine he was nervous about how this might affect their relationship, especially having Jules around the house all the time.

'What made you do it in the end?'

'It was actually talking to Luca about his graphic design work that did it, that time we spent the weekend sightseeing. I've decided I'm going to retrain as a graphic designer. I've enrolled on a course already, which will not only teach me all the skills I need but also help me put together a portfolio to help me get work at the end of it.'

'That's amazing, Jules!'

Luca seemed thrilled that he had had a part to play in her decision. 'I can help you with any of your coursework,' he offered.

'That would be incredible.'

'Two creatives amongst us... uh oh,' laughed Libby. 'Actually, make that three!' she realised, thinking about Angus and his art.

'I'm going to have the studio as my graphic design workshop,' Jules said.

'As luck would have it, I've just signed the contract to rent a much bigger studio down by the river,' said Angus. 'I don't have enough space to work from home any more; the whole thing is just taking off too fast. I need a dedicated studio without any home distraction.' His Lake District exhibition had been a raving success; every painting had sold and his list of commissions was growing rapidly. Libby was endlessly impressed with his achievements and extremely proud of him.

'Well that sounds like perfect timing,' said Libby. 'And it's probably best that you won't both be hanging around the house all day.'

'Yes, I think that is *definitely* for the best,' laughed Jules. 'You know what we're like at the best of times!'

Angus rolled his eyes. It was funny that they were the one couple she knew who frequently argued, despite the fact that Angus was usually one of the most easy-going of people. She suspected it was largely down to Jules knowing exactly which buttons to press to wind him up.

They had a happy evening at the pub, chatting to old friends. Everyone loved Luca and there were lots of excited congratulations and oohing and aahing over Libby's ever more visible baby bump. She was now five months pregnant. She couldn't believe how the time was flying.

She had told her employers a couple of weeks before, having arranged a meeting with the senior partner, as well as her supervisor. She had confided in Tammy and Sam at four months and had been sure it was perfectly evident to the whole company

– that it had been for quite some time, despite her best efforts to keep herself covered up – but, until she told her employers, they could hardly come out and ask her if she was expecting. They had taken it well, outwardly, though Libby could tell they were hardly thrilled. They had asked her when the due date was, and she had confirmed that she would be taking nine months' maternity leave, then returning to continue her training contract the following year. It was all becoming very real very quickly.

Not long after her birthday, Christmas rolled around the corner, in a riot of carols, twinkling lights and festive cheer. Luca and Libby found themselves back in Kent at her mother Miriam's house for the festive season. They had debated whether to stay in England or fly back to Italy, but Libby had argued that she needed to spend time with Helen while she was back from Hong Kong. She had told Luca he could go to Italy without her, but he had been reluctant to leave her should anything happen to her or the baby while he was gone. The good news was that Helen seemed to have completely come to terms with the fact that Libby was having a baby. She was clearly very excited when she put her hand on Libby's swollen stomach, trying to detect any small movement, and she was besotted when she saw the picture of the baby from their recent five-month scan. Libby was so relieved that her news hadn't caused a downward spiral in her sister's depression, as she had feared it might.

'It's actually starting to look more like a human now,' she said. 'That first picture you sent me looked more like a small alien!'

'I know. It's like a proper little baby now,' Libby beamed, resting her hand proudly on her bump.

'I should be back for the birth, you know,' Helen added casually.

'What do you mean? The due date is April the twenty-ninth.'

'I know. I've handed in my notice. I'll be back in March, for good.'

'That's wonderful news for us, darling,' Miriam said. 'But… are you sure that's what you want?'

'I'm not really enjoying myself over there, Mum. It's quite lonely. I miss having people I know who I can call up and see if I want to. And the work is hardly thrilling.' Helen was rarely this honest about her feelings, which Libby took to be an encouraging sign.

'That's great for us! So long as you don't mind babysitting,' joked Luca.

'I'm sure I could be persuaded. Though you might have to pay me! I don't know what I'll do for money when I get back.'

'Surely you can teach English over here? There must be plenty of opportunities now that you're qualified,' said Libby.

'Yes, you're probably right.'

Christmas had always been a tough time of year for the Saunders since losing Ronald, but this year had a different feel to it for the first time in a long time. It was lovely having Luca there to restore their depleted numbers a little and add a male perspective. They were all very excited that next year they would have a baby to spoil and fuss over; it would add to the fun enormously. There was something about having children around during the festive season that gave it a new dimension, some sort of purpose. Miriam in particular seemed to have a new energy about her. She had started knitting all sorts of blankets, tiny baby socks and cardigans, all in neutral colours that would suit either a boy or a girl. She was clearly going to be a wonderful granny. And though Libby was sorry that Helen's change of career and of scenery hadn't worked out as she had hoped, she was glad that Helen had decided to move back home. She was sure she would be an amazing aunt.

Chapter Thirteen

As Libby entered the third trimester of her pregnancy, her energy levels dropped right back to where they had been during those initial months of morning sickness. She felt sluggish and lethargic, not to mention extremely uncomfortable. The bed she was sharing with Luca seemed far too small, her constant tossing and turning – not to mention her constant trips to the loo – kept her up all night and frequently woke Luca too. She was also working long hours as well, which didn't help. Digby and Edwards weren't exactly going easy on her because of the pregnancy. In fact, she was expected to keep pace with the rest of the first-year trainees, pregnant or not.

'I can't believe our rotation is happening next month,' said Tammy, one rainy February lunchtime. The three of them had gone for a quick sandwich break together, a rare occurrence, as usually one or other of them had to drop out due to a last-minute call or meeting.

'I'm nervous to find out what we've got,' said Libby. 'Not that I've got much time there. I guess I'll do a few weeks at most and then that'll be it for nine months.'

'Will they put you back in the same seat after your maternity leave ends?' asked Sam.

'Yes, so I'm told,' said Libby. 'When do we actually find out? Do you know?'

'Next week,' said Tammy. 'I hope we get placed together again.'

'Sadly I think that's very unlikely,' said Sam.

'And I hope we get a nicer supervisor this time.'

'Jane won't be difficult to beat,' agreed Libby. It had been Jane who had assigned her to that horrific case a few months ago. She had then proceeded to make herself virtually impossible to track down whenever Libby needed to go to her for support or advice, to ask her an urgent question or to review her findings. As a supervisor she was elusive and unavailable, and every time Libby did manage to pin her down, she looked as though Libby was wasting her precious time giving the bare minimum in short, blunt answers. She was verging on plain rude.

The following week they found out their new seats. Libby would be in Contentious Trusts and Succession, Tammy in Wealth Planning, Family and Business, and Sam in Employment. It felt a bit like starting all over again, a new set of trainees to get to know, a new supervisor, and a new team above you to try and impress.

'You'll be fine,' Luca assured Libby. 'I'm sure they'll love you in your new department, and at least you don't have to work with Jane any more.'

They were sitting in their local pub, out for a celebratory lunch because Luca had secured his first contract with a London-based firm called Sicaro. It had been a long struggle for him to find work, and he was clearly over the moon to have finally secured a regular income to go alongside his Italian contract.

'Here's to your new job,' Libby said, proffering her ginger beer to clink glasses with Luca. It was great to see him in such a happy mood. He had been down in the dumps these past few months and she had been desperate for him to get some good news to cheer him up.

'It's going to be nice to have a reason to leave the house,' Luca said. 'As much as I love our little flat. I've been cooped up in there so long, with only my laptop for company, that I can hardly remember what it's like to be out in the real world.'

'It's ideal that it's only three days a week, so you've still got the other two free to work on Prospero.'

'Yes, it's actually the perfect arrangement.'

'Have you ever worked "in-house" before?'

'Not since Naples. It's going to be quite fun being part of the design team. This company is really up and coming and they have so many different clients. It should be really interesting.'

'How's Jules getting on? She said you'd been showing her some of the basic software she might be using this week.'

'It's been fun, actually. She's got a good eye and I'd say she's definitely got promise. I think she'll do really well once she's started her training.'

'It's so weird that both my boyfriend and my best friend are going to be graphic designers.'

'I keep telling you, it's the way forward! Nobody wants a serious job these days, to be a lawyer, an accountant… it's just too bloody hard.'

'Don't remind me,' Libby groaned. She was counting down the days until she could give up work. Even childbirth seemed appealing in comparison with the tedium of law. She didn't know what she'd been expecting exactly; she had hardly found her training fascinating. It was really only comparing herself with Tammy and Sam, who genuinely seemed to love the work, that made her realise how much she didn't. Up until then she had just assumed that all lawyers plodded through the day job without much joy, that earning their amazing salaries was enough of a reward, but she was beginning to suspect that maybe she needed more than just money from a job.

She missed the easy-going pace of life at La Casetta. The thought that perhaps one day she could open a bed and breakfast or a small guesthouse of her own had been gradually building in her mind's eye over the course of the last few months. She spent hours daydreaming about it, thinking through all the different elements she would need in place to set up a business, looking at potential properties on the internet and doing bits and pieces of research. It would mean she could look after the baby and work from home... it could be an ideal project. And, what was more, she knew she would really enjoy it. She would finally have found something she could work hard at, truly invest herself in and reap the rewards. Just then their food arrived, interrupting her daydreams.

As they tucked into their gourmet burgers and French fries, she chatted to Luca about the local football league that he had recently joined. He had met up with an old friend called Lorenzo from Sorrento. Lorenzo had moved to London at the start of the year for a new adventure with his girlfriend, and he had suggested that Luca joined the league he had signed up to. Lorenzo was football mad, and had wasted no time at all in investigating where he could play on a regular basis.

'They're a nice group of lads,' Luca said. 'It's quite fun to have a good kick-around. I'm not a natural footballer, but still... I can hold my own. And I'm getting better every time I play. It's also so nice to talk to an Italian. God, how I miss it... living in a second language just isn't natural for me.'

'We should meet up with Lorenzo and his girlfriend. It'll be good for us to hang out with some Italians more regularly.'

'Good idea.'

'What's she called again?'

'Giorgia.'

'Will you arrange something? Maybe a weekend is best, and before the baby arrives!'

'You know, I'm finally beginning to feel a bit more settled,' Luca said. 'I can't believe how long it has taken. I guess this is just such a different life to what I'm used to in Positano. Obviously it'll never be quite the same, but I'm trying my best to get used to it.'

'We will go and visit again this summer,' said Libby. She felt guilty that they hadn't visited yet.

'My family are desperate to see us. We should have gone at Christmas or at least for New Year.'

'I know. I'm sorry about that. I suppose it would have been sensible, but Helen is so rarely over that I needed to make the most of her being here and spend time with her. Mum loved having us both to stay too. It was good for her to get to know you a bit better. And at least I met your family lots while I was living in Positano.'

'I know, I know. But as soon as the baby is old enough, we should go.'

'I promise we will.' Libby bent across and gave him a kiss, having hauled herself out of her chair to go to the bathroom. She was also longing to get back to Italy. It was strange to think that their child would be just as Italian as he or she was British. She would do her best to make sure that their child grew up bilingual. What an amazing advantage to have in life that would be.

Chapter Fourteen

The next morning Libby woke up to find that she was bleeding heavily. She woke Luca in a panic. 'This shouldn't be happening,' she said. 'What do I do?'

'Don't worry, we'll call the midwife. They'll know what to do. Are you in any pain?' he asked, jumping out of bed and running over to the desk to find her maternity notes.

'No, no pain. Just heavy bleeding.' Libby sat down on the sofa, unsure of what to do with herself.

Luca dialled the emergency number to contact her team of midwives. Libby grabbed the phone off him, deciding she'd rather talk to them herself.

'Try not to panic. I'm just going to ask you a few questions,' the midwife said. 'Is the bleeding heavy?'

'Yes.'

'Any heavier than a period?'

'No, when I used to get a heavy period, it's probably about the same as that.'

'And are you experiencing any pain at all?'

'No.'

'OK, now I need you to stay calm and I'm going to ask you to call an ambulance to take you to A and E. The doctors will need to examine you to make sure that everything is all right.'

'Am I going to lose the baby?' Libby asked, her voice trembling.

'It is more than likely that the baby is absolutely fine,' the midwife reassured her. 'But you do need to get it checked as soon as possible.'

Luca phoned an ambulance and gave the emergency services their address. They waited nervously, holding hands on the sofa, too anxious to talk. When they arrived, the paramedics escorted Libby downstairs and on to a stretcher. Within fifteen minutes she was at the hospital, Luca walking by her side as they wheeled her in. A midwife called Sally introduced herself and took control of the stretcher, taking her into the labour ward.

'What's happening?' Libby asked. The panic was rising quickly; she was sure that she was going into labour too early and was desperate for somebody to do something to help her baby.

'We need to make sure that you are not having a placental abruption—' explained the midwife.

'What is that?' interrupted Luca.

'It's when the placenta separates from the uterine wall. If that is the cause of the bleeding, then you might have to have an emergency C-section.'

'Oh my god,' Libby gasped. Luca was deathly pale with worry; he held her hand and squeezed it tightly as the midwife set up the monitor to check the baby's heartbeat.

'The heartbeat is looking normal, so that's a good sign,' the midwife reassured them. 'And the doctor will be along shortly to examine you and find out where the bleeding is coming from.'

Libby tried not to worry while they waited for the doctor. Luca kissed her forehead and whispered, 'It'll be OK, *cara*.' She was so glad that she wasn't here by herself, that she had him with her. Several minutes later, the doctor arrived. She introduced herself and explained that she would be doing an internal examination.

'It will feel a bit like having a smear test,' she said as she inserted the speculum.

Libby held her breath and prayed for good news. Her heart was racing so fast she could hear the blood pounding in her ears.

'Right,' the doctor said. 'I can tell you that the bleeding is coming from the uterus, not the baby.'

'So the baby's OK?' asked Libby.

'Yes, the baby is fine. Uterine bleeding, though alarming, is usually nothing to worry about; it should settle down soon. We'll move you on to the antenatal ward for monitoring and we'll check you to see whether the bleeding stops.'

'Thank you,' said Luca, breathing a sigh of relief. 'How long will you keep her in for?' he asked.

'You'll need to stay here for twenty-four hours after the bleeding stops to make sure all is well, and then you can be on your way.'

The midwife came back and took her to the antenatal ward where she was monitored throughout the rest of the morning. The baby's heartbeat remained normal and, by late afternoon, the bleeding had stopped. Libby had never felt so relieved. She realised that she had taken her pregnancy somewhat for granted since making it through the uncertainty of the first trimester. Suddenly both she and Luca realised how desperately they wanted everything to work out, how much they were counting on the safe arrival of their baby. It had given them both a massive fright.

Luca stayed by her side for the night, going out the next morning to run some errands and collect the car so he could bring her home that afternoon. The hospital released her at around six p.m. and Luca was there to make sure she got home safely. He was suddenly reluctant to let her out of his sight, holding her hand as she walked along as though she might slip and hurt herself at any moment.

'I'm fine Luca, honestly,' she assured him.

'I know you are Libby, but still… I'm not going to let you lift a finger around here. You need to rest, rest, rest when you are not at work… and even when you are there I want you to try your best to take it easy. Stress is not good for you or the baby, and we need to make you and it our priority right now.'

Libby wasn't complaining about the special treatment. When they got home he ran her a bath and cooked her dinner. He had bought her a massive bunch of flowers, which were letting off their wonderful fresh fragrance into the flat. After her bath she put on her favourite baggy maternity dress and came in to find the table laid. A candle was flickering in the middle of the table and there was a little jewellery box in the centre of her place mat.

'Luca! Have you bought me a present?' she smiled.

'Maybe,' he responded. He was grinning from ear to ear, looking remarkably sheepish as he came over to the table to stand by her side. He took the little box and knelt down in front of her on one knee.

'Oh my god,' she said, as it dawned on her what he was doing.

'My darling Libby. In the last twenty-four hours I have realised just how much you and our baby mean to me. I know that I cannot live without you. I love you so very much. I wonder: will you do me the honour of becoming my wife?' He opened the box to reveal a single, solitaire diamond sparkling with all its might against the blue velvet lining.

Libby's heart had lodged itself somewhere near the top of her throat. She was speechless: shocked beyond belief and elated at the same time. Unable to get a single word out, both hands clamped over her mouth, she nodded. Her eyes filled with tears as he stood up and took her in his arms, holding her as closely as her bump allowed.

'Was that nod a yes?' he asked.

She nodded again, 'Yes,' she whispered. 'It's a yes!' She squealed with excitement as he carefully took the ring out of the box and slid it on to her finger. It fitted perfectly. She threw her arms around him and kissed him over and over again.

'I can't believe you just did that,' she laughed. 'I literally had no idea!'

'I can't believe you said yes! I am the luckiest guy in the world.'

'No, I am the luckiest girl,' Libby told him. They hugged and kissed until Luca realised that their dinner was burning and had to dash over to the stove to rescue the food. After they had eaten and toasted their engagement with a bottle of champagne, they telephoned their nearest and dearest to share the happy news.

Her mum had been particularly delighted. She had finally got the news she needed to be able to hold her head up high among her friends. No one could comment on the scandalous baby story now that the relationship was going to end in marriage. It was a happy ending all round. Except for Helen. Libby felt awful telling her. She might have got the order all wrong, boyfriend, baby, fiancé, but now it all seemed to be working out just as she would have hoped. Helen, on the other hand, was still single – and unhappily so. She was now thirty-nine, and Libby suspected it would be yet another bitter blow for her to hear that Luca had proposed, although she knew Helen would do her best to be happy for her sister. She would be coming back from Hong Kong in a month's time, and Libby was determined to do whatever it took to help her start to enjoy life again. She would encourage her to go on antidepressants, which Libby was sure would get her into a more positive state of mind, help her set up some good online profiles and encourage her to go on lots of dates.

Libby had been given the all-clear to go into work on Tuesday following her day of rest. She couldn't stop looking at her finger. 'What the hell is *that?*' shrieked Sam, clocking the ring within seconds of seeing Libby arrive in the office. 'OMG! Tammy, get over here, *now*,' she shouted.

Tammy clattered over in her high heels, a huge grin beaming across her lovely face as she realised what had happened. 'Congratulations,' she said, squeezing Libby around the shoulders. 'What incredible news!'

'What happened to you yesterday?' asked Sam. 'I thought you were off for medical reasons but now I realise maybe you were celebrating…?'

'No, I had to go into hospital. He only proposed last night.' Libby filled them in on the dramatic events of the weekend.

'What an incredible story! What drama,' Sam said.

'What a way to propose,' agreed Tammy. 'It's so romantic!'

'When will you get married?' asked Sam.

'We've decided not to set a date for the time being, just to enjoy being engaged. We certainly wouldn't do anything till after the baby comes, anyway, and then I hardly think we'll be in a position to be planning a wedding any time soon.'

'I think too many people rush into the wedding. I like to see engagement as another step between being boyfriend and girlfriend and husband and wife,' said Tammy, who herself had been engaged to Jake for quite some time and still had no date set for a wedding. Libby liked that idea. There would be plenty of time for all that later, but right now she was just glad to have a ring on her finger and the security that came with it. No more pitying glances for her as people clocked her bump and looked to her ring finger to see whether her pregnancy was planned. God forbid you planned a pregnancy out of wedlock, as many couples did these days. She was often tempted to tell people to mind their own business when she realised the assumptions they were making, but she knew there was no point. People wouldn't change their ways because of her.

Chapter Fifteen

Libby had decided to break the happy news to Jules and Angus the following Saturday, over lunch, preferring to tell them in person. Luca and Jules were meeting early so that Luca could show her how to operate some of the graphic design software she was struggling to figure out. Meanwhile Libby had persuaded Angus to take her on a quick tour of his new studio, which was just down the road. 'It's a lot bigger, isn't it,' said Libby as she looked around the huge space, which was north-facing and flooded with deflected light. 'Amazing.'

'It's just what I needed,' said Angus. 'There wasn't enough room to swing a cat in the last one. And it means I can experiment with some larger canvases, like this one.' He pointed to a huge blank canvas that stretched across one of the shorter walls.

'Is that for a particular commission?' Libby asked.

'It's for a Japanese client,' explained Angus.

'Wow, it's vast!'

'Yup! Luckily I'm not into lots of detail. The larger the canvas, the freer and more expressive I can be.'

'I can't wait to see what you do with it,' said Libby. 'What's the latest series going to be based on?'

'The Yorkshire Moors,' said Angus. He liked to use a different setting for each exhibition, saying that it kept the work fresh and gave him new inspiration each time.

'You're going to run out of good locations soon,' laughed Libby. A sudden thought struck her. 'You know, you should really go to Italy next. You'd never run out of beautiful scenery to paint there.'

'True. I'd love to paint there one day,' said Angus.

'You are so lucky, you know,' said Libby. 'To have found something that you really love.'

'It took a lot of hard work to make it this far though,' said Angus.

'I know. But it must be an amazing feeling to have a vocation. I can't believe I'm in yet another job that I don't enjoy – it's so frustrating.'

'Is there anything you think you'd like to do that you haven't tried yet?' Angus raised his eyebrows. 'I feel like you've explored plenty of different options since we left university.'

'Ha! You can say that again!' laughed Libby. 'As it happens I have been thinking about something recently. Something I think I would really enjoy…'

'Oh yes? And what is that?' Angus was curious to know.

'I've been thinking about setting up my own bed and breakfast somewhere. After the baby is born, I mean. I know it would be bloody hard work, but I loved working at La Casetta so much and I've always enjoyed meeting new people, interacting with travellers. I could find a quiet place in the countryside… I'm not sure the city really suits me too well. I think it would match my skill set nicely: a combination of admin, cooking and housekeeping. What do you think?'

'I think in theory it could be a great idea. But it would take a lot of work to get it up and running. And it would be a twenty-four-hour-a-day commitment. Running your own business is a whole different ball game. Being self-employed means you can never really switch off. But I agree I think you would be good at it if you are sure that law isn't going to work out. And it could be a good option to give you more time with the baby, provided you are able to employ someone to help with the work. I imagine if not, you'll hardly have a spare moment.'

They chatted for a while longer about the pros and cons of her idea. 'Do you think Luca would help you?' Angus asked. He clearly still had his doubts about the longevity of the relationship. She was aware of the engagement ring, which she had taken off shortly before arriving at the studio, burning a hole in the pocket of her jeans.

'Actually, yes. I think he is going to be around to help me. You see, I've got something to tell you.' Suddenly terrified of his reaction, but so desperately hoping he would be happy for her, she gingerly took the ring from her pocket. 'I was going to wait until we were with Jules too…' She slipped the ring on to the fourth finger of her left hand. The realisation of what this meant dawned across Angus's face.

'You're engaged?' he said, smiling at her, mixed emotions flickering across his face.

'Yes, Luca proposed! There's a whole story to tell which I will save for when we are with Jules, but yes, I'm engaged. And I'm so happy!' Angus gave her an enormous hug. He held her for much longer than expected, rubbing her back and squeezing her tightly. It was such a relief to feel as though things had finally settled back to normal between them. When he pulled away she noticed that his eyes were shining.

'Congratulations Libby,' he said, clearing a lump in his throat. 'I look forward to hearing all about it. In fact, we should probably make a move,' he said as he looked at his watch.

They walked, slowly, for Libby's sake, down to the pub that Angus had booked for lunch, overlooking the banks of the Thames. They found Luca and Jules already sitting at the table chatting. As Libby leant over to kiss Jules hello, Jules immediately clocked the dazzling ring on her friend's finger.

Grabbing her hand and twisting it around she said, 'Er, excuse me. And what do you call this?' Her mouth was wide open with shock. Libby burst out laughing and Luca laughed almost apologetically as he shrugged his shoulders.

'We're engaged!' Libby cried.

Jules yelped and gave them both a congratulatory hug. 'What amazing news! Congratulations!'

Angus leant over and shook Luca's hand. 'Congratulations, Luca,' he said. 'I'm very happy for you both. Libby told me while I was showing her round my studio.'

'I can't believe you told Angus before you told me,' shrieked Jules, shaking her finger at Libby.

'I know. I'm so sorry! I had planned on waiting until lunch, but I accidentally let the cat out of the bag.'

'We must get a bottle of champagne,' said Jules excitedly. 'Only a glass for you though,' she said. 'We'll just have to polish off the rest!'

When Jules returned from the bar and they had settled down with their drinks, Jules asked Luca to tell the story of the proposal. Luca talked them through it step by step. Libby still couldn't believe it. She knew she would never get bored of hearing the story. Neither would she ever get bored of looking down at her ring; it would be a wonderful distraction whenever she was losing the will to live at work.

After they had eaten their meal and ordered the bill, Jules suddenly remembered something. 'Libby, my sister mentioned something to me yesterday. I think you might find it an interesting proposition...'

'Very mysterious – go on!'

'Well, she has a work colleague called John who she is trying to set up.'

'Ooh yes!' Libby nodded enthusiastically. 'Helen will be back in the UK soon.'

'It's not actually for Helen. He is sixty-four.'

'What? For who then?'

'I was thinking maybe… for your mum?'

Angus laughed. 'Matchmaking Miriam are we now, Jules?'

'I think that's a great idea,' said Luca. 'Why not?'

'Well, I suppose it would be nice for her to meet someone,' Libby said thoughtfully. She hadn't even considered the idea of her mum dating but, now she came to think of it, why on earth shouldn't she? It had been years and years since her father had died. Plenty of women remarried and had a second chance at happiness. Maybe it was possible for her mum too?

'OK, so what do you know about this John?' Libby asked.

'I've seen a picture; he's really nice looking for an older man. Grey hair, smiley eyes. He looks absolutely charming.'

'Sounds good so far…'

'And he's apparently the most lovely guy. Megan thinks he's the best thing since sliced bread. He's got a great sense of humour and has asked her if she knows any nice women. His previous wife died quite some time ago and he's ready to get back out there.'

'What do you reckon?' asked Angus.

'I think we should do it. I'll call her later and see if she'd be up for it.'

'OK well, let me know what she says,' Jules grinned.

Later that evening, Libby phoned her mum and put the proposed date to her. She made sure that her description of John was right up her mother's street.

'A date? Darling, what on earth are you talking about?'

'Jules will give John your phone number and then he will call you to arrange a time and a place for you to meet up.'

'I see. Well, I can't say I've ever done that before.'

'I know, it's a strange idea. But it might be fun.' Libby wasn't sure how well this was going.

'You know what, darling; I think it could be rather fun to be taken out by a chap. It's been a jolly long time since your father died.'

Libby was amazed. 'Really, Mum? That's great. Good for you!'

'It sounds rather terrifying, I must admit, but it is probably about time I did something that puts me out of my comfort zone.'

'I must say, Mum, I'm very proud of you. I thought you'd tell me to get lost immediately for having suggested such a thing!'

'It's good to know I'm still capable of surprising my own daughter,' laughed Miriam.

She was amazed that her mother had sounded quite so enthusiastic about the whole idea. She sounded a little nervous too, but she hadn't said an outright no, which is what Libby had been expecting. Libby reassured her that it would be a very relaxed affair, maybe just lunch or a drink, and that she would help her choose what to wear. She then phoned Jules to give her the go-ahead for her matchmaking.

Miriam and John went on their first date one Saturday in early March. He drove out to Kent and took her out for lunch in a local pub.

'So, Mum, how was it?' asked Libby the next morning.

'It was wonderful,' said Miriam.

'Wonderful!' Libby laughed. 'Oh my goodness. So you like him?'

'Very much. We had lunch together and we just couldn't stop talking! We stayed there all afternoon chatting away and then we went for a walk along the beach. We didn't quite want to part ways just then, so we went to the Builder's Arms and had a couple more drinks and then John drove back to London.' It turned out Miriam had been utterly charmed by him from the first second she had laid eyes on him and, by all accounts, he seemed equally besotted with her.

To Libby's absolute amazement and delight, they began 'courting', as Miriam put it. By the beginning of April they had declared themselves an official couple. Libby had never heard her mother sound so happy. She was like a schoolgirl, giggling and laughing, full of a new lease of life. The two of them together were unimaginably sweet. They had found kindred spirits in each other and spent hours together gardening, doing the crossword and going to the theatre. Libby couldn't believe that Jules's matchmaking had worked – and so easily at that. It was an enormous weight off her shoulders to know that there was someone else out there who was looking out for her mother. The responsibility no longer rested entirely with her. For the first time since her dad died she could relax, comforted by the knowledge that her mother was in a safe, loving and capable pair of hands.

Chapter Sixteen

Helen had chosen a less than ideal time to come home. She had moved back in with her mother, only to be presented with John as a new member of the household. Despite having only known each other a month or so, Miriam and John were already practically joined at the hip. Miriam would come up to London for several nights of the week and John would join her in Kent for the rest, only having the occasional night apart from each other. Libby knew that for Helen this added insult to injury. Not only did Libby have a fiancé and a baby on the way, but now her mother had a boyfriend too. She knew that it must seem to Helen as though everyone in the world was coupled up and happy, except for her. Libby redoubled her efforts to include her, inviting her to any social occasions she could think of and phoning her often.

Libby's last week of work came and went; she had decided to stop three days before her due date. Tammy and Sam had taken her out for a celebratory glass of elderflower before returning swiftly to their desks; both of their new rotations were proving hard work. Libby had never been more relieved to be leaving. It had been an exhausting time: pregnancy and being a trainee solicitor had turned out to be a less than ideal match. The last few weeks in her new seat had been especially painful. There was so much to learn, yet at the same time little incentive for her to really knuckle down and make a good start when her maternity leave was approaching so rapidly.

Libby had managed to persuade Helen to come up to London and spend the day with her the following day. After having lunch down the road at a nearby café, Libby dragged Helen back to the flat so that she could set up a couple of online dating profiles for her.

'You really need to get back up to London.'

'Tell me about it. As much as I love playing third wheel to Mum and John…'

'Have you got anyone you could stay with for a while?'

'My old roommate Joni has a space, so I'm thinking of moving back in with her.'

'That's perfect! When does your job start?'

'A week on Monday.'

'So you'll move in next weekend?'

'Yes, I think so.'

'At least you'll be able to afford your rent.'

'Only just. It's not very well paid.'

'You'll just have to get all your dates to take you out for dinner!'

'I'll try my best. I'm determined to get back out there, Libby. I mean, if Mum can do it—'

'Exactly, of course you can.' She showed Helen the photo that she had selected to be her profile picture. 'What about this one?'

'Go on then. I'm so useless at this. It's up to you. You're clearly an expert in attracting the opposite sex.'

'Perhaps not in my current state!' Libby said, gesturing to the laptop that was balancing on top of her bump. They both laughed at the sight. Soon she was clicking the submit button so that the powers-that-be could make Helen's profile live. She started browsing through the lists of suitable candidates, Helen shrieking at some of her suggestions as she got extremely trigger-happy with the mouse. She 'liked' a good fifty profiles as a starting point, making Helen promise that she would message back anyone who sent her an opening gambit. Libby was full of hope that her efforts would pay off. Surely it was about time Helen's luck changed.

'Have you thought any more about going on antidepressants?' Libby asked tentatively. She was wary of broaching the subject.

'I don't know, Libby. I hate the thought of being on some kind of pill.'

'So many people take them. I can count handfuls of friends that do, and they're all perfectly happy while they're on them.'

'I just don't like the thought of artificially regulating my emotions. I want to experience whatever I am meant to be experiencing.'

'But that's the thing – when you are depressed, you aren't experiencing what you should be. You're only feeling the bad stuff. Antidepressants help lift your mood so that you can enjoy the good bits too.'

'Well, when you put it like that it doesn't sound too bad.'

'Will you promise me that you'll at least talk to the doctor about it?'

'OK. I'll make an appointment this week.'

'Amazing. And you'll call me straight after to let me know how it goes?'

Helen promised that she would.

True to her word, Helen called Libby later on that week. She had agreed to start a mild dose of antidepressants, as recommended by her doctor. Libby was delighted; she felt so proud of her big sister for taking such a big step forward.

'Have you had any luck on Lovestruck yet? Or eHarmony?' asked Libby.

'I have been messaging a couple of guys following your "liking" campaign.'

'And…?'

'Not sure. They're probably weirdoes.'

'Helen, you can't have that attitude. They're probably just normal people, looking for a relationship just like you.'

'Well I'm still messaging them. And I've been looking through profiles every day, "liking" anyone who looks interesting.'

'That's brilliant. You need to go on some actual dates, though.'

'I know. It's impossible to know if you fancy anyone until you see them face to face. As soon as I move in to Joni's, I'll start arranging some dates. I can't wait to be back in London and out of the love nest.'

'I bet. I'm so happy for Mum, though! It's so great. I can't believe that it actually worked out.'

'I have to admit I never would have believed she'd get a boyfriend.'

'Do you like him?' Libby had met him a couple of times and thoroughly approved. He was softly spoken and unassuming.

'I do, actually. He seems like a good person.'

'What a turn-up for the books!' laughed Libby.

'So... it's not long to go now,' said Helen. 'The baby is now officially late.'

'I'm telling you I'm *desperate* to get it out. It's the most uncomfortable thing in the world. It's like a watermelon is pressing on your bladder; even my pelvis feels bruised from the pressure.'

'Hopefully it won't be much longer.'

'It bloody better not be.'

She was fed up with being so enormous. The pregnancy seemed to have gone on forever and she was dying to get her body back, to reclaim it as hers and hers alone, free from lumbering around like a beached whale, able to jump up from the sofa in a flash or lie on her tummy if she wanted to. It was just so restrictive.

As Libby hung up the phone, Luca came through the door carrying several large bags of shopping. He had decided to cook a load of meals and freeze them in small batches for after the baby's arrival. Her emergency bag was packed and waiting by the door; there was nothing left to do but sit and wait. She had read that eating a curry could induce labour, so she had requested a curry for dinner.

Ever since the scare, Luca had been nothing but the doting fiancé. He fetched her cold glasses of water, he rubbed her feet or her aching back upon request, and he ran her baths, helping her get in and out of them without slipping. She felt much happier about their relationship now that they were engaged. The problems hadn't disappeared; Luca was still finding life away from Positano tough and she was still acutely aware of everything he was sacrificing, but she could tell that he was making much more of an effort to make things work. She was sure that he would be a similarly doting father. He had been so kind recently. She knew that he had spent a lot of his free time helping Jules with the initial stages of her coursework, and she was very grateful for him for doing so. He and Jules got on really well; it was nice for Libby that they had become such good friends.

Four days later, Libby's contractions finally started. Because her waters hadn't broken, the midwife advised her to stay at home for as long as possible. She only needed to go to the hospital when they were three minutes apart and lasting about sixty seconds each. She used an app to time her contractions, doing her best to keep her mind off the pain that was growing in intensity with each passing minute. When she was nearing three-minute gaps they set off in the car to the hospital, making sure they had everything they needed for Libby while she was there and also for the baby when it arrived.

Her waters broke soon after arriving. Libby had never known pain like it; she thought she might pass out from the force of each contraction. She held her breath and counted backwards until the pain stopped, sucking huge gulps of gas and air into her lungs.

After what felt like an eternity, the midwife finally instructed her to push. Luca was holding her hand and she crushed it in hers as she gritted her teeth and pushed as though her life depended on it. As the baby came out she listened for its cry as she collapsed back on to the pillows behind her. A piercing wail filled the room and Libby laughed in relief at the sound.

'It's a beautiful little girl,' said Luca, tears glistening in his eyes. 'You did it, Libby! You are incredible, she's perfect.'

The midwife put the baby on Libby's chest straight away, getting skin-to-skin contact as quickly as possible while she clamped and cut the cord. As she gazed at the baby, feeling its heartbeat against her skin, she felt an overwhelming wave of love course through her. She couldn't believe it was all real.

'I can't believe you're finally here,' she said to her daughter. Tears of joy sparkled in her eyes. 'You are the most beautiful baby I have ever seen.' She dropped kisses on the baby's head, covered in the softest downy hair, and placed her finger in the palm of her tiny hand as she curled her fingers around and gripped tightly.

'We've been waiting a long time for you,' said Luca, tracing the minuscule toes with his finger. 'She is so impossibly small, and so perfect,' he said, turning towards Libby and kissing her. 'You are so amazing, my darling.' They just couldn't take their eyes off their precious new arrival, entranced by every tiny feature.

Later the midwife weighed and measured the baby before returning her to Luca and Libby with a little wristband naming her Morelli. Luca watched over both of his girls, leaving Libby to sleep when possible between breastfeeding.

The next day they were allowed home from the hospital. Miriam and Helen were their first visitors. John had politely declined the invitation, not wanting to invade Libby's privacy too early on. The proud grandmother and aunt took turns to cuddle the precious new addition to their family.

'We've decided on a name,' Libby told them.

'Have you? What have you chosen?' asked Helen.

'Isabella,' said Libby. 'Isabella Morelli.'

'Lovely,' said Miriam. 'That works just as well in England as it will in Italy – it's just perfect.' Both Helen and Miriam were clearly besotted, as was Luca. He couldn't stop taking photographs and his phone was vibrating like crazy with all the responses from his family as he sent them more and more pictures of his pride and joy.

Jules and Angus came the following day, laden with gifts for the baby and a huge bunch of flowers for Libby. Jules said all the right things and cooed appropriately over Isabella but it was Angus's reaction that really moved her. He seemed to fall in love with the baby at first sight as he picked her up and cradled the tiny bundle against his shoulder. He was so tall and broad that Isabella looked impossibly small against him. It was a truly heartbreaking sight and Libby's heart swelled with love for them both as she watched them, her daughter and her oldest friend, so desperate to become a father himself. He even seemed reluctant to part with her when it was time for Libby to feed her. Jules and Luca chatted in the kitchen making everyone cups of tea, while Angus asked her all about what her plans were in terms of establishing a routine for the baby. She loved how interested he was. It made it all the more clear just how wonderful he would be as a parent. She knew that it must be hard for him, that he was genuinely happy for her, despite his regret that he wouldn't experience it himself unless Jules had a serious change of heart.

Jules and Angus didn't outstay their welcome, for which Libby was extremely grateful. She was so exhausted from the birth itself, not to mention the fact that she had barely slept a wink since. She was feeding Isabella every three hours and trying to nap when she could. She thanked god that Luca was there to do all the housework. He was a good cook but laundry and cleaning were not his area of expertise. Libby usually took care of all the jobs that kept the household running. Watching Luca struggle through, asking countless questions as to the whereabouts of basic cleaning products made them both realise just how much Libby did around the house. Not that she minded: having a fully functioning, well-stocked house was important to her and she enjoyed it. But now that Isabella had arrived there was no time for any of that. Feeding seemed like a full-time job in itself; as soon as she had finished, it was time to start the process all over again. Her mind boggled at the thought of how anyone coped with having twins.

Chapter Seventeen

The first two months of motherhood seemed to pass by in a blur of sleep deprivation, breastfeeding and laundry. Libby didn't know if she was coming or going, and she would have been hard pushed even to guess what time of day it was. When Luca's two weeks of paternity leave were up he had gone back to work, leaving Libby to cope for three days at a time without him. She had become increasingly dependent on his support, so his leaving had felt like an enormous wrench. She had burst into tears as the door closed behind him, looking at the clock to work out how long she would be alone with the baby until he came back. This was extremely unlike her; normally she relished restoring order to her home and she was usually pretty good at coping with only a little sleep, but the hormones had clearly taken their toll. Thankfully Miriam and Helen had really stepped up to the mark. Miriam usually came to visit during the day, staying with John at night now that the spare room had become the nursery, while Helen took to popping around at weekends and even for the odd evening, giving Libby and Luca a much-needed break.

'I saw Henry again last night,' Helen said one morning as she sorted out the latest load of washing to put in the machine.

'Ooh really! He's the one who took you bowling, isn't he?' Libby's baby brain was just about keeping abreast of the developments in Helen's dating life. Her sister had stayed true to her word and was determined to get herself back out there. The dating sites she was on were proving an excellent method for meeting new men. The past few weeks had seen her date a

Mancunian plumber, a South African dentist and an IT consultant. The latter had apparently been worthy of a second date.

'So, what do you think? Do you like him?' asked Libby, who was flat out on the sofa enjoying a brief moment of respite while Izzy slept.

'He's not devastatingly handsome or anything, he just sort of looks normal. But he's a nice guy, we get on well…'

'There's a lot to be said for normal, Helen.'

'That's very true. Alan was anything but…'

'So where did Henry take you?' Libby was intrigued. It felt like a long time since she had been on a proper date.

'We went to a restaurant called Circus in Covent Garden. It was quite cool actually; there are loads of awesome acts to watch while you eat: trapeze artists flying overhead, fire eaters and cabaret singers, that sort of thing.'

'Wow, that does sound cool! He seems like an interesting guy… Did you kiss at the end?'

'Not really. He kissed me on the cheek. I think he wanted to kiss me properly, but I didn't have the guts so I just said goodbye and went off to the Tube.'

'Third time lucky perhaps?'

'Yeah, maybe. I think we'll see each other again. He sent me a nice text this morning saying that he'd had fun.'

'Did he pay?'

'We split the bill. But he did offer.'

'You should have said yes!'

'I know! I can hardly afford it. But I didn't want him to think I was scrounging off him.'

They took Isabella out for a walk around the park. Luca had escaped for his Saturday morning football with Lorenzo, and it was nice for Libby to have Helen's company as they wheeled the pram along the pathways. July was fast approaching and the summer sun was finally making an appearance. She couldn't believe it had nearly been a year since she had started at La Casetta. It was crazy to think about how her life had changed because of that place. She would never have met Luca without it, and she certainly wouldn't have Izzy. She owed so much to Floriana and Tonio for giving her that job.

Luca and Libby had booked their flights to go and visit Positano in September, deciding that Isabella should be able to cope with the travel by then. Though Libby realised it was actually more them than Isabella who would need to do the coping! She just hoped their daughter would behave herself on the flight. Overall she was a pretty good baby, but she certainly did have her moments. There were times when Libby just wanted to ram earplugs in her ears for the level of decibels emanating from her. Quite how such a tiny person could make such a loud noise never ceased to amaze her.

Soon August arrived, and with it came a glorious heat wave. Libby and Luca, often joined by Jules and Angus, took Isabella to the park at weekends for sunny picnics. Miriam went away on holiday with John for a week in the middle of August. Libby and Luca took advantage of having an empty house and spent the week there, enjoying the British countryside, as well as Miriam's beautiful garden. During the weekdays, while Luca was at work, Libby would often walk down to Angus's studio by the river. It gave her a decent walk and saved her from feeling cooped up inside the flat all day. Angus would break for lunch and they would sit overlooking the river, eating sandwiches and chatting while Izzy slept.

'Do you think Jules is coming round to the idea of having a baby now that she's seen Isabella?' asked Libby.

'Sadly not,' Angus replied. 'We've actually had some pretty intense conversations recently. She refuses to budge. It's almost worse now that she's so passionate about retraining in graphic design. All her energy is devoted to that and she doesn't want any distractions. I almost wish she'd stayed in accountancy. At least then she might have thought of maternity leave as a welcome break.'

'It's a pretty terrible situation for you Angus. I'm so sorry it has to be like this.'

'I just feel like I'm meant to be a dad. I can't help but feel resentful that she is refusing to give me the chance.'

'I understand,' Libby said, giving his hand a squeeze. 'In fact, now that I have had Isabella, I think I can understand even better.'

'At least I've got Izzy, my beautiful goddaughter. She'll just have to do for now.' Luca and Libby had decided to make both Jules and Angus godparents, along with Gian Matteo back in Italy. Angus was a dream with Isabella and he clearly adored spending time with her. Libby knew she could call him if she needed help and Luca wasn't around. His art was becoming increasingly in demand as word of his talent spread across the art world, yet he always made time for Libby when she needed him.

By the end of August, Libby was over the moon to hear that Helen and Henry had become an official couple. She felt personally responsible for bringing them together. To celebrate the news, Libby invited them both around for dinner, having finally gained Helen's permission to introduce herself to the lucky man.

'Henry,' said Libby as she flung open the door. 'It's wonderful to meet you! Nice to see you too, Helen.' She kissed them both and ushered them inside. 'Izzy has just gone to sleep, thankfully. Let's hope she stays that way so we can eat uninterrupted.'

Luca came over to shake Henry's hand and kiss Helen hello. Libby was cooking one of Antonio's recipes, a huge mushroom risotto, and the flat was filled with mouth-watering smells.

They had a lovely evening, covering a wide range of topics from politics to travel.

'This is absolutely delicious,' said Helen as she tasted the risotto. 'Is it an authentic Italian recipe?'

'Yes, it's one I learned while I was in Positano,' said Libby. 'I'll give you the recipe if you like.'

Henry accepted a top-up of wine from Luca. 'Do you miss Italy?' he asked.

'Terribly,' said Luca. 'Though London has its advantages, of course. But there is no place like Positano.'

Libby hated hearing him say that. It reminded her of just how much he had given up to be with her and Izzy. She knew that his heart would always lie in Italy, and that London would never be able to make him anything like as happy as he was back home.

Henry seemed like a very nice guy. He was jovial, polite and interesting to talk to. Libby thought he would be extremely good for Helen – a steady, calming influence on her, which was exactly what she needed. She just hoped that it would work out. There had been too many guys who had let her down, too many disappointments. Another one would probably be too much for her to handle. She was glad that her antidepressants seemed to have had such a positive impact on her, and was so grateful that Helen had been brave enough to give them a try.

Chapter Eighteen

In September, Luca and Libby set off for Italy, their suitcases stuffed to the brim. A large amount of baby paraphernalia was crammed into Libby's hand luggage to help them survive the journey. They arrived in Naples in good time, and were greeted at the airport by Luca's parents, Mario and Chiara, who were waiting with open arms to embrace their son, his fiancé and their baby granddaughter.

'Oh my goodness, she's so beautiful!' cried Chiara. 'More beautiful than in any of the photos.' She hugged Libby and looked at her ring. 'I can't believe we haven't seen you all for so long. Congratulations; so many congratulations! The engagement, the baby – we have so much to celebrate!'

'Hello little granddaughter!' said Mario, peering at Isabella's sleeping face, content in her pram. 'And Libby, it's fantastic to see you too. We're so happy to have you!'

'We've got your bedroom ready. We've borrowed a cot from Antonia and it's all set up waiting for you,' said Chiara as she led them out to the car.

'That's so kind, Mamma, thank you,' said Luca.

'I'm so excited to get back to Positano,' said Libby. 'I have missed it all so much. London just doesn't compare—'

'You should move back,' announced Mario, getting a shove from Chiara with a pointy elbow. 'Sorry, sorry! I am under strict instructions not to put any pressure on you...'

'I don't think I've ever been away this long,' said Luca. He seemed so happy to be back on home turf; it was clear just how much he had missed it, something Libby was only too aware of.

They piled into Mario's car and set off along the coast, Izzy sleeping peacefully beside Libby. She had cried on and off for most of the flight, much to the irritation of their fellow passengers. Libby had been worried that the change in air pressure was hurting her ears, but she seemed to be fine now, so any discomfort must have only been temporary. Soon they were whizzing along the open roads, drinking in the scenery and chatting away, catching up on all of each other's news. It felt amazing to be back. After about an hour they arrived at Mario and Chiara's house. It was cool and spacious, with wonderful views overlooking the sea. They both ran to the balcony and gulped in huge lungfuls of sea air, feasting their eyes on the jewel-bright sparkling water, the pastel houses and the familiar backdrop of coastline that stretched as far as the eye could see. Luca hadn't looked so happy all year… he whooped loudly and kissed Libby on the cheek, spinning her around in delight.

After a delicious lunch of cold meats, mozzarella and salad, Luca strapped Izzy to his back and they set off for the beach. As soon as they got down to the sea front, Luca wasted no time getting straight into the water. After he had had a good swim, they swapped over. Libby swam out into the deep water and turned back to look at the beach. She watched Luca with Izzy. He was so sweet with her. He bounced her on his lap, rubbed sun cream into her pale white skin and made sure she had enough shade, chatting away to her all the time. Later Chiara and Mario joined them. Mario's hip was suffering after so many years of climbing up and down Positano's steep steps; he could no longer get down to the beach that way without a great deal of pain, so Chiara and he took the bus to the centre instead and walked from there. The five of them spent a happy afternoon on the beach. Chiara and Mario were just as besotted with their granddaughter as their son was, and Libby had the luxury of a nap in the sun with so many willing babysitters to entertain her daughter.

The rest of Luca's family were all meeting them that evening for dinner, as well as a few of his closest friends. Antonia and her husband Matteo were hosting the party because they had the biggest terrace and enough space to accommodate the whole group. Before arriving at Antonia's, Luca and Libby dropped into La Casetta to see Floriana and Tonio and introduce them to Isabella. 'It's so good to see you!' said Floriana, having given both Luca and Libby enormous hugs. 'And this must be little Isabella?'

'Yes it is,' said Libby, unclipping her from the pram and passing her over to Floriana for a cuddle.

'She is divine!' Floriana cooed over the baby as they were joined by Giulia and Maria, both of whom greeted them warmly. It seemed Giulia had finally accepted Luca and Libby as a couple; perhaps the baby and engagement had convinced her that Luca wasn't about to mess Libby around. Or maybe she had just moved on from whatever residual feelings she might have been harbouring. She seemed genuinely happy for them, and both Giulia and Maria were absolutely sweet with Isabella. Tonio cracked open a bottle of prosecco to toast the engagement and the baby.

'To our first La Casetta marriage,' he said, his blue eyes crinkling with happiness.

'To Isabella,' added Floriana.

'She is beautiful,' said Maria, as she bounced Izzy up and down on her hip. 'Congratulations guys!'

It felt strange to be back at La Casetta after so long. Libby remembered the first time she had laid eyes on Luca on her very first day there. She would never have guessed she would end up marrying him. She remembered sitting in the bathroom next to her little bedroom doing the pregnancy test. Looking at Isabella now, it was so strange to think of how it all began. 'It's so weird to think how much we owe to this place,' she said to Luca as they closed the yellow front door behind them.

'Just imagine – if you had never taken the job here, we would never have even met!' Luca kissed her. 'Thank god you came into my life. Otherwise we would never have had you, would we?' he said to Izzy, bending down and kissing her cheek as she sat in her pram looking quizzically up at him.

Luca pushed her up the hill to the main road and they continued walking further up the steep slope for a good twenty minutes or so, until they reached the steps that led down to Antonia and Matteo's. Luca carefully carried the pram down the precariously steep steps. Not for the first time, Libby realised what a nightmare it would be living in Positano with a baby.

There was a huge cheer as they opened the door and came inside the house. All of the family were gathered together, a noisy gaggle of a party that appeared to be in full swing already, with the prosecco and beer flowing. Izzy was swept into a tide of hugs and passed from one aunty or uncle to another. Libby left them to it, always keeping half a watchful eye on her daughter to make sure she was all right.

'Darling Libby, I have missed you so much,' said Nicola. 'This is Francesco,' she introduced Libby to her new boyfriend, who seemed lovely and who also happened to be extremely good-looking. This was unsurprising considering how beautiful Nicola was. They made a very striking couple indeed. Luca came over to introduce himself to Francesco and the girls left them to chat. 'No doubt Luca wants to give him a good grilling,' laughed Libby.

'I'm sure he'll want to make sure he is up to his exacting standards!' agreed Nicola. She caught Libby up on all the local gossip. Antonia and Giovanna soon came bustling over to join the conversation, keen not to miss out on a moment of their future sister-in-law's company.

They all enjoyed a culinary feast, courtesy of Matteo, who was a chef at a local restaurant. They had so many courses: starters, pasta, meat and pudding, that by the end Libby thought she might explode. Isabella had been well and truly worn out by all the new faces passing her around as though in a game of pass the parcel. She had gone to sleep without protest in Antonia's spare room.

As they ate, Libby watched Luca from the opposite side of the table. Seeing him here made her realise that he just wasn't quite himself in London. This version of Luca, so comfortable in his own skin and so relaxed in the company of his family and oldest friends, was the true Luca, the Luca that she had fallen in love with. It saddened her that he still wasn't quite settled in the UK. There was something about being back home that suited him immensely. There was a new sparkle to his eyes, a spring in his step. He didn't complain that often but it was obvious to her now just how much he missed being here. She vowed to herself that she would make more effort to come over. It was unfair on him to be away for too long. Selfishly she was worried that London would seem all the worse to Luca now that he had been reminded of just what he was missing. She hoped he wouldn't struggle when they got home, especially now winter would be kicking in.

Libby was determined that they would enjoy their holiday to the hilt, and they certainly did, packing in as much as they could in the time that they had. They took Izzy to the beach every day; they ate long lunches and dinners at friends' houses and in their favourite local restaurants; they went out on the boat several times with Gian Matteo, who was just as besotted by Izzy as the rest of Luca's family. They gorged themselves on gelato, pasta and pizza, getting their fix of authentic Italian food while they had the chance, and they drank plenty of delicious local wines and prosecco. It was a blissful week – fun but also somewhat exhausting due to all the socialising with so many friends. A week later, they returned to London, nicely bronzed from the sun and a good few pounds heavier.

As the autumn progressed, Luca did seem a little down, as Libby had suspected he might. She could understand why. He seemed to retreat inside himself somewhat, withdrawing from her and frequently seeming lost in his thoughts. Libby had no idea what to do. She tried to get him to talk to her but it didn't seem to help. She hoped that in time he would feel as happy in London as he did in Positano, but she had a sneaking suspicion that they would never quite match up in his eyes. Positano was one of the most beautiful places in the world; she couldn't blame him for missing it. She missed it like crazy herself and she had only lived there for a few months. For Luca it was well and truly home.

That December they flew back to Italy for the run-up to Christmas as well as Christmas Eve and Christmas Day. They then flew back home to Kent on Boxing Day to spend the rest of the festive period with Miriam, John and Helen. Henry was with his own family and Helen seemed lonely and a little lost without him. Having Isabella around did a lot to lift her spirits. Luca found it very hard to tear himself away from his family to board the flight back home. He would clearly rather have stayed in Positano, but Libby had insisted that Miriam should be allowed to share in some of Izzy's first Christmas too.

'Did you know that John's sister-in-law lives in your area of Italy, Luca?' Miriam asked as they all sat enjoying a feast of cold meats and jacket potatoes on Boxing Day.

'Really?' asked Luca. 'Whereabouts?'

'What a coincidence!' said Libby.

'She lives in a small village called Tremento. It's about an hour's drive west from Amalfi, up in the hills,' explained John. 'About twenty minutes to the nearest beach... I've forgotten the name.'

'I've heard of Tremento,' said Luca. 'I bet it's very beautiful up there.'

'Have you been to visit?' asked Helen.

'Not for quite a few years,' said John. 'When Julie became sick, we stopped travelling abroad. But we did visit Lizzy a couple of times over the years. She is married to an Italian chap called Giuseppe. She runs a bed and breakfast.'

'How wonderful!' said Libby. Her mind immediately darted to her own dormant but ever-present plans to run her own bed and breakfast one day. Maybe she could open one in Italy? That was an idea that hadn't occurred to her before. Perhaps she should bite the bullet and leave law completely, move back to Positano with Luca and start a business. That way maybe they could both be happy. She wanted so badly for him to be his sparkling, usual self, and she knew things weren't quite right between them in London.

'So how was Positano?' asked Helen.

'It's almost unrecognisable at this time of year,' said Libby. 'The waves are pretty rough; they have dismantled all the beach restaurants for the winter.'

'Do they do that every year?' asked Miriam.

'Yes, they have to rebuild them for the start of each season, it's exhausting!' explained Luca.

'I'll bet!' said John.

'It's quite beautiful, though; the clouds hang low over the hills above and the whole place has more of a mystical feel to it.'

'I prefer the summer,' said Luca. 'But it was great to be home and to see all my family.'

'You must miss them terribly,' said Miriam.

'It was my first Catholic mass on Christmas Day,' said Libby, trying to change the subject. 'I didn't understand a word!'

'They all adore Izzy, of course,' continued Luca.

'She is looking impossibly sweet at the moment,' said Miriam. 'I know I am biased, but I do think she is the most gorgeous little girl I've ever seen.'

'Well I'm not biased,' said John. 'She really is the most beautiful little thing!'

Luca and Libby spent a happy few days making the most of having such willing babysitters on hand to go for walks together, watch movies and generally relax. She was glad of the opportunity to spend time with him. She wanted more than anything for him to be happy and she felt like some of the distance that had built up between them since their holiday in September was beginning to break down. It was a much-needed break for them both as they gathered strength for the new year to come.

As January dawned, Libby suddenly began to dread the approaching end of her maternity leave. 'I can't believe I'm going back to work at the end of the month,' she said to Luca. She just couldn't bear the thought of leaving Izzy.

'Nine months have gone by very quickly, haven't they?' said Luca. 'We need to sort out what we're going to do with Izzy once and for all.' They had lined up both a nursery and a child-minder who lived locally as possible childcare solutions, but they had yet to decide which option they would choose.

'I think we should go with the child-minder,' Libby said. She had been weighing up both options for quite some time.

'Nurseries won't accept babies if they have even the slightest sniffle, and I can't be off work every time she has a cold.'

'I'm happy with that. I can't just drop everything either. But I do think we need to pay for the child-minder for four days a week. I can do the fifth day of childcare, but I need at least one of my days off from Sicaro to work on my freelance stuff.'

'OK, so if we put her in care from Monday to Thursday, are you happy with that? It needs to be the same days every week.'

'Yes, that sounds perfect. Shall I phone the child-minder?' offered Luca.

'No, don't worry, I'll do it. It's going to break my heart leaving her,' she said miserably.

'I'm sure you'll get used to it. It'll be like ripping off a plaster. You've just got to take the plunge, and then when you're back in the flow of working it will be fine.'

'I don't even enjoy my work, though. At least if I was passionate about what I was doing, it would seem more worthwhile. How am I supposed to leave Izzy, the one person in the world that I love more than life itself, to sit in an office staring at a computer for eight and a half hours a day?' The only reason she was determined to stick at her law conversion was to provide for Izzy's future. The money was so good she knew it was the responsible thing to do. As much as she would love to start her own bed and breakfast, to move to the countryside or back to Positano, she would never be able to reach anything like the earning potential she would by staying in law. She knew she should give Digby and Edwards her best shot. If she didn't get an offer from them at the end of the training contract, then she would have to rethink. She knew she owed it to Izzy, and to herself after all the hard work she had put in so far, to give it one final shot.

She had negotiated her hours to start at nine and leave at five thirty so that she could be home with Izzy by quarter past six for her bath and bedtime. She was determined to stick to her guns about her leaving time. There was no way she was willing to miss out on Izzy's bedtime routine; it was her favourite time of day and in her mind it was completely non-negotiable.

Soon enough, Libby's first day back at work dawned with an early alarm call. She left the house, having handed Izzy over to the child-minder with a thousand last-minute tips and instructions, tears shining in her eyes. It was one of the strangest days of her life. She had dressed in a smart navy dress and heels, the first pair of heels she had worn in as long as she could remember. She arrived at Digby and Edwards at nine o'clock on the dot, walking through the huge swivelling doors and breathing in the familiar smells of wood polish and coffee. Nervously she had made her way to the Contentious Trusts and Successions Department. She had a meeting first thing with Derek, her supervisor, who welcomed her back and explained that she would be completing the remaining five months of her seat in the company of the new round of first-year trainees. She met the two trainees who would be sharing her placement, Imogen and Rajid, both of whom had already settled in well to their new roles in the department.

Strangely, against all expectations, she actually quite enjoyed being out of the house and having a purpose other than childcare, as rewarding as that was. It was refreshing to use her brain and engage in adult conversation for such large parts of the day. The work itself seemed dull to her, but it felt good to be back in a buzzing office environment.

As spring flew by, Libby was happier than she had thought she would be to be back at work. Izzy seemed to adore Zoe, her child-minder, which certainly helped. It was a wonderful relief having such a reliable and kind person to leave her daughter with. Libby had liked her instantly. She had come highly recommended from a local family, who had employed her for both of their young children over the last five years, sadly letting her go now that they were both old enough for primary school. Libby felt happy with the arrangements that they had made and soon settled into her new routine, relishing the precious evenings and weekends that she spent with her daughter. Both Luca and Libby were so busy at work that they hardly seemed to see each other. He would sometimes get back late from client meetings as apparently Sicaro was keen for him to win new business; this – coupled with his football matches and other social engagements with Lorenzo at the weekends – meant that they weren't spending nearly as much time together. During the weekdays, when Libby had got through the bedtime routine, she often collapsed into bed, desperate for an early night after a long day at work. Juggling work, relationships and motherhood wasn't easy, but she felt as though she was trying her best. She felt proud of herself, for once, for persevering when the going was tough.

Chapter Nineteen

At the beginning of May, it was Izzy's first birthday. Luca and Libby had organised a birthday tea to celebrate. Miriam, John, Helen and Henry were all invited, as were Angus and Jules as godparents. They were having tea and cake in the flat. Libby had been slaving away over a birthday cake decorated in pale pink icing and masterfully carved into the shape of Peppa Pig. 'Perhaps I should enter *The Great British Bake Off*? What do you think?' she asked.

'I think we should taste it first!' Luca teased.

'Oy, how dare you? It's going to be delicious!'

'Of course it will. I'm only joking! You are a fantastic baker. What time is everyone coming over?' he asked, looking at his watch. He seemed a little on edge for some reason.

'Three o'clock, hopefully.' She wondered if he was finding it as hard to believe as she did that it had been a year since Izzy had arrived. The memories of going into labour and their brief stay in hospital weren't far from her mind. They laid the table, and sooner or later the guests arrived bearing gifts wrapped in brightly coloured paper for the birthday girl.

'I cannot believe she is one already,' said Miriam, cuddling her granddaughter and planting a kiss on her rosy cheek. She was such a chubby little thing, her brown eyes like little round conkers in her angelic face as she beamed her most dazzling smile at her grandmother.

'How time flies,' agreed Angus. They cut the cake and sang 'Happy Birthday' to Izzy, who had no idea what was going on but seemed delighted with all the attention she was getting nonetheless. Libby and Luca opened her presents; she had been spoiled with lots of wonderful toys and some lovely new dresses.

'What a lucky girl you are,' Libby told her as she kissed her on the top of her head. As the others chatted, sipping their tea and eating their cake, Libby noticed that Jules was being rather quiet.

'Everything OK?' she asked, going over to her friend.

'What? Oh yes, fine! Fine!' Jules replied, a false brightness to her voice. 'Sorry, I'm just a bit tired. I've been working hard on my coursework... I was up late last night.'

She had been acting a bit strangely lately, not responding to texts and calls and seeming a bit out of sorts generally. Libby had asked Angus whether everything was OK with them, and he had told her that she had been a bit distant with him.

'That's weird,' Libby had said. 'That's exactly how I feel she's being with me.'

'Mmmm. I'm not sure what to do about it,' Angus had replied. 'I'm just giving her space. To be honest, I'm so busy working on my latest exhibition, I haven't really been around much. I'm practically living at the studio trying to get it all done.'

Libby had been mulling this over for some time. She wondered what was going on; she knew Jules well enough to know that something was up. Perhaps she was finding the graphic design course harder than she had expected. Maybe she was regretting having left her job as an accountant.

Libby decided to arrange lunch with her the following weekend, just the two of them. After they finished eating, she decided to bite the bullet and tackle Jules's strange behaviour head on.

'Jules, what's going on? You seem very quiet recently, not yourself... I'm worried about you.'

'Nothing's wrong,' she said. Libby noticed that she was looking very pale.

Suddenly a thought popped out of nowhere into Libby's mind. 'Are you pregnant?' she asked.

'No!' Jules said sharply. 'What on earth makes you think that?'

'You just don't look quite right, that's all. Are you ill?'

'Not that I'm aware of...' Jules tailed off.

'You would tell me, right? You know you can talk to me about anything – anything at all? Are you struggling with the course?'

Jules took a deep breath and sighed. She was staring blankly out of the window. Libby noticed there were bags under her eyes. She clearly wasn't sleeping well. 'Is it you and Angus?' she tried, taking a different approach. 'Is everything OK between you two?'

Jules didn't say anything, but Libby felt as though she was on the right tracks. 'Is the baby issue becoming too much of a problem? I know how much he wants a child, and how much you don't...'

Jules shook her head.

'What is it?' she asked again.

Suddenly a solitary tear rolled down Jules's cheek. She wiped it away quickly.

'Come on, Jules, you have to tell me.' Libby leant across the table and took her hand.

Eventually Jules whispered, 'I've done something stupid,' so quietly that Libby could barely hear her.

Libby's heart plummeted. Oh my god, she thought. Jules had had an affair. Suddenly she knew it; it all made perfect sense. 'Have you cheated on Angus?' she asked. She could tell from the look on Jules's face that she was right. She had hit the nail on the head.

Jules nodded, ever so slightly.

'Oh my god! Jules! How could you? Poor Angus!' Libby knew this probably wasn't what Jules wanted to hear, but her heart broke for him. She felt absolutely furious with Jules for hurting him, and at the same time shocked beyond belief that Jules could consider doing such a thing. What the hell was she thinking?

'Who was it?' she asked. All she could think of was Angus's face: how hurt, shocked and humiliated he would be if he found out.

'I can't tell you,' Jules replied. She couldn't make eye contact with Libby.

'Do I know him?' Libby's mind reeled with potential candidates; she scanned through all their mutual friends, wondering who on earth it could possibly be. Jules wouldn't answer the question.

'Is he married?' she asked. Her pulse was racing with anger on Angus's behalf.

Jules nodded again, just a fraction, but enough to confirm what Libby had suspected.

'*Jules!*' Libby's mind was reeling. She didn't know what to say. This was the most awful news she had ever heard.

'Don't tell Angus,' Jules said. 'You have to swear you won't.'

She looked so miserable and so fragile sitting there opposite her, her eyes begging Libby to agree to protect her secret. Libby wanted to reach out and hug her. But she was too cross.

'I don't know, Jules He's just as close a friend to me as you are.' Her heart swelled with emotion at the thought of him.

'It will kill him,' Jules said simply. 'It'll destroy our marriage. You can't. Not even Luca. Promise me you won't say a word.'

Slowly Libby nodded. She was right; it would destroy Angus. What a position to be put in. She wished she had never asked. How was she ever supposed to face Angus again knowing this secret? And why should she choose Jules over Angus? There was no way out of this without betraying either one of her best friends. Her head spun with the reality of what she had heard.

'When did it happen?'

'I don't want to talk about it. I'm sorry, Libby. I feel sick with shame; I couldn't help myself. I can't say anything more.'

Libby didn't know what to do. They sat in awkward silence for a while before Jules tried to change the subject, asking Libby about work. Libby responded to her questions automatically, but she was too shocked and upset with Jules to really engage with her.

She left shortly after, walking all the way home. She couldn't believe her best friend was capable of having an affair, of being the potential cause of the destruction of not only her own marriage, but someone else's. No wonder she looked so terrible. Living with the guilt must be awful. Libby couldn't help but think that Jules deserved to feel so bad. Every time she thought about Angus she wanted to cry. He was the kindest, loveliest man she knew and the last person on earth who deserved to be treated like this. Not only was Jules denying him the chance of having a family, despite knowing how much it hurt him, she had now shown utter contempt for him and their marriage vows by acting so despicably.

For the rest of the day, Libby's thoughts raced. She held Izzy close and rocked her gently, thanking god for her own little family. Her and Luca's relationship certainly wasn't perfect. They weren't as close as they once had been, and she knew deep down that Luca wasn't entirely happy with their life together here in London, but she trusted him and she was grateful for that.

Chapter Twenty

Libby felt terribly burdened by the awful secret that, against her will, she was helping Jules to keep. She tried to persuade her to do the right thing and tell Angus what she had done, but Jules was adamant that she couldn't. She begged Libby to keep her silence. Libby felt torn to breaking point.

Luca noticed something was up and asked her if everything was OK. 'Yes, everything's fine,' she lied. 'I'm just a bit stressed at work at the moment.' He seemed worried about her all of a sudden, fussing over her and looking at her with concern. Work was her go-to cover for feeling a bit low. She had used exactly the same excuse when Angus had asked her the same question. She was clearly not as good as she would have hoped at acting normally around him. She was terrified she would blurt out the truth at any second, and yet she was equally tempted to do exactly that. It wasn't right that Angus was sacrificing the chance of being a father to stay with someone who had been unfaithful to him. Jules didn't deserve him.

One evening later that week, Luca went out to the shops saying that they were out of milk. His phone had been buzzing in his pocket on and off over dinner, but he kept ignoring it, despite her asking him repeatedly whether he was going to answer the call. He had shrugged his shoulders vaguely and ignored her. As he walked down the stairs, the door banging shut behind him, she heard him answer the phone. She wondered who it was.

Not long later, the key turned in the lock and Luca came back in. His entire body language had changed. He had no milk. He hadn't been gone long enough to go to a shop. A combination of panic and worry clouded his face.

'What's the matter?' Libby asked him. 'Has something happened back home?' Her heart began to pound as she took in the tension in his body. She knew that he must have had some horrific news.

He stood frozen to the spot as he closed the door behind him. He turned to face Libby. She saw the nervous expression on his face and in an instant she knew he was about to confess something. Something he was terrified that she would find out.

'Libby, I'm so sorry.' Tears filled his eyes and he trembled with emotion. He looked like a lost little boy half his age.

'What is it?' she breathed. 'Who was on the phone?'

'It was Jules.' Luca couldn't look at her; he was staring at the floor.

'Jules?' What could Jules possibly have said to make Luca react like this? Surely she hadn't told him about her affair? 'Luca. Talk to me! What's going on?'

He took a deep breath and forced himself to look at her.

'Angus just found out that Jules and I have been having an affair,' he said. 'He found messages on her phone—'

'*What?*' she asked, completely unable to process what she had heard.

'I'm so sorry, Libby. I'm so ashamed of myself. I don't know what I've been thinking… I couldn't help myself…'

Time stopped as his words slowly sank into her consciousness. She felt as if a bomb had exploded inside her. Her senses reeled.

'You?' she whispered. 'I knew she had had an affair but…' She tailed off in disbelief.

'You knew?' he asked.

'A couple of weeks ago I practically forced her to tell me. I could tell something was wrong…'

'Oh my god,' he said, rubbing his temples.

'*You?*' she said again. 'It was *you*? It can't be. It *cannot* be true.' She shook her head, desperate to block out the unthinkable images that were flooding her mind of the two of them together.

'When?' she said. 'When did it happen?'

'It started a few months ago—'

'A few *months* ago?' Libby shouted, wide eyed. 'You mean this wasn't just a one-off?' She was still desperately trying to make sense of what he was telling her.

'No. It wasn't. I'm so sorry.'

'How many times?'

'I don't know Libby.'

'*Tell me!*' she yelled, suddenly overcome with anger. 'Tell me right now.' She had to know the extent of their betrayal. Her fiancé and her best friend. How could this possibly be happening?

'I don't know – maybe thirty?' he said weakly.

'Thirty times? You have had sex, with my best friend, *thirty* times. You BASTARD!' she screamed, running over to him and pounding her fists against his chest. Her cheeks were flushed and she felt herself shaking with shock. 'How *could* you?'

A million questions flashed through her mind. 'Did you sleep with her here? Did you sleep with her in our bed? What the hell were you *thinking?*'

'I'm sorry, Libby, it just happened…'

'It *just happened*…' Libby repeated. 'You are the father of my child, you are engaged to *me*, or had you conveniently forgotten that?' She wrenched the ring from her finger, suddenly desperate to get it off. Her eyes were hot with tears. She flung it at him.

'You can take that back, you arsehole! To think that I could even have considered marrying you. You cheating, lying, conniving bastard! You haven't changed one bit, have you?' Her voice was dripping with disgust. 'I can't believe I thought you could, that I believed you.'

'I wish I had been able to, Libby. I was sure that you were different... that this time it would be different.' He shook his head.

'But it wasn't. You can't control yourself, can you? You are so pathetic. And Jules... how she could have done this is beyond anything I can understand. Even if you were attracted to each other, how could you act on it? Where is your loyalty to me? To Angus?' Libby collapsed into a sobbing heap on the floor. Luca came over to her and she shoved him away, choking on her tears.

'I'm so sorry,' Luca repeated, again and again. 'I am so, so sorry.'

'Sorry isn't good enough, Luca,' she said eventually. Barely able to ask the question she whispered, 'Do you love her?'

Luca nodded his head slowly. 'I have feelings for her. I can't deny it.'

'Do you love her?'

'I think I might – I don't know.'

Suddenly Libby saw red; she couldn't stand it a second longer. 'I can't even look at you right now. I want you to get out of my house. Get out! Get *out!*' She got up to her feet and pushed him and shoved him, hitting him and lashing out, tears streaming down her face, hysterical sobs rising up her throat and choking her. She thought she might vomit. She forced Luca out of the door and slammed it shut behind him.

Sitting on the floor, she wailed a harrowing cry, screaming in agony. The noise woke Izzy who began to whimper softly in the next-door room. Blind with tears, Libby stumbled over and opened the door, picking up her daughter and cradling her against her chest, comforting her as she tried to make sense of it all.

How could Jules do this to her? To Angus? How could she possibly have done such a thing? They had grown up together. They had known each other nearly all their lives. There was no one apart from Angus who knew her better. What kind of person would sleep with her best friend's fiancé, the father of her best friend's child? It was unthinkable. Like something you read about in a magazine, not real life. Not Jules. Not her and Jules.

And Luca... how ironic that she had thought he had changed. She realised now that her first impressions of him had been accurate. She wanted the earth to swallow her up as she realised just how naïve she had been. She had fallen under his spell, revelling in the attention he gave her, glorying in his affection, sure that it would last forever, that he had changed his ways. The truth sounded so tragic: Luca the great womaniser, trapped in a relationship because of an accidental pregnancy, all the while desperate to escape. Had there been anyone else, she wondered? Probably. *Oh my god*, she thought. *What an idiot I have been. What an absolute idiot.*

He had never changed; it had all just been a pretence. Why the hell had he even bothered proposing? He clearly had no intention of being faithful. She remembered all too clearly how he had explained that monogamy was for fools, right back when they had first met; that it was unnatural for a man and a woman to be anything other than friends; that even if he fell head over heels in love with someone, sooner or later he would get bored and stray. She felt partly responsible. She had chosen to ignore that; chosen to ignore the alarm bells that had rung in her head. She had hoped that he would be different for her, that she could change him. How could she have been so stupid? She should have listened to her instincts; she should have taken Giulia's advice on that very first day at La Casetta. She thought of Angus, what he would be thinking right now, and her heart went out to him. They had both been betrayed by their other halves, betrayed by their friends.

Izzy settled in Libby's arms as her sobs turned to streams of silent tears and her breathing became more even. Izzy's sleep-suit was wet from her tears. She kissed her peacefully sleeping face and carefully laid her back in the cot.

She went back into the sitting room. Her phone was ringing. It was Jules. Suddenly overcome by an anger so fierce she was frightened by its strength, she picked up the phone and answered the call.

'Libby... I'm so sorry. Luca told me that you know. He had to tell you, Angus found messages on my phone from Luca and he figured it out... I knew that Angus would tell you so I called Luca. I wanted him to be the one to tell you first. I-I don't know what to say... I'm so, *so* sorry.' Jules desperately pleaded for forgiveness. Libby listened to her in silence, she sounded so pathetic. Eventually she could stomach it no longer.

'You bitch,' Libby said, her voice steady and ice cold. 'How *could* you? You lied to my face; you had every opportunity to tell me. You slept with my fiancé, the father of my child. I will never, *ever* forgive you. You are dead to me. I never want to see you again. Stay the hell away from me. Do not contact me again.' She hung up the phone. This couldn't be happening.

Suddenly her breathing came in jagged spurts as the momentousness of the evening's events hit her like a ton of bricks. She felt as though she couldn't get any air into her lungs. She felt choked for breath, as though she was suffocating. She ran over to the window and flung it open, taking in gulps of fresh air. She needed to stay calm but the shock was too much. She knew that from the moment she had heard those words, her life had altered its course irreversibly. She would have to rethink her entire future. Izzy would not grow up living with her father. Libby would be a single parent, and would have to go through the rest of her life without her best friend. There was no way she could even consider forgiving either of them for what they had done.

Later there was a knock at the door. Libby had fastened it with the chain. When Luca opened the door with his key, it only opened an inch. 'Libby? Let me in. Please let me in. I have to talk to you. I have to know that you are OK.'

She didn't reply. She just stared at the door from her position on the sofa, unable to move.

'Libby, please. I know you are there. I have to try and explain.'

As she listened to him talk, she noticed that he never asked for her forgiveness. He didn't tell her that he loved her and would do anything to make it up to her. He just wanted to explain, to justify his actions to her, and to himself, so that they didn't seem so bad. He didn't want to make her feel better, he wanted to comfort himself. She refused to say a word, sitting mutely as she let his words wash over her. He was crying now, pleading with her to let him in, to see Izzy.

Eventually, realising it was pointless, he gave up. He closed the door and walked slowly down the stairs. She had no idea where he would go. She didn't want to know. She continued to stare at the door, utterly broken. She felt as though she might be losing her mind.

Chapter Twenty-One

Her voicemail beeped as the message echoed down the line once more. 'Libby, I wish you would answer your phone. I want to see how you are, how Izzy is. Please… Look, I am with Jules. We are in Sussex. I'm sorry but I do really care about Jules and we've decided to be together. We wouldn't have done this to you or to Angus if we weren't serious about each other. I hope one day you can forgive us. I'll let you know when I'm back in London so we can arrange when I can come and see Izzy. I'm sorry. I wish things had worked out differently. You are an amazing person.'

Angus passed back the phone. Tears shimmered in his eyes. She couldn't bear to see him like this. Libby had listened to the message so many times that she knew it off by heart. Jules had told Angus face to face that she was leaving to be with Luca, but Libby had refused to see him, to have any contact with him, so he had left her a voicemail instead.

'I just can't believe it,' he shook his head again. 'What kind of people are they?'

'They certainly aren't who we thought they were,' Libby said. Her eyes were swollen from all the tears she had cried. Angus looked shell-shocked; they both did. Deep bags shadowed his blue eyes.

'I think I would find it easier if it had been *anyone* else,' Angus said. 'I just feel so ashamed of her; I can't believe she could do that to you… To me, yes. I could have seen it coming. Things haven't been great between us for quite some time, but neither of us knew what to do about it. It was almost inevitable that something would break us. Not that it makes this any less difficult. I thought about ending it myself, you know. I almost did once. I wanted to start over with someone who could give me a family. I felt desperate to have a chance at becoming a dad... But I just couldn't do that to her. I couldn't walk away from all those years of marriage. I would never have broken my marriage vows; to me that just was never and never would be an option.'

'I know it doesn't seem like it now, but I think this is probably going to be a good thing for you, Angus.' Libby took his hand and turned to face him. 'The fact that Jules could do that to you, and to me, just shows what kind of a person she is. She has clearly got no loyalty, no principals; she's just so selfish that all she cares about is herself, what *she* wants.'

'I think you're right.' He took a deep breath, putting his head in his hands and rubbing his temples.

'You deserve so much more than that; you are the best person I know. And some day you're going to make an incredible dad.' She rested her head on his shoulder as they sat side by side on the sofa, partners in their misery. Tears rolled down her cheeks once again and she turned to rest her face against his chest. It felt as though they were grieving. Angus stroked her hair and held her closely. She breathed in the familiar, comforting smell of him and felt her sobs subside; she could feel the rhythmic beating of his heart against her cheek.

'Thank god we've got each other,' she said. 'I don't know what I'd do without you.'

It was all slowly starting to sink in.

'When do you think this all started?' Angus asked her.

'I've been thinking about that, going through any possible clues that I might have missed. Luca was clearly an expert at covering his tracks. Not that *that* should surprise me, given his history. God, I feel so naïve…'

'I guess I just wasn't paying much attention to Jules. I've been so engrossed in work. I preferred spending time in the studio alone to coming home to more arguments.'

'I bet it was all that time they spent working on Jules's portfolio.'

'It must be.'

'Luca said it had only been a few months. I've been thinking – maybe it started as far back as that weekend they spent together? When I asked Jules to entertain Luca because he was so bored and lonely? How bloody ironic. She certainly took that request to heart, didn't she?'

'Where do you think they did it?' asked Angus, wincing at the thought even as he asked the question.

'Don't! I can't bear thinking about it.' Libby still couldn't get her head around the fact that they had actually slept together.

'Do you think they did it in our beds?' he asked.

'Probably.' She shook her head in disbelief. The thought made her feel physically sick.

'I can't stop trying to piece it all together. I knew Luca wasn't happy, but I thought it was just him missing Italy. I can't believe how trusting I was.'

'It's not your fault, Libs.'

'There were so many clues, so many times when he was down or distant… I just left him to it.'

'I feel the same… I never thought she would cheat on me. It genuinely never crossed my mind.'

'I should have known these client meetings he'd started having in the evenings were a load of crap. Him suddenly making plans at the weekends—'

'Libby, please… Don't be so hard on yourself. You are not the one at fault here. Luca is. I never really trusted him, you know. I never thought he was good enough for you. I'm sorry about the way I behaved when I found out you were pregnant. You know I think I was jealous in some way, that you were having a child when I wanted one so badly. That this random guy could just click his fingers and have you, a family, the kind of life that I wanted so much – and after such a short fling… I couldn't bear it.'

'He only stayed with me because of the baby,' said Libby. 'If it hadn't been for Izzy, we never would have lasted past the summer. We certainly never would have got engaged. None of this would have happened if I hadn't fallen pregnant…'

They sat in silent contemplation on the sofa, slowly processing it all, allowing it all to gradually sink in.

Chapter Twenty-Two

As the dust slowly began to settle, Libby was forced to piece together a new routine for herself and Izzy. Zoe had kindly agreed to extend her childcare days to five days a week so that Luca could be excused from his parental responsibilities on Fridays. Apparently Luca and Jules were still in Sussex. He had been phoning her frequently since the night he left, but it had taken her a good three weeks until she felt able to answer the phone.

'Luca,' she said, her hand trembling as she finally clicked the icon to receive the call.

'Libby, thank you for answering,' he said, relieved to have finally got through. 'How are you?'

'Fine.' She couldn't talk to him about what he had done, about her feelings. It was too raw and too painful.

'I'm so sorry—' he began.

'Don't.' Libby interrupted him. She took a deep breath. 'I'm not answering the phone so that we can have a conversation about what you have done, Luca. I'll talk to you about Izzy, but that's it.'

He paused. 'I understand,' he said. She could picture him so clearly, her heart hurt at the thought. She wondered whether Jules was by his side, listening, and she hardened her heart once more. 'How is she? I miss her.'

'Then you shouldn't have left her.' She couldn't help it; tears smarted in her eyes. Calming herself, she gave him a cursory update to let him know that his daughter was all right.

'Will you let me see her when I get back to London?'

'Are you still in Sussex?'

'Yes.'

'Jules too?' It pained her to even say Jules's name.

'Yes.'

She waited for a minute, knowing what the right thing to do was but reluctant to agree to it. 'I'll let you see her,' she said.

Despite everything he had done, she knew that she didn't want Izzy to miss out on having a good relationship with her father. Her own dad had meant the world to her, and nothing Luca did could alter the fact that he was Izzy's father. She would have to put up with his treatment of her for her daughter's benefit, even though all she really wanted to do was cut him out completely from her life and delete him from her memory. But life was never that straightforward. She didn't have to see Jules, though, and she told Luca that when he was with Izzy she did not want Jules to be there too. He agreed, promising that he would see Izzy alone. She had hung up the phone before her resolve crumbled, too proud to let him hear the emotion in her voice, and then given way to the inevitable tears.

The days continued to roll by. With each day that passed, Libby regained a slither of her former independence, but at night, as she lay alone in bed, she was all too aware of the empty space beside her. Luca had vacated their home, and the lack of his presence left a gaping hole. She felt as though she had been plucked from the security of her relationship and dropped into the middle of an ocean. She was paddling manically to stay afloat, to juggle everything that was required of her at work, and to look after Izzy without her partner's support. She felt incredibly isolated. She imagined it must feel similar when your partner died; the decision was entirely out of your control, but here you were, alone, and with no choice other than to somehow keep going, to acclimatise to your new circumstances the best you could.

Libby missed him, yet she could barely contain the rage she felt at his and Jules's betrayal. It took all her strength to try and remain civil when they spoke on the phone. How she was going to manage it when she saw him face to face she had no idea. She had shed so many tears, crying herself to sleep, going over and over events in her mind, reliving the happy memories she had shared with Luca in Italy when it all began. She combed through her memories obsessively to try and find some telltale sign she had missed, glances between Luca and Jules as they'd plotted and schemed behind their backs.

Libby felt Jules's betrayal most bitterly. Luca had been in her life for two years, but Jules had known her for nearly all of her thirty-four years. Their friendship had been sacred to Libby. If she could have named one person she knew would never, ever do something like this to her, it would have been Jules. She felt unbelievably foolish that she had trusted her so deeply and implicitly. She couldn't get her head around the fact that Jules was capable of such deceit. It seemed unthinkable.

She thought back to the early days when she had first started seeing Luca. She remembered Giulia's warning. She should have listened to her. It was clear now to Libby that Giulia hadn't been jealous of her, she had been genuinely concerned. When was she going to learn? Her character judgement was clearly way off track. She needed to stop being so naïve and trusting. She was determined not to let anyone close to her, and to Izzy, again.

She thought about Helen, how she had once said that everything came so easily to Libby. How wrong she had turned out to be. Or maybe she had been right. Perhaps it was Libby herself who was at fault. She should have taken the time to really get to know Luca before rushing into things. She should have paid more attention to the signs that things were not quite right between them, that they hadn't been these past few months. She should have seen Jules for what she really was.

Jules called her often, desperate to explain herself, to apologise and try to make amends, but Libby couldn't have been less interested. Her blood boiled at the mere sight of her name on the screen of her phone, and she knew that she would never forgive her. Her days seemed an awful lot emptier without them, but life ploughed on with its unstoppable force, oblivious to the dramas that trailed in its wake.

Helen and Miriam rallied around her with a stoic show of support. Libby was grateful that Helen was in so much happier a place.

'Of all the people,' Miriam said, giving her daughter's hand a squeeze. They were sitting at the kitchen table drinking cups of tea.

'It is quite unbelievable,' agreed Helen, who had known Jules for just as long as Libby had. 'How are you holding up?'

'Better now that I've had some time to get used to it. I'm sorry I've been so hard to get hold of. What with getting my head around all this, work and looking after Izzy, I've just needed to focus on getting through each day one by one.' She hadn't wanted to see her family immediately.

'I understand completely,' said Miriam. 'It's been a shock for us all. It's just so unexpected.'

'Have you seen them?' asked Helen.

'No, they are in Sussex apparently,' said Libby.

'Sussex? So they really are together then?' asked Miriam.

'It would appear so. They have "serious" feelings for each other, according to Luca, so that justifies their actions apparently. They would never have run off together unless it was the real deal…' Libby laughed ironically. 'Clearly being engaged and married respectively was not the real deal – who would have thought it?'

'How's poor Angus coping?' asked Helen.

'Do you know what, he has been amazing,' said Libby. 'A complete rock for me and Izzy, despite everything he is going through.'

'You said they hadn't been in a great place for quite some time,' said Helen. 'Perhaps that helps.'

'It doesn't make it any easier, but I think deep down he suspects that it might be for the best. It's just so shocking, though. To think of them going behind our backs like that…' Libby trailed off, shaking her head in disbelief.

'How could they?' Miriam was clearly disgusted. The scandal of the affair had been the talk of Kent. She was glad that she had John by her side to help her deal with all the gossiping locals. 'What are you going to do about Luca seeing Izzy?'

'Well, that's the hardest part in a way,' said Libby. 'The fact that I can't just forget about him and move on. I have to accept that we will be in touch for the rest of our lives because of Izzy. I suppose that that's just what happens when a relationship ends and a child is involved. The sooner I face up to him, the better.'

'So you'll see him as soon as he comes back to London?'

'Yes, I'll have to.'

'Will you talk about it?'

'We'll see. I'm not sure how I'll feel. But yes, I suppose we should. I need to force myself to be civil towards him for Izzy's sake, and the sooner I do that the better.'

'You're so brave, darling,' said Miriam. 'I'm so proud of you.'

'You've handled this amazingly well,' said Helen. 'I honestly don't know what I would have done if it had happened to me…' She gave her sister a big hug.

Later they left Libby as they headed back to Henry and John. Libby couldn't help but envy them their happy relationships, and wonder if she would ever find happiness like that again. It would be very hard to trust someone after all this. She felt as if she had clamped a metal cage around her heart and she knew that it would be incredibly difficult to open it. She was doing what she had to do to stay strong for her daughter, though, and for Angus. But she was terrified that her resolve would fail and she would end up in a pit of despair so deep that she would never be able to climb out.

Chapter Twenty-Three

Libby's heart skipped a beat as she heard the knock on the door. She had been dreading this moment. She looked at herself in the mirror. She knew it was pointless, but she wanted to look her best when she saw him. Her long brown hair was pulled back off her face in a low ponytail. Her green eyes stared back at her as she took a deep breath and walked calmly over to the door.

She pulled it open. Luca was standing outside looking sheepish. She was relieved to see that Jules was nowhere to be seen.

'Libby,' he said. He came inside and moved towards her to kiss her – or hug her, Libby wasn't sure. She took a step back to avoid contact, resisting the urge to throw herself into his arms as she had done a thousand times before.

'Luca,' she said. Her heart was thudding against her breastbone but she refused to let him see the inner turmoil he was causing her. 'Izzy will be awake any moment now.'

'I can't wait to see her,' he said. 'I've missed her terribly. I've missed you too…'

Libby didn't know what to say. It was so strange to see him, to have him back in the flat.

'I've packed up all your things,' she said, pointing at the pile of suitcases and bags next to the door. 'You can take them with you.'

'Thank you,' Luca said. 'I've got a car here so I'll get them out of your way tomorrow if that is OK?'

Libby nodded and sat down on the sofa. She felt numb. Luca came and sat next to her, careful not to sit too close. He put his set of house keys on the table. 'Libby, I feel awful about how this ended. I owed you more respect than to go behind your back. I should have been honest with you.'

'You should never have slept with my best friend.' Her eyes filled with tears despite her intention to remain aloof. 'If you weren't happy you should have told me. I would have understood. But this was just the worst possible thing you could have done.'

'I'm so sorry,' he said.

'I've had to cope with losing my fiancé and my best friend at the same time. It's not fair…'

'I know. I'm sorry, Libby. It just happened… and suddenly it was too late, I was in too deep and I couldn't stop myself.'

'You could have, Luca.'

'It's hard to explain.'

'I'm not interested in your excuses or explanations. Are you still seeing each other?'

'We are.'

'Is she here?'

'No. She's in Sussex.'

'Where are you staying?'

'We're staying in a flat in Lewes that belongs to friends of Jules's. They've let us house-sit while they're away travelling. It's an hour on the train from London, so I've been able to get into work.'

Libby wished she'd never asked. She realised that the less she knew the better.

'I don't want to talk about it,' she said. 'You told your family…' She had received sweet messages from his sisters, clearly upset with Luca for his behaviour, and she had been grateful for their kind words.

'They think I'm mad,' he said, that cheeky, helpless smile that she knew so well settling across his features. It would have made her stomach flip in usual circumstances, but now it just hurt her.

They talked a short while longer before Izzy roused from her sleep and began to chatter away to herself in her bedroom.

'Can I?' asked Luca, clearly longing to see his daughter. Libby nodded her head and he went into her room. She listened to him call out to Izzy and talk to her in Italian, and her heart twisted with sadness as she heard the delight in her daughter's response at seeing her father after so many weeks apart.

He carried her back out into the sitting room. The sight of the two of them, so similar with their brown hair and hazel eyes, caused tears to fill her eyes once again. She bit her lip and turned away; distracting herself by fetching the travel cot and the bag she had packed for Izzy. Luca asked whether there had been any changes to her routine, and checked he had everything he needed for the weekend with his daughter. He was staying in a hotel down the road so they wouldn't be far away, but it still pained her to think of their imminent separation. Libby had to stop herself from crying as she kissed her goodbye, breathing in the sweet smell of her and holding her closely. Her heart wrenched as she let them go. She knew she would have to get used to it, but it felt so unnatural, so wrong for them no longer to be the tight family unit that they had been since Izzy had arrived.

As soon as the door closed behind them, she picked up the phone and called Angus. 'Have they gone?' he asked, answering on the first ring.

'Yes,' she said, tears spilling down her cheeks.

'Do you still want to come over?' he asked.

'Yes please,' she said. She wanted to get out of the flat as quickly as possible. She needed a distraction. It was horrible not to be with her daughter at the weekend. She worked so hard during the week that she treasured more than anything the time she got to be with Izzy on her days off. Luca was taking that away from her and she felt incredibly alone; she needed company. She watched him drive off, then waited a few minutes before setting off for Angus and Jules's house. It was a relatively cool day for June, for which Libby was grateful, considering the physical labour ahead.

Angus answered the door and wrapped her in a huge bear hug. There was a cobweb in his auburn hair. Libby reached up to remove it.

'What is it?' he asked.

'A cobweb.'

'I've been in the cellar bringing up the packing boxes,' he said.

'Well, your helper has arrived,' she said. 'I am at your service.' She was looking forward to some hard work to take her mind off Luca.

'Thanks so much for coming,' he said. She was pleased to see that his bright blue eyes had regained a hint of their usual sparkle. The idea of moving house and having a fresh start seemed to have given him a small spring in his step. This house belonged to Jules. Angus hadn't had enough money to contribute towards it as a struggling artist, and she had been given a helping hand by her parents to buy it. Now that Angus was doing so well with his art, he was earning more than enough to rent his own place and had wasted no time in doing so. He had collected the keys to a small flat near his studio by the river the previous day.

'I can't wait to see the new pad,' Libby told him.

'Well, depending on how long you want to stay and help, you can,' he laughed. 'I'm planning on packing for a few hours and then moving straight in.'

'Is it furnished?'

'Fully. Most of this stuff belongs to Jules anyway, so it shouldn't take me too long to pack up my possessions and get out of here.'

They taped the flat-pack boxes together and began to fill them with piles of Angus's belongings.

'How do you feel about leaving?' asked Libby.

'Do you know what, it's strange, but I feel quite good. There are so many happy memories from this place, of course, but there are also so many terrible ones. It feels like the right thing to do. I know it's going to take a long time, but I think I'll be able to move on much better in a new flat. Plus Jules could come back at any moment, and there's no way I'm sticking around to be here when she does…'

'Definitely not.'

'How was it seeing Luca?' he asked.

'Weird,' she said. 'I literally hadn't seen him once since I kicked him out. It was hard seeing him with Izzy. They are so alike. It's strange getting used to the idea that we will never be a family, all three of us, again.' Realising she had welled up yet again, Libby wiped her eyes with the back of her T-shirt sleeve. It was so hard to talk about it without getting emotional.

'I'm so sorry, Libby.' Angus came over and gave her a hug. She loved his hugs; they were so warm and reassuring. She loved the smell of laundry powder that clung to his T-shirt and she held him closely as she breathed it in.

A couple of hours later they stopped for lunch. Angus made them cheese and pickle sandwiches and they sat in the garden to eat them, enjoying some fresh air after their hard work. Libby tried not to think about Izzy and Luca, but she couldn't help checking her phone in case he had tried to call. There were no messages, so she had to assume that everything was fine.

Later that afternoon they loaded up the car with as many boxes as would fit and drove over to the flat.

'I love it!' cried Libby as she walked around taking a good look at his new place. There was a large bedroom and a small boxroom off to the side, which Angus was intending to use as a study. The walls were painted a bright off-white throughout, which added to the sense of light and space. A large galley kitchen was separated from the sitting room by a breakfast bar. The flat was furnished with comfortable sofas, a table and chairs, and there was a huge double French door which led from the sitting room on to a spacious balcony. 'It's got such a nice feel to it.'

'That's exactly what I thought,' said Angus. 'It's very light and airy.'

'And the view of the river is amazing.'

'It's not bad,' agreed Angus. He looked pretty pleased with his new home. It was in a newly built block of flats overlooking the Thames, and was fully fitted with all the mod-cons you could hope for.

They carried all the boxes up the stairs and into the flat, repeating the journey several times until there was nothing left in the old house that belonged to him. As they stood in the hall of the home he had shared for so many years with Jules and looked around for one last time he said, 'I can't believe this is it.'

'Are you sure you're ready?' Libby asked, taking his hand and giving it a squeeze.

He nodded. 'It's time.' He shut the door and locked it, placing his keys into an envelope and sealing it shut before posting it through the letterbox. They took a step back and looked at the bright red door. So many memories raced through her head as she stood there; she could only imagine how many must be tumbling through Angus's mind. They stayed for a few minutes in silence, alone with their thoughts.

Eventually Angus walked away, opening the car door and climbing in without a backward glance. Libby joined him in the passenger seat. Angus looked at her and raised his eyebrows. She smiled at him and nodded her head. He turned the key in the ignition and they set off for Anglesea Road and his new home, leaving all the memories behind them. They were in the past now… where they belonged.

Libby helped him unpack the first few boxes. The radio was blaring out some classic eighties tunes. They had stopped to buy some cold beers from the corner shop and they sipped their drinks as they worked.

Later that evening, Angus ordered some Indian food and they sat on the balcony and watched the sun go down as they ate. Libby's mind had been put to rest when Luca texted her a photograph of Izzy sleeping peacefully in her travel cot.

'To new beginnings,' said Angus, chinking his bottle against Libby's.

'To your new home,' added Libby. 'And a fresh start.'

'It feels good,' he said. 'Strange, but good. I'm glad you're here with me, Libs.'

'I'm glad I'm here too,' she smiled.

Chapter Twenty-Four

Luca came to see Izzy several times in June and July. Sometimes he would take her for the day on a Thursday or a Friday when he had the day off, and sometimes he would take her for a weekend. Each time Libby became a little more used to his coming and going. She managed to spend the first night in the flat by herself without Izzy and, though she hated it, she survived. She knew that it would take her a long time to get used to her new circumstances yet, slowly but surely, her new reality was becoming the norm. She was able to see Luca without being filled with regret. She realised that he truly hadn't been happy in their home together, as much as she had wished that he was. He was near the sea in Sussex and he seemed to have regained a little of his lost *joie de vivre*. She hoped it had less to do with Jules and more to do with his freedom from London and the accompanying claustrophobia of city life.

Jules herself pitched up outside Digby and Edwards, determined to talk to Libby face to face and fed up with her lack of success getting through on the phone. Knowing that she would have a better chance of catching Libby off guard on her lunch hour she hung around outside the entrance waiting for Libby to come outside. As Libby walked out of the office to head to the usual row of sandwich shops, she heard a familiar voice call her name. She knew instantly who it was. She looked in the direction of the voice and, sure enough, was confronted by a somewhat drawn-looking Jules.

'Libby, please stop; I just want to talk to you,' she pleaded.

Libby set off at a quickened pace in the opposite direction, feeling her cheeks flush with rage at the mere sight of her. Unfortunately there wasn't much she could do to avoid her. Jules caught up with her in no time and grabbed her arm. The last thing Libby wanted was a scene in front of her colleagues or, worse, her clients, any number of whom could be within earshot.

'Jules, I've already told you. I've got nothing to say to you.' Libby spoke through gritted teeth.

'I know, I heard you, but I have to try and talk to you… I have to try and explain.' Tears swam in Jules's eyes, and for the briefest second Libby felt a flicker of pity for her former best friend. She stopped walking and said, 'I'll give you five minutes.'

'Thank you.'

Libby crossed the busy square and sat down on an empty bench, Jules following close behind her. She turned to face her.

'I know you must hate me, but I miss you so much. I can't bear what you must think of me.'

'Really?' said Libby frostily. She found it extremely hard to feel sorry for her and really wasn't in the mood for self-pity. 'This was your choice, Jules. You did this.'

'I know, I know. And I'm so sorry. I just fell for him, Libby, that's all. It wasn't planned, I couldn't help myself…' This sounded familiar; Luca had given her the same sob story.

'I'm afraid I just don't buy the "I couldn't help myself" line, Jules. Yes, you might have found Luca attractive, yes he might have reciprocated, but you certainly didn't need to act on it. Having the thought and actually going ahead and sleeping with someone are two very different things. If you had a single moral in your body, you would never have been able to do that to me. Luca was my fiancé – and don't even get me started on Angus…'

Jules pulled anxiously at the sleeve of her top. 'I feel very guilty about it all,' she said. 'I know I was selfish and that I only thought about myself, but I felt so trapped in my life, so trapped in my marriage. Luca was a breath of fresh air; he made me feel like myself again.'

'Jules, I really couldn't care less how he made you feel.' Libby was trying her hardest not to raise her voice, but she couldn't stomach listening to Jules's pathetic excuses for a second longer. 'You completely destroyed two relationships because you were too selfish to think about anyone else but yourself. The two of you deserve each other: in fact you are perfect for each other. I'm glad that you've finally shown me your true colours and that I've realised that you are not even worth wasting a second of my thoughts on, a second of my time. To think I used to call you my best friend. You are *nothing* to me. I mean it. *Nothing!*' Libby stood up and started walking back to the office; she had lost her appetite completely. She couldn't bear the needy look on Jules's face, so desperate for Libby to accept her insincere apologies.

'Libby please, don't! I'm so sorry. I hope one day you can forgive me—'

'I will never, *ever* forgive you, Jules. And I never want to see you again. Don't show up at my work, don't show up at my flat – stay the hell away from me.' With that she turned on her heels and walked away without so much as a backward glance, fuming at Jules's audacity in turning up out of the blue like that.

Back in the office, she buried herself in the huge mound of paperwork that awaited her at her desk, determined to distract herself from unpleasant thoughts of Jules. Her run-in with Jules had left a distinctly sour taste in her mouth. She needed the monotony of sorting through case files to steady her nerves and calm her rampaging emotions. Never before had she had to confront someone she had loved so much after such a horrific betrayal. It had been a horrible experience and one she would rather have avoided. She had known seeing Jules would make her feel even worse, and that was part of the reason she had been so desperate for it not to happen in the first place.

Life at Digby and Edwards was as hard as ever, but Libby was doing her best to keep on top of her to-do list. She resolutely stuck to her guns, making sure that she left on time each day to collect Izzy from Zoe, her child-minder. She was nearing the end of her training contract and would soon be finding out whether Digby and Edwards would offer her a permanent place in the firm. Unlike Tammy and Sam, who had both been snapped up at the end of their training, she was ninety-nine per cent sure that they wouldn't keep her on. It was a competitive firm at the best of times, and she knew that she didn't put in anything like the hours that some of her colleagues did. She found it increasingly hard to care. There was no way that work could ever be her priority now that she had Izzy. A career in law would only ever take second place.

She started to dream more and more about what she might do instead. She began to seriously contemplate leaving law altogether and starting up her own bed and breakfast, her own version of La Casetta. It would be a totally different pace of life. She could be her own boss. Despite the relentless schedule of cleaning, cooking and catering for her guests' every whim, she knew that overall her quality of life would be better, that she would get more time with Izzy. It certainly sounded tempting. She had started compiling a folder with all her research on her laptop. She found herself spending more and more time on her new project; hours would fly by as she scoured the internet for potential properties. She wanted a place that would be big enough to turn a decent profit but not so overwhelming that she wouldn't have any time to spend with Izzy. She also found out exactly what kind of insurance she would need and she researched the relevant building regulations. She planned and practised cooking scrumptious breakfasts which she intended to prepare using only the freshest local produce. She jotted down marketing ideas, and dreamt of exactly how she would make her B & B stand out from the crowd. She was slowly beginning to see exactly what steps she would need to take. The prospect terrified and thrilled her in equal measure. She felt exhilarated at the thought and ready for the challenge. She knew that if she committed to it, she would have no choice but to make it work. It would mean selling her flat and moving, yet she realised that she was no longer afraid of the intense amount of hard work she would need to put in to make it a success.

That August, Angus and Libby decided to go away on holiday together. Neither of them had made any plans for the summer, and Libby had been delighted when Angus suggested it, knowing that it would have been hard to go away by herself with Izzy, yet feeling desperate for a long overdue break.

'Where shall we go?' Libby asked, her mind racing with possibilities.

'Well, I'm planning on going to Devon at some point for my next series of paintings, so it might make sense to go there?' suggested Angus.

'That's a fab idea!' Libby said. 'Devon is beautiful and it'll be much easier to stay in England than to travel abroad. We can just load all of Izzy's stuff into the car and set off.'

In the end they decided that Angus would go down a week early to get all of his painting done before Libby and Izzy arrived. Libby would drive down and join him and they would spend the second week together. Angus took control of the planning and found a little house to rent on the coast called Acorn Cottage.

Soon enough Libby was pulling into the drive, getting her first glimpse of the house. It had stone walls that were covered in climbing roses. Libby fell in love with it in an instant. The garden was full of flowers in blossom. Fat honeybees flew sleepily from bush to bush, drunk on nectar. At the end of the garden a sandy pathway sloped down to a golden beach, winding its way through dunes and wild hedgerows. It was the perfect spot for a holiday and she felt herself relax instantly. This was just the kind of place she had been looking at during her bed and breakfast research. The thought of living somewhere like this full time one day filled her with excitement once again.

Angus came out as soon as he heard the car pull up in the drive. He showed them around and helped Libby unload their luggage. The walls were stacked with small canvases covered in sketches of the local area; he had clearly had a productive week. He had also stocked the fridge and the larder with supplies ready for Libby and Izzy's arrival.

'Look, Izzy, it's the sea!' Libby said, bouncing her on her hip. 'I can't wait to get down to the beach!'

She prepared a round of sandwiches for lunch, banana for Izzy and fresh crab for Angus and her. They sat out on the patio to eat. The air tasted salty from the sea spray and the sun shone brightly. Libby felt the happiest she had felt in a long time, the week stretching luxuriously out ahead of her. 'This is bliss! You are so clever to have found this place.'

'It was total fluke. Literally the first place I looked at on the Devon rentals website. We're lucky it was free; apparently it was a last-minute cancellation.'

'I bet it's always fully booked in the summer, it's such a beautiful area.' Libby took a bite of her sandwich. 'Tell me about what you've been doing so far.'

'I've been out every day with my easel and paints. I moved about quite a bit, sketching and drawing as I went, taking note of the changing light. It's amazing how the sea changes under the sun; it has an almost macabre feel under cloud cover, but practically radiates light when the sun comes out. I feel very inspired here.'

'That's good. You've definitely chosen some amazing places so far.'

'I certainly have. I feel as if I've almost run out of places in the UK, though. It might have to be somewhere abroad next time…'

'Such a hard life! Are you happy with what you've got so far? Do you think you'll need to do much more this week?'

'I think I've made a very good start. I'll definitely do a bit more here and there and take lots of photographs. But I won't be slaving away. I want to spend time with you and Izzy.'

'I'm glad to hear it.' Izzy emitted a loud gurgle of pleasure. 'And so is Izzy!'

His blue eyes softened as he looked at them both and Libby's heart filled with affection. He looked very handsome; his face had tanned well in the sun. It always surprised her how brown he could get, despite his auburn hair. She noticed that his crow's feet were ever so slightly paler than the rest of his skin. He must have been squinting as he painted; either that or smiling away to himself as he worked. She was pleased to see him looking so relaxed, so happy. She couldn't think of the last time he had seemed so at ease with himself. Being away from Jules was having a wonderful, liberating effect on him. In that moment a tiny part of her was grateful for what had happened, for allowing Angus to move on and have a chance of real happiness without Jules.

'OK, are you sure we've got everything we need?' Angus was laden down with bags, an umbrella, and he also had Izzy strapped to his back.

'I feel as if you're carrying it all and I've got nothing!' Libby said. She had a beach bag and that was about it.

'Well that's what I'm here for… your personal packhorse. Isn't that right, Izzy?' She gurgled on cue and they set off down the path towards the sea. They made a little camp below the dunes and spread out rugs, towels and the umbrella to give Izzy plenty of shade. Angus slathered sun cream on Libby's back, and she rubbed it all over herself to make sure that she didn't burn. The sun was lovely and hot, with a pleasant sea breeze ensuring it wasn't unbearable.

'Can you do mine?' Angus asked. Libby squirted cream all over his freckly, tanned back, marvelling at how huge it was.

'Have you been working out?' she asked. 'You're so muscly!'

'No more than usual,' Angus replied. Perhaps she hadn't noticed before, but he really was in impressive shape. He was built like a rugby player, tall and broad and muscular. She seemed incredibly petite standing next to him in her bikini, and she wasn't short at five foot eight. As she rubbed the sun cream in she felt a peculiar stirring in the bottom of her stomach. She immediately checked herself, telling her mind not to be so ridiculous – this was Angus; how mortifying! But it was undeniable; she was definitely feeling the familiar flicker of desire. What was wrong with her?

She felt herself blush and sat down quickly; giving him back the sun cream and hoping that he wouldn't notice her ridiculous reaction to his semi-naked body. She glanced at him as he bent over to pull his towel out of the bag. Now that her mind had started to go down that particular route, she couldn't help but notice his enormous thighs, straining against his board shorts, and the blond hair that covered his tanned calves. It was as if she was suddenly seeing him for the first time. She looked away, studying the horizon with determination. She seriously needed to get some action soon – look what was happening to her, she was ogling her best friend.

'Are you OK?' Angus asked.

'What? Yes fine, thanks… just soaking up the view.' He looked at her quizzically, an amused expression on his face. She hoped he hadn't noticed her blushing. What would he think?

'You know that green really suits you,' Angus said. 'It matches your eyes.'

'This old thing!' she pinched the material of her bikini. 'It's probably lost its elastic completely; I haven't got around to buying a new one for years.'

'Right, I'm going for a dip,' Angus said, standing up and stretching.

Libby watched him walk down to the sea and wade into the water. She remembered him saying that she had beautiful eyes once before, all those years ago, when they had kissed on the beach as teenagers. She wondered how much he had meant it when he had confessed his feelings for her, and what would have happened if neither of them had been so awkward about their kiss. What if they had given themselves a chance instead?

He got to waist-deep and then dived under, swimming quickly out into the deeper water before turning to wave at her. As she gave him a wave back, he turned to swim parallel to the shore. She lay back on her mat and reached for her book, soon losing herself in the words on the page, keeping half an eye on Izzy who was sleeping peacefully in the shade beside her.

Later they took Izzy down to the water and dipped her toes in the sea. She shrieked in surprise. The water was cold, so they paddled around in the shallows with her. Angus snapped photographs of them both on his camera. She imagined they looked like any other happy family on their summer holiday. At tea-time they packed up their belongings and walked back up to the house. Angus had bought scones, raspberry jam and clotted cream, so they indulged themselves with a cream tea while Izzy had her dinner. He helped Libby bath her and put her to bed, clearly enjoying every second of his godfatherly duties.

'She is so gorgeous,' he said as they turned off the light.

'You're so good with her. She really loves you,' Libby told him.

'Now why don't you go and run a bath while I cook?' he said.

'I'm happy to cook tonight if you'd prefer?'

'No, don't worry, I've got it all lined up. Are you happy with fish? I got some lovely-looking sea bream at the fishmonger's this morning. I thought we could have it with asparagus and new potatoes?'

Libby's stomach rumbled at the thought. 'That sounds utterly perfect. My turn tomorrow, though.'

'Deal.'

She luxuriated in the hot bath water, listening to Angus pottering about in the kitchen and singing along to the radio. Soon delicious smells were making their way through the gap in the door. Libby dried herself off and pulled on a wraparound dress.

'Do you want a glass of white?' Angus asked as she joined him in the kitchen.

'I'd love one, thanks.' She accepted the cold glass and sipped the dry white wine. They ate on the patio, making the most of the warm evening. The wine was the perfect accompaniment to the sea bream, cooked to perfection by Angus. They had treacle tart and raspberries for pudding and then sat and chatted under the stars. Libby noticed that they had stopped talking so much about Luca and Jules. As if by mutual agreement, they had decided to move on from that chapter of their lives as best they could. It seemed as though they were both looking to the future rather than to the past.

The following day, Izzy woke Libby up bright and early. Having given her some food, she strapped her into her car seat and set off for the local village. She wanted to buy some sausages and eggs so that she could cook them a proper English breakfast. Angus would tell her whether it was up to scratch for potential paying guests in the future. The village consisted of a post office, a butcher, a baker, a hardware shop, a fishmonger and a grocer. It had everything you could possibly need, all from local producers. It was Libby's idea of heaven. She went from shop to shop, filling several bags full of goodies before loading them into the boot. She had decided to cook spaghetti with prawns for dinner. It was one of Luca's traditional family recipes, passed down through the generations. He had cooked it so many times that she had learned it off by heart, another addition to her by-now-impressive collection.

By the time Angus woke up, the house was full of the mouth-watering smell of sausages. Libby had made a fresh pot of coffee and they sat outside, looking at the sea, while they ate their sausages and fried eggs.

'What do you want to do today?' Libby asked.

'There's an amazing little beach that I found on one of my walks last week that I think you might like. Seeing as it's another beautiful day, we could take a picnic and spend the day there?'

'That sounds perfect. What's it called?'

'Coomber Cove.'

'Coomber Cove it is!' They cleared up breakfast, made sandwiches for lunch and loaded the car with their beach stuff. After a short drive they found the turning. They parked at a small farmhouse and followed the footpath up the hill through a rickety old gate. It led them through sun-bleached cornfields peppered with poppies and lined with dry-stone walls overgrown with wild flowers. At the end of the fields, the sea loomed below them, seemingly quite a long way down. A well-trampled path lay partially obscured by long grass, leading the way to the hidden beach.

'You did some good exploring to find this!' laughed Libby as they set off through the grass. 'I'm not sure I would have ventured this far!'

'It's worth it, I promise,' said Angus.

The path was steep but not dangerous, yet Libby was still glad that Angus was carrying her daughter. She trusted him not to lose his footing much more than she trusted herself; she had always been slightly clumsy in that respect. Angus had disappeared at a sharp bend to the left ahead of her. As she turned the corner to follow him, she gasped. A deserted sandy beach lay below. The sea rivalled that of Positano, sparkling for all its worth, and as clear as could be, thanks to a large outcrop of rocks that stopped the tide fifty metres or so out to sea and left the water in the cove mostly undisturbed.

'It's absolutely stunning,' cried Libby in amazement. Angus had turned to watch her reaction and was chuckling to himself, clearly proud of his discovery. They climbed down the rest of the path, Angus holding his hand out to steady Libby on the steeper sections. She jumped from the ledge safely down on to the sand and ran straight to the water's edge, dipping her toe in. 'I can't wait to get in the water, it looks irresistible!'

They set up camp in the middle of their own private beach, secretly hoping that no one else would appear and that they could keep this hidden paradise all to themselves for the day.

Izzy was having a nap, so they left her in the shade and stripped off their clothes.

'Race you?' Angus said.

Libby rose to the challenge and sprinted as fast as she could into the water, trying her best to get a head start. The water was freezing but refreshing. She splashed her way as far out as she could before Angus caught up with her, tumbling her into the sea with a rugby tackle. 'Got you!' he laughed as she found her feet and pushed herself up to the surface, gasping.

She wiped the salt water from her eyes. 'You bastard!' she laughed as she splashed him in revenge. She stayed close to the shore so that she could keep an eye on Izzy, while Angus swam out to sea. After a few minutes Izzy started to cry, so she swam back, grabbed her towel and dried herself off. She scooped Izzy into her arms and walked her around the beach until she settled. When she had stopped crying and was once again playing happily, Libby came to lie in the sun next to Angus, who had returned from his swim.

They spent the whole day lounging on the beach, swimming to cool off, paddling in the rock pools with Izzy and reading their books. It was totally idyllic. When the time came to pack up and take Izzy home, they were both glowing from the sun and covered with sand in every orifice, far more relaxed than they had been in a very long time. Angus gave Izzy her bath while Libby showered, then they put her to bed and Libby began cooking their dinner. She laid the table out on the terrace and picked some flowers from the garden to put in the middle of the table. She found a candle in the sitting room and lit it before pouring them both some wine.

'I'm seriously impressed!' Angus said as he ate the spaghetti. 'This is really delicious.' She had cooked the prawns in plenty of garlic with a squeeze of lemon and some fresh chilli; it was a great combination.

'If Luca served one purpose it was teaching me his family's secret recipes!' laughed Libby.

'And fathering Izzy,' said Angus.

'True! We mustn't forget that. It's funny, isn't it, how everything seems to happen for a reason. If I hadn't met Luca, then Izzy would never have been born, but I know that she is meant to be here; there is no way she was just an accident. And Jules, if she hadn't run off with him then you would never have a chance to start over, to be a father one day, and you are such a natural I just know that is what is meant for you too.'

'I hope so,' Angus said.

'Cheers to us,' Libby said.

'To the future!' said Angus. They clinked glasses once again. 'So, what do you think is next in store for you? It's not long now till you find out if Digby and Edwards will make you an offer.'

'I'm fairly sure they won't. And I don't really know if I want them to anyway, if I'm honest with myself. I've actually been doing a lot of thinking about the future recently,' Libby said. 'Do you remember I once told you that I'd like to start up my own bed and breakfast?'

'That does ring a bell.'

'Well, I've been doing a lot of research. I'm seriously considering it… I've even started drawing up a business plan.'

'Wow, I had no idea. Tell me more.' They spent the rest of the evening discussing Libby's plans. He asked her hundreds of questions and seemed impressed with how seriously she had considered the answer to each one, how careful her research had been. This did not seem to be yet another hare-brained scheme that Libby was dreaming up to escape her current job. There was something more to it this time. In fact, Angus seemed to think it was a fantastic idea, in particular because of the benefits it would have in terms of childcare. He even suggested getting involved, perhaps helping her to get the business up and running, as an investor of sorts.

There was plenty for them to talk about, and they continued to discuss the options throughout the remainder of the holiday, which was full of similar lazy, sun-drenched days on the beach. They went for walks along the coastal paths, Izzy strapped to Angus's back; they swam in the sea, ate amazing food, barbecued on the beach and drank plenty of wine. They were so relaxed in each other's company and they got on so well that they both agreed it was one of the best holidays they had ever had.

When Libby returned to London a week later, she felt a dull ache at their separation. She had become so used to Angus's company, it was as if he was part of their little family. Back in her flat that evening, she picked up her phone and hovered over his number, stopping short of calling him just to check in and hear his voice. She knew that she needed to make sure she retained her newfound independence. She had promised herself that she would never rely on any man for support again, and whilst she knew he was different to 'any' man, he still counted. She had to admit, though, the idea of having Angus's input and backing into her potential new business venture was extremely appealing. It was definitely worth considering. He had such a good eye, and he already had all the experience of starting up his own company, not to mention of being self-employed. She knew she needed to give it all some extremely careful thought over the next few months, when her final review would take place at Digby and Edwards.

Chapter Twenty-Five

One rainy Saturday morning in October, Libby's phone began to ring. She rummaged around before finally locating it under a pile of laundry on the bed. She was surprised to see that it was John calling.

'Hello?' she said as she answered the call. It was probably Miriam having forgotten her phone.

'Libby, it's John.'

'John! What a surprise! Is everything OK?'

'I'm afraid not…' His voice sounded tight and strained. 'It's your mother. I don't want you to worry, but we're in hospital. She has had a heart attack. She's in surgery at the moment and the doctors are doing the best they can, but I think it's a good idea if you get here as soon as you can.'

Libby felt the blood drain from her head. She sat down on the bed. She couldn't believe what she had just heard. 'A heart attack? My god, poor mum. Of course, I'll come straight away. Where are you?'

John gave her the details of the hospital and she hung up the phone. Helen and Henry were away in Florence on a long weekend. John had tried calling her first but hadn't been able to get through. Trying to fight the rising panic that was coursing through her veins, Libby grabbed the phone once again. She knew that Angus was working on his paintings, but she didn't know who else to call.

'Libby?' Angus picked up the phone on the third ring.

'Hi Angus. I need your help.' She started to cry at the sound of his voice.

'What is it? What's happened?' he asked, his voice immediately full of concern.

'It's Mum. John just called. She's had a heart attack.'

'Oh my god. Is she OK?'

'I don't know. She is in surgery. I need to get to the hospital straight away. I hate to ask, but can you come and look after Izzy?'

'Of course. I'll jump in the car now. I'll be with you in five. Libs, don't worry, she'll be OK.'

'Thank you so much,' Libby said. She grabbed a few things and stuffed them into an overnight bag, her head spinning. Her mother had always been so healthy. She had never had a scare like this before. Memories of her dad dying came flooding back and her eyes smarted with tears once again.

A short while later there was a loud knock on the door. Libby opened it to see Angus standing there in a grey T-shirt with spatters of paint in his hair and on his cheek. At the sight of his concerned expression, she collapsed into his arms and let him hold her as she sobbed. He stroked her hair and rubbed her back. 'It's going to be OK,' he said.

When she had gathered her composure she pulled herself away, running through a list of instructions for the day in terms of looking after Izzy.

'Just call me if you have any questions,' she said.

'I will. We'll be just fine, don't worry about us,' he said. 'You just go and look after your mum.'

'I don't know how to thank you, dropping everything to come and have Izzy. You really are the best…' She kissed him on the cheek and hugged him tight. She had to pull herself away. She kissed Izzy goodbye and grabbed her bag and her keys, dashing off down the stairs.

A couple of hours later she was running through the hospital corridors looking for her mother. As she turned the corner she saw John, pacing up and down. Her heart went out to him as she saw the worry on his face. They sat side by side and waited for news from the surgeons. Eventually a doctor came to find them.

They stood up as soon as they saw her approach. Time seemed to slow down as she walked towards them down the brightly lit corridor.

Libby's heart was pounding. Her palms were sweaty and she tried to steady her breathing, to stop panicking.

John reached for her hand and gave it a gentle squeeze. Libby was moved to see how hard he was trying to fight back his emotions. She could tell it was taking him all his strength to retain his outward appearance of calm.

'Doctor,' said John. 'Is there any news?'

'How is she?' Libby asked, desperately scanning her face for any clues.

The doctor smiled at them both. 'I'm pleased to say that Miriam is in a stable condition,' she said.

Relief coursed through Libby as she grabbed hold of John and squeezed him tightly.

'Thank god!' she said.

John exhaled slowly; he must have been holding his breath.

'We were able to repair most of the damage,' explained the doctor. 'But she will need to stay in hospital to be closely monitored for a few days until we are completely sure she is stable. When we discharge her, she will need to rest and allow herself a slow and complete recovery, avoiding physical exertion.'

Libby and John thanked the doctor and hugged each other, tears of relief falling down their cheeks.

As soon as Miriam had come round from the anaesthesia they went into see her. Libby was shocked at how tiny and pale she looked, dwarfed by her gown and the hospital bed. It was amazing how vulnerable illness made you seem. 'Mum,' Libby said as she took her hand. 'It's me, Libby.' Miriam opened her eyes and smiled weakly at them.

'How are you feeling, darling?' asked John, bending down to kiss her forehead.

'Pretty awful,' Miriam replied, her voice groggy from the anaesthetic. Libby knew that she must be feeling bad, as her mother never usually admitted to any discomfort.

'I'm going to be your full-time nurse,' John said. 'I'm under strict instructions not to let you lift a finger until you are completely better, and I am more than happy to oblige.'

'Thank you, darling,' Miriam said to John. She turned to Libby. 'Does Helen know I'm here?'

'Yes, I just spoke to her,' said Libby. 'She is with Henry. She's fine. She sends you lots of love and she's going to come and see you as soon as she gets back from Florence.' They stayed by her side until she fell asleep again. Then Libby went to phone Angus.

'Thank goodness she is OK,' he said as soon as he heard the news.

'I know. It's such a relief. It just doesn't bear thinking about the alternative. How's Izzy?'

'She's fast asleep. I'm just about to tuck into a takeaway pizza and watch one of your DVDs – that is, if I can find one that isn't too girly!'

'Honestly, Angus, you really have been amazing. Thank you so much.'

'It's my pleasure. It really is. Now take your time, spend as long as you want at home. I can cope with Izzy, no problem;

we'll go to the shops tomorrow and get some food, go for a walk in the park. It's all under control here.'

It was such a relief knowing that Izzy was in his capable hands. She didn't know what she would do without him. He really was the most incredible guy. She reminded herself once again just how lucky she and Izzy were to have him in their lives.

Libby spent Sunday by her mother's side with John, making sure that she was all right. She drove back to London on Monday afternoon in time to collect Izzy from the child-minder, who had relieved Angus of his duties earlier that morning. As Zoe handed her over, Libby held her daughter close and hugged her, appreciating for the first time that the bond between mother and daughter that she experienced so strongly with Izzy was the same as the bond connecting her to Miriam, and quite what a special and unique thing that was.

She drove over to Angus's flat and rang the bell, laden with cans of beer and bottles of wine to thank him for his babysitting. She was disappointed to find that he wasn't in. Somebody buzzed her into the building and she climbed up to his flat, balancing Izzy on her hip. She left the bags on his doorstep with a note, surprised at the force of her disappointment. It occurred to her that he might be on a date. She hadn't asked him about his love life recently; maybe he was dating again and he just hadn't mentioned it to her. For some unknown reason she felt slightly sick at the thought. She felt absurdly close to tears. Suppressing her emotions, she walked back down the stairs and strapped Izzy into her car seat before driving home.

A few hours later a text pinged on her phone. 'You didn't have to do that! You know how much I love Izzy! I would happily look after her every weekend. But thank you. And so glad your mum is OK xx'

She was confused at her reaction to his absence earlier that evening. She wondered if she was becoming too dependent on him. She knew she should be careful. After Luca had left them, she had vowed to herself that she wouldn't get herself into that situation again. But Angus was different; he had always been there for her. The thought occurred to her that if he did meet someone new and start a family of his own, that would no longer necessarily be the case. Jules had been her friend, too, but maybe next time – with a new partner – it would be different. Her eyes welled up at the thought of Angus not being in her and Izzy's life. She loved him so much as a friend, she realised just how much closer they had become over the last few months. Perhaps it was a good idea to go into business with him: that way she could ensure that she would never lose him as part of their lives. Plus, she couldn't think of anyone she would rather have by her side for such an important venture.

Chapter Twenty-Six

It was Angus's birthday in November, a month before Libby's. She couldn't believe that they were turning thirty-five. Six months had gone by since Luca and Jules had left them. Libby wondered whether the rose-tinted glasses through which their exes saw each other were beginning to fade. She had heard reports of arguments from a mutual friend, and had been secretly pleased at the news. Apparently Jules was keen to move back to London now that Angus was out of her house, but Luca was reluctant. On Sunday they met up for a birthday lunch in Angus's local pub. After their meal they settled down to read the papers by a roaring log fire. Izzy was playing happily with her toys on the sofa next to Libby.

'So, I had my final review on Friday…' Libby said. She hadn't told him that it was happening earlier than expected. 'I didn't get offered a place.'

'Oh Libby, why didn't you tell me?' Angus said.

'I knew I was seeing you today… It's hardly come as a surprise.'

'So you aren't too disappointed?' Angus asked.

'No, not really. There are many more deserving people than me. Do you know I am actually quite relieved? Law isn't the career for me, but at least this time I can truly say I stuck at it for once. I didn't give up when the going got tough.'

'I know you didn't and I'm so proud of you for that,' Angus said. This praise from her oldest friend and occasional toughest critic meant an awful lot to Libby.

'Thanks Angus.'

'So what next?'

'I've decided to go ahead with the bed and breakfast business. I've got a meeting scheduled for December with the bank and I'm going to get the ball rolling.'

'It does sound like a fantastic idea. Imagine if you found somewhere like Acorn Cottage – wouldn't that be amazing?'

'Exactly. Living in the countryside, in the peace and quiet… maybe on the coast somewhere.'

'You could keep Izzy at home with you.'

'Until she starts at school, and even then I could make sure I was there to pick her up every day. I would see so much more of her than I've been able to at Digby and Edwards.' She took a deep breath, nervous to ask the question that had been at the forefront of her mind. 'Are you still interested in being involved?'

Angus paused for a moment. 'I've been thinking about it myself recently, wondering if you were still scheming away. I think I'd love to be involved. Are you sure you want me?'

'Definitely sure. You'd bring so much to the table on top of your investment. You'd be completely invaluable to me.'

They spent the rest of the afternoon back at Libby's flat. She showed him all her research and her proposed business plan. Her legal background gave her an impressive starting point; she had drawn up a contract that would protect their separate investments and assets should their circumstances change in the future. They went through the portfolio of potential properties that Libby had compiled, and they brainstormed and hatched plans for the kind of business they would like it to be.

Libby felt energised and excited about the future. She was thrilled that Angus was interested in coming on board. He said he could relocate to the bed and breakfast if there was space for him to have a studio, at least while the business was getting started. He was only renting his flat by the river, so there was no long-term commitment there. He was extremely flexible, and Libby had nothing stopping her from relocating apart from the sale of her flat. He accompanied her to the meeting with her bank manager and they began to discuss the necessary paperwork. Suddenly it all felt very real.

Angus and Libby went their separate ways for the festive season, ready to start their business plans in earnest in the new year. They both headed to their respective homes: Angus back to Middlesex to the Lockhart family home, Libby and Izzy to Kent. Libby parked the car outside the front of the house. The front door was decorated with a festive wreath. The door opened and John and Miriam came out to greet her.

'Hello, darling, how was the journey?' Miriam asked. 'And how is my darling granddaughter?' She waved at Izzy who was sitting in her car seat, tears streaming down her face. 'Oh dear! Not looking too happy! Happy Christmas, little one!'

'Izzy's upset that we've stopped moving. She loves motion and has taken to crying each time we stop at the traffic lights – which makes travelling anywhere very peaceful, as you can imagine!' Libby laughed as she picked her daughter up, kissing her on the cheek.

'Let me help you with all these bags,' John said. 'Miriam, you go inside and rest; we will sort this out.'

'I won't touch anything, I promise, I'll be good!' laughed Miriam. John had clearly taken his role as her nurse very seriously.

Later on they were all seated at the kitchen table with steaming cups of tea and huge chunks of coffee cake when a loud commotion at the door signalled the arrival of Helen and Henry. They had been on yet another mini-break, this time to the Christmas markets in Berlin, and were laden with even more bags and presents. After kissing everyone hello and settling themselves down at the table, Helen announced that she had some news. Libby and Miriam waited on tenterhooks for her to tell them, though the beaming grin from ear to ear had given them some idea as to what might be about to come.

'I'm pregnant!' said Helen. 'And Henry and I are getting married!'

'*What?*' shrieked Libby. 'Oh my *god! Congratulations!*'

'You're pregnant?' said Miriam. 'And engaged? How absolutely wonderful, darling! I can't believe it!'

'Congratulations,' said John, smiling with delight. 'My goodness me! I'd better see if I can find a bottle of champagne.'

'Miriam, can I please ask your permission to have your daughter's hand in marriage?' Henry asked. 'I realise it is a little late—'

'Of course you can, you silly boy! Not that you need it,' laughed Miriam. Tradition had gone out of the window and she couldn't have cared less. She was so delighted that her eldest daughter had finally got engaged, and pregnant to boot! They all knew how desperately Helen wanted to have a child.

'How far along are you?' asked Libby.

'Twelve and a half weeks,' beamed Helen. She got her phone out of her pocket and passed around the photograph from the twelve-week scan.

'Gorgeous,' Miriam cooed.

'Look Izzy,' Libby said. 'This is your little cousin!'

'We didn't want to say anything until we knew that I had passed the danger zone, what with my being slightly older,' explained Helen.

'And then we knew we were seeing you for Christmas, so we thought we might as well tell you in person,' added Henry.

'And then Henry proposed outside this beautiful church in the snow last night in Berlin!' Helen took the ring box out of her pocket. 'I took it off so I didn't give it away the second I walked in the door, but look, here it is! Isn't it beautiful?'

'Wow, darling,' Miriam said.

'It is absolutely stunning!' Libby gasped. A huge blue sapphire sat elegantly between two sparkling diamonds, catching the light from the string of fairy lights that hung above the Aga.

They listened avidly as Henry and Helen told the story of the proposal, toasting the happy couple with the champagne that John had whisked out of the fridge. Libby was so thrilled for her sister; she barely recognised this glowing, radiant person sitting opposite her from the sister who had left for Hong Kong all that time ago. She was so grateful to Henry for making her this happy. She knew he was going to be an excellent brother-in-law.

Not wanting to steal any of Helen and Henry's limelight, Libby waited until Boxing Day before telling them about her new business venture.

'I've actually got some news of my own,' she announced. 'I've decided what to do next now that my contract is ending with Digby and Edwards.'

'Oh really darling, that's fantastic,' said Miriam.

'Are you going to continue with law?' asked Helen.

'Well, you know I've been thinking about setting up my own bed and breakfast or guesthouse?' Libby said. 'Well, it's official. I am going to start my own business. The plan is already in motion. And, what is even better, Angus is going to be my business partner!'

'Angus? Wow, that is excellent news. I had no idea he'd be interested in something like that,' said Helen.

They asked her lots of questions and were intrigued to hear about the research she had done so far. She was pleased with their reaction to the news. They all seemed thrilled for her, and the idea of Angus being involved certainly did a lot to alleviate any worries they might have had about Libby taking a project like this on all by herself. They could see it made sense for Libby in terms of looking after Izzy, and they knew how hard she had found life in the law firm.

That evening Libby phoned Angus. 'How did they take it?' he asked.

'They actually think it's a wonderful idea, especially knowing that you're going to be involved. Of course, Mum wants me to buy somewhere in Kent so she can be close by! What about your family? Did you mention it to them?'

'They're very supportive. So it's official: we're business partners. Everyone knows except for Jules and Luca…'

'I couldn't care less about them. They can find out when they find out, though I must say I'd quite like to see the look on their faces when they do.'

'Me too!' laughed Angus. 'How's Helen feeling?' She had told him about the pregnancy a couple of days before.

'She didn't really have much morning sickness, lucky thing,' Libby said. 'She just seems glowing. Being pregnant really suits her. And she and Henry are so loved up, it's adorable.'

'I'm so happy for them! Have they set the date yet?'

'Not yet. I think they're going to have a registry office ceremony in London somewhere in the next couple of months. They don't want a big white wedding, and Helen doesn't want to wear a traditional wedding dress anyway with her baby bump. I think it'll happen fairly quickly and be a very relaxed affair.'

'Sounds perfect. I can't believe there's going to be another baby in your family.'

'I know! It's going to be so sweet watching Izzy with her little cousin.'

That weekend Libby and Angus spent New Year's Eve together. Neither of them had made any plans. They had dinner and watched television, slowly getting drunk on champagne. A year ago neither of them would have ever been able to predict quite how much their lives would change over the following twelve months. As the countdown to midnight began and the fireworks exploded on the screen, they toasted the new year. 'To new adventures!' Angus said as their glasses touched.

'To the best year yet!' said Libby, sipping the bubbles. She had a feeling it might be just that.

Chapter Twenty-Seven

When Libby woke up on New Year's Day, she felt slightly hung over from all the champagne that she and Angus had consumed the night before. It had been her favourite New Year's Eve yet, just the three of them: low-key but perfect. She padded into the sitting room, saying 'Morning' as Angus lifted his head from the pillow – he had decided to sleep on the sofa after one too many drinks.

She looked at her phone and noticed several notifications from her FaceTime app. 'Three missed calls from Luca,' she said.

'What can he want?' Angus grunted sleepily.

'I'll call him back,' Libby said as she pulled on her dressing gown and went back into her bedroom, shutting the door to leave Angus undisturbed. '*Ciao*, Luca,' she said as he came into view. She recognised his backdrop instantly. He was on the balcony of his and Nicola's flat in Positano. She felt an instant pang of longing for Italy at the sight.

'Hi Libby, how are you? Happy New Year. And Happy New Year to my little Izzy – is she awake?'

'She is, I'm just about to give her some breakfast. I'll take you through in a sec. Is everything OK?'

'Yes, yes it's OK. I just wanted to talk to you…' He was looking tired; there were shadows under his eyes.

'What's up?' she asked.

'I've ended things with Jules. I realise you don't want to hear anything about our relationship, but I know you were worried about Jules seeing Izzy, so I thought I would tell you that it is no longer going to be an issue.'

'Right. Thanks for letting me know,' Libby said. Inside her heart was racing at the news, but she was determined not to let Luca see that it had had the slightest impact on her whatsoever.

'As you know I've been in Positano for Christmas and New Year. I've decided to stay here. I can't be away any longer. I just miss my life here so much. I miss my family, my home...' Libby wasn't surprised at this; she had been expecting it for quite some time now. 'I told her last night that I wasn't coming back, and when she offered to come and join me I said no. Things just weren't really working.'

'What about Izzy?' she asked, less interested in hearing about their break-up and more concerned about how his change of circumstances would affect their daughter.

'That's the one thing I can't bear the thought of: being in a different country from my own child. But I need to be true to myself. I will come and see her often, if that is OK with you... and I'd like to bring her to Italy sometimes too, if you agree?'

Libby's heart wrenched at the thought of being in a separate country from her daughter, even for a short period of time, but she forced herself to think of it from Luca's perspective. She realised it was only fair if she let him have her with him every now and again. It was important that she knew Italy as well as she knew England; she was half Italian, after all. 'I'm sure we can work something out,' Libby said bravely.

'Thank you. I know this is less than ideal for us in terms of co-parenting, but I suppose it was never going to be easy having parents from different countries.'

'Unless those parents were still together,' Libby said.

'I know. I'm sorry Libby... I wish it could have worked out.'

She was suddenly annoyed with herself for having said that. She didn't want him to get the impression that she was sitting here pining for him, when in fact the total opposite was true.

Instead she changed the subject, moving on to talk about her and Angus's plan to set up a bed and breakfast together. Luca seemed surprised but he was supportive. If anyone knew how much she had loved being at La Casetta, and just how much she had struggled with law, it was Luca. A few minutes later she took the phone next door so that Luca could see his daughter. She held the phone while he chatted away to her in Italian.

After ending the call she went through to the sitting room and dropped the bombshell. 'Guess what! Luca has dumped Jules,' she said. 'Can you believe it?'

'No way! When?' Angus was clearly shocked.

'Yesterday. He's decided to move back to Positano for good. Apparently when he told Jules she offered to fly over and be with him there, but he said no. He had grown tired of the relationship, surprise surprise, and so that's that! Luca goes back to his old ways and Jules is left alone…'

'Well that certainly is a turn-up for the books.'

'I know. I wonder if Jules will get in touch with you now that she is on her own again. She had better not try and get hold of me. I hope she got the message the last time she showed up out of the blue.'

'I need to talk to her anyway,' Angus said. 'I need to tell her that I want a divorce.' They had discussed this last night, and Libby agreed that it was the right thing to do, to give him the clean slate he so clearly needed and deserved. Libby didn't know quite how she would feel about the two of them seeing each other. She realised it wouldn't be easy, though she wasn't sure why it bothered her so much.

Sure enough, later on that week Jules telephoned Angus telling him that she needed to talk. He agreed to meet up with her, just the two of them, the following month. He wasn't going to drop everything and see her immediately. She could wait until he was ready.

When the day came that Angus and Jules were scheduled to meet, Libby woke at the crack of dawn with a knot of dread in the bottom of her stomach. She was worried that seeing Jules might have a strange effect on him; that he might suddenly change his mind about their business plans. She had no doubt that now she was single and alone, Jules would try her very best to wheedle her way back into Angus's life. What if he suddenly realised that he still loved her, that he wasn't over her? What if it really was Jules he was meant to be with all along? What would she do then? The thought of him getting back together with Jules was so unbearable she felt her eyes fill with tears. She knew she could never forgive her, so where would that leave her in terms of her friendship with Angus?

She phoned him that morning.

'What time are you meeting?'

'At one thirty,' Angus said. 'What have you got planned for today?' Having left Digby and Edwards the previous week, she was still getting used to her unemployed status. It felt strange being able to choose what to do with her days once again.

'I've got an agent coming around to value the flat at midday. Shall we meet this afternoon to finalise the paperwork and start arranging some viewings?'

'Good plan.'

'See you later then,' Libby said. 'I hope it goes well with Jules.'

'So do I. I'm not exactly looking forward to it.' She could tell he was anxious.

'It'll be fine,' she said. 'Stay strong.'

The agent came around to view the house. Libby found herself buzzing with excitement: the plan was actually in motion once and for all. He told her his valuation and she was pleased with how much the flat had gone up in value since she had bought it. It wasn't far off her estimate, and the money she could get from selling it, coupled with the money Angus had proposed to invest, would give them a substantial deposit. She couldn't wait to start viewing some real properties. She wished Angus would hurry up and get here so they could get the ball rolling.

She knew that she watned to find a place relatively near the coast, that there needed to be space for Angus's studio, and that she would rather inherit a business that was already set up and running than start one from scratch.

Time seemed to be moving painfully slowly. She kept checking her watch. Why hadn't he called? She couldn't stop thinking that Jules had got her way; that Angus had capitulated and would soon be ringing her to tell her that they were back together. The thought made her feel anxious. She didn't know what was wrong with her. Why was she having such a strong reaction to the idea?

Libby's nerves were so on edge that she decided to get out of the house as a distraction. She took Izzy to the park and walked around it, trying to stop the onslaught of images that were running through her mind: Jules declaring her undying love for Angus. Jules pleading for forgiveness, telling him it had all been a moment of madness. Jules begging him to stick to his wedding vows, promising to give him the baby he had always longed for… Her head spun. She tried to focus on the scenery around her instead. She checked her phone frequently in case Angus called her. She hoped that he would ring straight afterwards, just to put her mind at rest.

She walked all the way around the park and then via the shops on the way home, picking up some groceries. She set Izzy on her play mat and unpacked the shopping.

Just then she heard a knock on the door. She opened it and Angus walked in.

'So how was it?' She felt her breath catch in her throat as she waited for his response.

'It was weird seeing her after all this time. She looks terrible. She has moved back into our old house and she's found a job. She tried to tell me that she had ended things with Luca, that she had realised it had all been a big mistake and that she wanted to try and work things out between us.'

'Oh my god, she is such a liar!'

'Thankfully I already knew that it had been Luca's decision, so knowing that she was lying to me yet again just made it easier to ignore her fake tears and ask for a divorce.'

'You asked her?'

'I certainly did.'

'And what did she say?'

'She tried her very best to talk her way out of it. There were lots of tears, apologies, and undoubtedly more lies, but I stuck to my guns and remained unmoved. I think she was quite shocked at how insistent I was.'

'Did you tell her about the B & B?'

'Yes. I actually thanked her for leaving me for Luca, for making it possible for me to have a new life without her.'

'How did she react?'

'You should have seen the look on her face: it was priceless!'

'I bet! What did she say?'

'That was when I stood up and said goodbye. I told her that I wished her the best of luck, that there were no hard feelings, and then I walked out. I left her speechless sitting at the table, mouth open.' Libby couldn't help but giggle at the thought.

Chapter Twenty-Eight

Angus had shelved plans for any future exhibitions for the time being, in order to focus on the B & B project. His newfound success meant that his last three exhibitions had completely sold out, and he still had plenty of commissions to keep him ticking over in the meantime. The following week Libby and Angus travelled from place to place, viewing a variety of properties. They particularly liked an old mill house in Sussex, not far from the coast, which had a functioning water wheel. Libby and Angus had decided that they were happy to invest in a property that needed some work, so long as it was structurally sound. It was more important to them that the location was excellent and that there was plenty of potential.

On Thursday they visited a charming old farmhouse in Kent, not too far from the Saunders' family home. This had predictably led to huge levels of excitement from Miriam. Unfortunately it was a complete shambles. There was a roof partially missing in one of the outhouses, it hadn't been running as a B & B for years, and the whole place would need gutting. It had been a fairly immediate no for both of them. They had driven straight over to have lunch with Miriam and John after the viewing, still in high spirits despite their unsuccessful morning.

'I'm glad it's a no,' said John. 'If it had been a yes I was banned from saying what I'm about to tell you.'

'John, I never said you were banned. I just wouldn't want to encourage my daughter and my granddaughter to be so far away from me if they had liked the B & B down the road!' Miriam laughed but Libby could tell John was probably telling the truth, though about what she had no idea.

'This sounds most intriguing!' she laughed.

'Do you remember a while ago I told you about my sister-in-law Lizzy?' asked John.

'About her B & B near Positano? Where was it again?'

'Yes that's right, in a village called Tremento. Well sadly her husband, Giuseppe, died last autumn. She closed the bed and breakfast when he died, and it has remained closed ever since.'

'How awful,' said Angus.

'He'd been unwell for quite some time,' said John. 'She is all right, but she has decided to sell up and move back to England. I just thought I'd mention it in case it would be of any interest. It's quite a successful business, from what I hear. It's just too much for her to manage on her own and she thinks the time has come to find someone to take over.'

'Wow. Italy!' Libby exclaimed. She hadn't even thought about that as an option. 'It would certainly make sense for me and Izzy in terms of Luca…'

'But Angus, you wouldn't want to be involved in a business in Italy, would you?' asked Miriam, an element of pleading in her voice.

Libby looked at Angus, intrigued to see how he would react to the idea.

He paused for a while before answering. 'It wouldn't actually be a bad idea. I can see how sensible it would be for you, Libby. And I'm slightly running out of beautiful locations to paint here. It could open up a whole myriad of possibilities for me in terms of my work. In fact, I've been dying to paint the Amalfi coast for years – never more so than after having seen all Libby's photos from her time there. It's certainly an interesting thought…'

They discussed it as much as they could with John's fairly limited knowledge. It was called The Lemon Tree – L'Albero di Limoni – which Libby loved. They all peered at the screen of Miriam's laptop and scrutinised as many photographs from the website and TripAdvisor as they could. It looked idyllic. Libby could feel the excitement levels begin to build within her. She had a really good feeling about this. The best thing was that Lizzy hadn't put the business on the market yet. There would be no competitors; Libby and Angus could have first refusal. They arranged to call Lizzy the following day to talk things through in more detail.

Back in London, Angus and Libby had written a long list of questions to discuss with Lizzy. They called her on Skype from Libby's kitchen and spent over an hour on the phone. She sounded absolutely charming and answered all of their questions patiently and thoroughly. It was clear that she had run the business side of things herself and she was extremely clued up on profit margins, incoming and outgoing costs, and the legal requirements of running a guesthouse. Libby started looking into the legal aspects of buying property in Italy and made some phone calls to several ex-colleagues to make initial enquiries. Once again she was grateful she had stuck out her training contract. Her legal background was going to come in useful time and time again, of that she was sure.

Convinced that the business would be a viable opportunity for them both, and drawn to the idea of relocating to Italy, Angus and Libby decided to book flights to go and see the B & B for themselves at the beginning of March. They left Izzy with Miriam and flew to Naples before hiring a car and driving through the picturesque countryside to Tremento.

It was a cool but crisp day; the sky was perfectly clear and a bright, cerulean blue. Angus marvelled at his surroundings. He seemed inspired already, and Libby could tell that he was experiencing the same sense of building excitement and nervous anticipation as she was. They followed the instructions from the website to find L'Albero di Limoni, a short drive from the centre of the village. As they wound their way up the twisting track, the guesthouse slowly came into view. It was everything it had appeared to be in the photographs online, and more.

'I love it!' squealed Libby, as she drank in the golden stone, the rambling wisteria that climbed up the sides, the slightly topsy-turvy-looking walls and painted window shutters. Lemon trees lined the driveway, and brightly coloured flowers spilt over the sides of terracotta pots of all shapes and sizes. The guest rooms, in a separate block from the main house, were covered in tumbling bougainvillea. To the back was an enormous barn that they were hoping would be perfect for Angus's studio.

'It looks even better in real life,' agreed Angus, unable to stop grinning with enthusiasm.

Lizzy welcomed them into a large farmhouse-style kitchen. Libby noticed photographs of Lizzy with a handsome man on the large wooden dresser that stood to one side of the room. Presumably it was her husband, Giuseppe. Libby couldn't imagine how awful it must have been to lose first her sister and then her husband. Her heart went out to her as she realised how emotional the thought of selling this place must be.

'Thank you so much for having us to stay,' Libby said.

'It's a pleasure!' said Lizzy. 'You have to test out the rooms for yourself, naturally... and it's far too far to come for a day trip.'

They chatted easily, passing on news of John and Miriam to John's sister-in-law as they sipped cups of tea and ate some delicious homemade lemon drizzle cake. Libby was dying to have the grand tour, but she was also intrigued to meet Lizzy, and was more than happy to enjoy a tea break after their early start that morning.

Afterwards, Lizzy showed them around the rest of the house, opening each room and every door, allowing them to explore each nook and cranny. She showed them the guestrooms as well as the extensive grounds. Finally they visited the barn. Angus could immediately see the potential for a studio… it was a vast space, but they would need to ensure that it was structurally sound for conversion. It had to be north-facing, and large panes of glass would need to be installed to allow the controlled, indirect light to stream in. Lizzy had organised for a local architect to meet them at the house that afternoon to discuss the possibilities. Luckily he seemed to think there would be no problem converting the building into the studio Angus described. He said he could draw up some initial plans and send them electronically back to England over the course of the next couple of weeks.

Lizzy left Libby and Angus to explore the house again, this time unaccompanied, and they took their time revisiting each room, discussing options for décor, layout and any work that would need to be done. They decided it would probably take a few months to get the property fully into shape, as they wanted it. They were both happy to get stuck in with painting, and they had budgeted enough to employ local carpenters, electricians and decorators to help them as needed. Like any house that had been lived in for years and years, there were areas that would need touching up. They would need to replace carpets and some of the bathroom fixtures and fittings, which could do with updating.

The whole place seemed to be continually flooded with light that streamed through the windows. It had such a wonderful, homely atmosphere. Giuseppe and Lizzy had clearly been extremely happy and settled here, and Libby could imagine herself and Izzy being very happy there too. And Angus – for as long as he stayed with them.

The best thing about being on the Amalfi coast was the guarantee of a constant stream of tourists. It was such a popular tourist destination, and the village of Tremento itself was becoming firmly lodged on the tourist track as the secret of its existence slowly spread. It was a small village with a couple of local shops and one or two trattorias. Just enough to keep the bed and breakfast guests happy and well fed.

Over dinner, Lizzy explained how they had found the place back in the seventies; how they had lovingly built it up into the successful business it had become. They hadn't been able to have children, which had always been a huge regret for Lizzy. She was clearly delighted at the prospect of Izzy growing up in the home she had always known would be ideally suited to the pitter-patter of small footsteps.

The next day, as they made their way back home, Libby and Angus talked and talked and talked. They discussed all their options in minute detail. Angus played devil's advocate and Libby explained any legal ramifications of a move abroad, compared with staying in England. They thrashed out ideas and debated the pros and cons of all the places on their shortlist. It became very clear to them that L'Albero di Limoni was their outright favourite. They would be hard pushed to find something more ideal. Libby hadn't wanted to get Luca's hopes up, so she hadn't discussed the idea with him yet, but she had to admit it made perfect sense. When they finally made their minds up to go ahead with the sale, she phoned him. He was absolutely over the moon. He couldn't believe his luck, that Izzy would be so close to him. It was almost as though everything was working out somehow – that from the wreckage of her failed relationship, she was managing to make a life for her small family unit, a good life for her daughter. She knew that it was largely Angus that had given her the confidence and the strength to make these momentous decisions. She was so grateful to him for being by her side. As she looked at him sitting across the table from her, talking to Lizzy on the phone, her heart swelled to bursting point with emotion. She felt like crying. She didn't know what she would do without him. He had been her best friend for as long as she could remember. As she drank in his familiar features, his handsome, rugged face with those deep blue eyes, she had a sudden urge to jump into his arms and hold him close.

Chapter Twenty-Nine

Libby found a young, newly married couple to buy her flat. After thirty-odd unsuccessful viewings she had begun to give up hope until they suddenly appeared on her doorstep. They had clearly loved the space and she had managed to negotiate the full asking price out of them. The sale was able to move fairly swiftly, thanks to Lizzy's flexibility with the purchase of L'Albero di Limoni and the couple being chain-free. She was glad that she liked the look of the buyers. There was something strangely personal about selling your home. She hoped that they would be happy there, that they would enjoy living in her home as much as she had. Angus had terminated the contract on his flat and they had started researching moving companies that would come in and pack up their possessions to send them ahead to Italy. The paperwork for the B & B was coming along nicely, and soon they found themselves signing on the dotted line. It was all happening very quickly. Libby had never felt so excited about anything before. She felt energised and full of life, her imagination spilling over with ideas. She had to keep turning her bedside light on in the middle of the night to scribble them down on her notepad lest she forget them. It was wonderful to feel so inspired. She had never experienced it before, so used to being either in a dead-end job with no prospects, or lately bogged down in a world of terminology and paperwork that made her see stars in front of her eyes. She and Angus were never far apart; they plotted and schemed together with Izzy by their side.

Spending quality time with Izzy was the biggest perk. It was a true joy for Libby to see her daughter every day. She didn't know how she had managed for so long without it. She was growing so quickly, and finally Libby didn't have to miss a thing. Luca had come over to visit a couple of times, taking Izzy for the weekend. No one was more excited than him at the thought of Izzy and Libby's imminent translocation, and he had offered to do anything they needed to help things run smoothly on the Italian side. It was definitely proving useful to have a local around when they needed him.

Angus's lease terminated at the end of April. As planned, all of his possessions were being shipped ahead of them to Italy, along with the majority of Libby and Izzy's belongings. Angus was staying at Libby's for the last couple of weeks until she exchanged with the buyers and handed over the keys. As a final farewell they had decided to throw a dinner party, inviting Angus's parents as well as Helen, Henry, Miriam and John. The Lockharts and the Saunders had known each other for years, with their children having grown up together, but it was nice for the Lockharts to get to know John a bit better and to meet Henry for the first time. Eight people was a rather tight squeeze around Libby's dining table, but it seemed a fitting send-off for Angus and Libby as they set off on their new venture.

Before she knew it, the last day that she would ever spend in her little flat came hurtling around the corner. It felt like the end of an era. She could hardly believe that the next day they would be driving out to Italy, no looking back.

To celebrate their last night in London they ordered a takeaway and drank a bottle of red wine, toasting new beginnings. They curled up on the sofa and watched a movie. At the end of the evening they got ready for bed, both of them feeling a little nervous and full of anticipation about what was to come. Suddenly feeling emotional, Libby asked Angus if he would sleep next to her in her bed. 'Would that be weird? I just don't want to be by myself tonight. Besides, you shouldn't have to sleep on the sofa on your last night… and you've got a big day of driving ahead of you. There's plenty of space for two…'

'Of course I will,' he said, ruffling her hair in the same way that he had done since they were young teenagers. They brushed their teeth before climbing into bed. It had probably been a good twenty years since they had last slept in the same bed.

'Night, night,' Libby said as she turned out her bedside light. She rested the side of her head against the pillow, her head spinning with dreams of their new life in Italy.

'Night Libs,' said Angus. She felt him move a bit closer to her. He pulled himself up and reached over to plant a kiss on her cheek. He was about to roll back over to his side of the bed when she took his hand and pulled him closer, so that the length of his body curled against her back like a big spoon. She placed his arm around her and rested her hand against his forearm. It felt so good to have him next to her; she could feel the weight of his muscular torso pressing into her back against the fabric of her pyjamas. She felt a swell of love for her oldest friend, his presence calmed and reassured her as she felt the rise and fall of his chest behind her. His steady, rhythmic breathing soothed her and, for the first time in weeks, she fell asleep with a deep sense of peace.

Chapter Thirty

It had been a long and exhausting few days. Izzy had done remarkably well coping with the journey. They made sure they had regular stops to take her out of her car seat and get some fresh air, enjoying the spectacular scenery as they made their way south. Angus had been a real trooper, doing the majority of the driving, keeping Libby entertained with chatter, and generally providing excellent company. She couldn't believe her luck that he was here by her side; that they were doing this together. She truly couldn't think of anyone in the world she would rather be there with as she took this extraordinary, life-changing step into the unknown. As they drove through the picturesque Italian countryside, Libby's heart soared.

'I can't believe we are actually here for good,' she said. 'This country is our home for the foreseeable future. Isn't it crazy?' she laughed.

'It is the craziest thing we've ever done,' Angus said. 'That's for sure.'

'It's so beautiful…' Libby sighed as she stared out through the window.

'Impossibly so,' Angus agreed. 'I can't wait to start my first series.'

'I can't wait to see what you do. We'll have to have your work all over L'Albero di Limoni.'

'Definitely… I might get some sales and commissions that way too.'

'Good idea,' Libby agreed.

'Do you feel weird having left England?' Angus asked her.

'A bit. It's so exhilarating, though, to have a change. I think it's all too easy to get stuck in a rut, in the same old existence. It feels pretty liberating to leave it all behind and have a fresh start, don't you think? Even though I know it's going to be incredibly hard work at the same time,' Libby added.

'I agree,' Angus smiled. 'I feel over the moon. Terrified, but so excited at the same time.'

When they eventually arrived in Tremento, they were greeted by Lizzy, who was staying for one more night to do a final handover and exchange before she flew back to the UK. She was leaving her car behind and flying back with just a couple of suitcases. All her other possessions had been shipped on ahead, except for any furniture and fittings that Libby and Angus had decided to keep as part of the sale. The house was full of boxes ready and waiting for them to unpack. They decided to wait until Lizzy had left before tackling them. They both realised how hard it must be for Lizzy to leave the place that was so utterly steeped in memories of Giuseppe.

Lizzy had cooked a delicious meal for them and they toasted the exchange with champagne, finding out all about her plans for the foreseeable future. She would be staying with John for a while to give her a chance to find her feet and decide where she might settle down. It was an emotional goodbye the following morning as they waved Lizzy off in her taxi.

'Poor thing,' Libby said. 'It must be utterly heartbreaking leaving this place.'

'So many memories.'

'Perhaps it'll be good for her.'

'I hope so.' They had offered her permanent visiting rights should she ever want to come back and stay, which she had gratefully accepted. Libby wondered whether she would take them up on their offer one day.

Izzy was toddling around the place happily within no time. She seemed to love exploring, and thought the packaging boxes were wonderful playhouses. Luca came over frequently to see Izzy, taking her back to Positano for his agreed days of shared custody. They had worked out a schedule that suited them both, heavily weighted in Libby's favour.

The first few weeks flew by as they unpacked, sorted and explored the local area, working out where the shops were, the supermarkets, the DIY stores. Libby sourced suppliers for local produce to ensure she could provide the freshest and best-quality ingredients for her breakfasts. She would serve pastries and bread from the bakery as well as homemade fruit tarts and traditional breakfast cake. The butcher would ensure a regular supply of cooked meats, milk, eggs and bacon, and she would get fresh fruit, jams, and honey from the farm shop several miles down the road.

They had inherited a charming older lady called Francesca from Lizzy. She had been at L'Albero di Limoni for years as a cleaner and housekeeper, and she had instantly taken a real shine to Izzy. It was great to have someone so reliable to help look after her. Francesca's daughter Simona had agreed to help with childcare when the guests started to arrive, especially during the busy mornings when both Francesca and Libby would be rushed off their feet. There were lots of meetings with local carpenters, decorators, electricians, and the architect in charge of converting the barn. The first priority was sorting out their living area, redecorating the parts of the house which would be their home, and so that was where they started. As each room was completed, they began to feel more settled, a little more at home.

It was Izzy's second birthday not long after they arrived. It was hard for Libby to believe how the time had gone by. They spent the day with Luca and his family in Positano, having a birthday lunch in a local restaurant. It was the first time that Libby had been back there since she and Luca had split up and, while it was lovely to see Mario and Chiara and the rest of the family, she had never been more grateful to have Angus by her side. She could tell that Nicola, Giovanna and Antonia were watching them carefully, trying to figure out whether or not they were together. She was more than happy to let them come to their own conclusions. As she watched Angus chatting to Luca's family, she could see how they would be impressed with her taste. He was deeply tanned and so tall in comparison with the Morellis. His charm was completely different to Luca's, much more rugged and less groomed; his masculinity was earthier and less manicured. At first it felt strange to be there with Luca's family, but by the end of the meal it had begun to feel more natural. Luckily enough time had passed, and enough had changed for Libby, both in terms of her circumstances but also her self-confidence and self-esteem, that she found she could handle the situation much better than she would have given herself credit for.

'Thank you so much for coming with me,' she said, as Angus drove them back to Tremento.

'It was my pleasure,' he replied. 'They seem like a really nice family, to their credit.'

'They are… It wasn't as bad as I thought it would be, seeing them.'

'I'm glad. They must think Luca is insane to have left you. I could tell.'

'I think they think *we* are a couple…' said Libby.

'Let them!' laughed Angus. 'It'll do them good!' An image of Angus kissing her flashed into her mind and she blushed to the roots of her hair. She turned to check on Izzy in her car seat, distracting herself from the inappropriate thoughts that were attempting to flood her imagination. Once again she was grateful that Angus couldn't see into her mind.

In June Helen's baby was born. Libby left Izzy with Angus and flew back to the UK to meet her nephew. As she pulled away from the drive in the taxi with her small suitcase by her side, Izzy wailed and wailed. Libby couldn't bear leaving her, but she was longing to meet her little nephew. She looked at Angus, standing by the front door holding her daughter, and she felt overcome with emotion. He looked so handsome in his decorating clothes, paint-spattered jeans and a crumpled T-shirt. She knew she was going to miss them both immensely, even if it was just for a couple of days.

Back in the UK, Henry opened the door to their little flat. 'Libby! Welcome! It's so good to see you…' He gave her a big hug and took the huge bouquet of flowers from her. 'Wow, this is the biggest bunch of flowers I've ever seen! You shouldn't have…'

'It's not every day you become an auntie,' laughed Libby. 'Where are they? I'm dying to meet little Archie.'

'They're in the bedroom,' replied Henry, leading her down the corridor.

As Libby entered the room, her eyes filled with tears at the sight of Helen, plumped up with pillows and cradling her tiny newborn baby in her arms. Miriam was sitting on the bed next to her, gazing besottedly at her newest grandchild.

'Oh my goodness Helen look at him – he's adorable!' Libby cried. 'Congratulations!'

'Libs, it's so good to see you,' Helen smiled. She looked exhausted but elated at the same time, clearly head over heels in love with her much longed-for little baby.

'Darling,' said Miriam, getting up to give her daughter a kiss. 'Isn't he perfect?' she said.

Libby kissed Helen and stroked Archie's impossibly soft cheek. 'He's tiny! I'd forgotten how small they are when they are born. Can I hold him?'

She picked up the tiny baby, as light as a feather, enjoying the feeling of him nuzzling into her shoulder as she caught up with Helen and Miriam. She found out all about the birth, and in turn told them all about their first month in Italy. They sat on the bed talking while Helen fed the baby, leaving her to doze when the baby slept, making themselves useful cooking and tidying up, doing loads of washing, and generally giving Henry and Helen a chance to rest. At night Libby stayed in the spare room while Miriam went back to John's house.

The weekend flew by and, though she missed Izzy and Angus terribly, it was wonderful to spend some time with her family. She was already missing not being able to see them so regularly.

'Please will you come and stay soon?' Libby asked as she said her goodbyes.

'We are planning on coming this August,' Miriam said. 'Is that OK?'

'We'd love that! I doubt the guestrooms will be finished till the end of August, but we've got a spare room in the main part of the house which will be ready by then. We decided to prioritise our living quarters in terms of building work to make sure Izzy felt settled as quickly as possible. What about you, Hels? Do you think you'll be able to come and stay with the baby?'

'Maybe when he's a little older?' she said. 'But definitely – try and stop us! I'm desperate to see it, it looks so beautiful.'

'You'll probably find it hard to get rid of us,' added Henry, smiling.

'Great… come and live nearby,' Libby clapped her hands.

'Oy… I can't have both my daughters abandoning me!' cried Miriam.

'Don't worry, Mum,' laughed Helen. 'Henry's job is based here so we won't be jumping ship any time soon.'

'He's going to be so big by the next time I see him.' Libby was reluctant to leave her nephew. 'Promise to FaceTime every day, and send me millions of photos please…'

As she got on the Tube back to Heathrow, she couldn't help but smile. She was so happy for her sister. It was amazing how well things had worked out for her. Helen had come such an unbelievably long way since those dark days after breaking up with Alan. It felt like a huge weight off her shoulders that both her mother and her sister were so happy, and so well looked after by their other halves. Once again she thought about Angus. The possibility of him leaving her popped into her mind, of him meeting someone else… She couldn't bear the thought. Her heart wrenched at the idea. She suddenly realised just how much she needed him. His smiling face, always so kind, so reliable, so even tempered, had become as familiar to her as her own daughter's. She couldn't imagine life at L'Albero di Limoni without him. She realised that she didn't ever want to know what that would be like.

Back in Italy, the months of June and July flew by. Work on the barn was going ahead at full tilt and the house was nearly finished. Work was due to start on the guestrooms and they had an estimated completion date set for the end of August. The bed and breakfast was officially opening at the start of September. They had agreed to wait until the builders had left to ensure their guests could have uninterrupted nights. It had also given them plenty of time to get settled with Izzy before work began to take over their lives. The first bookings were starting to roll in through the website, which Luca had helped Libby and Angus revamp. They had started to make some local friends, inviting the odd couple around for a drink or a barbecue. Luckily most of them spoke English, but if not Libby translated for Angus. His Italian was getting pretty good. He had studied Spanish at school, which helped – the languages were so similar – and he was having regular Italian lessons too.

It felt to Libby as though they were settling in to their new life remarkably well. Miriam and John came out to visit, as promised, in August, as did Angus's parents, his sister and her husband, along with their two children. It felt wonderful to be able to show the place off. They loved everyone's reactions as they took them to the best beaches, the best trattorias, the best gelaterias. They drove them around the countryside exploring, had picnics and barbecues, and sampled the local wines. It gave them great pleasure to see their families looking so relaxed and so happy, so in awe of the new life that they had created for themselves. It made them realise just how lucky they were.

Chapter Thirty-One

As the last vestiges of summer rolled by and autumn came creeping in, it dawned on Libby that perhaps she was feeling more for Angus than she should as a best friend. It had happened so slowly that she had barely noticed it at first, but the stronger her feelings became, the harder it was to ignore them. She had always loved him dearly, but now she found herself thinking about him in an entirely new light. She had always thought he was handsome, but now she was feeling attracted to him in a way she had never imagined possible. Ever since Jules had declared her interest in him all those years ago, Libby had forced the part of her brain that had considered him a prospect – the part of her that had kissed him – to shut down completely and, she had assumed, irreversibly. But something was happening now that was beyond her control. She was falling for him and there was nothing she could do about it.

Libby had started dreaming about Angus kissing her; the same dream recurred over and over again. They were in the cottage that they had rented in Devon, standing on the patio. He had his arms wrapped around her and was pulling her close, kissing her. Sometimes her dreams would go further; they would be lying in bed together, making love. She would suddenly wake up in a fluster, her heart pounding, shocked at herself but unable to get the images out of her mind. She was absolutely sure that Angus would be horrified if he could see inside her head. He thought of her as a best friend but nothing more. She was determined that he would never find out her secret. She couldn't risk spoiling their friendship; it was the most important relationship she had. She felt like a teenager once more, pining for him; her heart longed for him to be hers and hers alone. She felt confused and agitated by the strength of her feelings towards him. Ever since she had allowed herself to admit how she felt, they seemed to have blossomed and grown, making her act awkwardly around him in a way she hadn't in years.

Luckily, she had plenty of other distractions to keep her mind occupied during daylight hours: business was booming at the bed and breakfast as word spread that L'Albero di Limoni had reopened. Libby was thrilled with how the rooms had turned out. Each one had its own theme, inspired by the five-star hotel she had stayed at with Luca. She had kept some of the brickwork exposed and had chosen beautiful floral fabrics for the curtains and bedspreads. She filled the rooms with fresh flowers from the garden each day, took care of the laundry, which they were doing themselves for the time being to save money, and made sure each room was sparkling clean and spotless. Angus and his DIY skills were put to good use whenever something broke down or needed a quick repair. The local suppliers delivered fresh produce each day for the breakfasts and Libby had invested in a top-of-the-range coffee machine just like the one at La Casetta. Each time a guest departed, she asked them to write a review on TripAdvisor. She thought she might burst with pride as more and more four- and five-star ratings appeared on her page throughout the months of September and October. She was immensely proud of her achievements, as was Angus. Every time he told her just how proud he was, she felt as though her heart might burst with love for him.

It was becoming clear that she was going to have to do something about it soon, to say something to him about how she felt. She had no idea how he would react, but it was becoming harder and harder for her to hide her feelings. Every time she saw him she wanted to kiss him, to hold him close and never let him go. Every time he brushed past her or ruffled her hair she would have a physical reaction to the contact that took her breath away. It was becoming impossible to bear.

Angus's studio was nearly complete, and he had already built up a huge bank of sketches and photographs in preparation for getting started on his first Italian-inspired series of canvases. She found his passion and talent so attractive, adding to her feelings for him all the more.

Before she knew it, November had rolled around the corner, and, along with it, Angus's birthday. 'So what do you want to do for your big day?' asked Libby.

'I was hoping we could go out for dinner, maybe?' Angus suggested, looking up from the article he was reading.

'Just the two of us?'

'Yes. Unless ... you want to bring someone?' he asked, looking somewhat worried at the prospect. God knows who he thought she would want to invite!

'No, no! Of course not!' Libby laughed. The look in his eyes had ignited a flicker of hope deep inside her, but she was quick to extinguish it, not wishing to give her vivid imagination an ounce of encouragement.

'Great,' Angus smiled.

'Let me choose where,' Libby said. 'It'll be more of a birthday treat if it's a surprise. I'll see if Francesca can babysit.'

'OK. That would be lovely,' Angus said.

Libby spent a lot of time choosing where to take him. For some reason it seemed a big deal to her that she got it right. She almost felt as if she was planning a date, but she was incredibly out of practice at doing that. She looked through the list of recommended local restaurants that she had been collecting so as to be able to advise her guests. Lizzy had told her about a place that she was particularly keen to try. She had described it as an indoor garden, full of plants, candles and fairy lights. She thought it sounded right up their street.

On the evening of Angus's birthday, Libby changed into a new teal dress that complemented her green eyes perfectly. She had teamed it with gold jewellery and some flat pumps, not wishing to look as if she'd made too much effort. They had booked a taxi so they could enjoy a few drinks, leaving Izzy tucked up in bed under the watchful eye of Francesca. When they arrived they went straight into the restaurant to find their seats. It was perfect. Candles glowed softly from the centre of each table; the ceiling was covered with fairy lights that twinkled amid a canopy of ivy. Libby looked up from her menu and her heart flipped as she saw Angus looking at her, his face creased into the smile she loved more than any other.

The waiter poured them a glass of prosecco each. 'Happy birthday!' she said as she chinked her glass against his. She gave him his present, a book of beautiful prints by a local artist that Angus had been admiring of late.

'Thank you,' he said, leaning across the table to kiss her. She could smell the trace of a new aftershave lingering against his skin. It was slightly spicy. The combination of the scent of his aftershave and being in such close proximity to him had catapulted her heart around her ribcage like a trapped bird making a bid for freedom.

'Thanks, Libs. What a place! It's like the secret garden – I love it!' he said. His eyes shone brightly as he took in his surroundings.

'I hope you like the food too. There are only a few things on the menu.'

They placed their orders: pasta to start and a local speciality beef dish for their main course. They chose a bottle of red wine to go with their meal.

After their starters had been cleared away, their beef arrived on a huge carving board. Angus sliced it up and shared it between their plates. They had a selection of sauces to accompany the meat, which was tender and pink and perfectly cooked.

'This is absolutely delicious,' Angus said as he devoured his plateful of food.

'A good recommendation from Lizzy,' Libby agreed. They ordered a mixed plate of desserts to share for pudding, including panna cotta and chocolate fondant, along with another bottle of wine, this time a sweet pudding wine. Libby was beginning to feel a little tipsy. When they had finished their pudding, she leaned slightly closer to Angus across the table. Emboldened by the wine, she decided to ask the question that had been lingering on her mind all evening. She knew that Angus had signed his divorce papers that week. The whole process had taken a long time to complete since that initial conversation with Jules. Libby and Angus hadn't really talked about it, and Libby was dying to find out how he felt about the whole thing.

'How was it… signing the papers? Does it feel weird knowing that it's finally over?' She hesitated as soon as she asked, not sure whether it had been a good idea to bring up the topic of Jules and Angus's failed marriage. She was worried that it might spoil their lovely meal. Angus paused and rolled the wine around the balloon of his glass, watching the amber liquid rise and fall as he did so.

'Do you know what, Libs, it made me think about everything that happened last year. I sort of tested myself to see how I feel and … I think I've finally made peace with it all.'

'Really?' Libby asked.

'Yes, I think so. It's so strange. If Jules hadn't left me, I doubt that I would have had the courage to do anything about it. I like to say it's because I wouldn't want to have broken my wedding vows, but I think it also comes down to a fear of the unknown. I wasn't really happy and I hadn't been for some time. I knew it, but I was unwilling to admit it fully to myself because then I would have been forced to do something about it. And that would have caused so much upset, to Jules, or so I naïvely thought, that I'm not sure I would have had the courage.'

'I can see that,' Libby said.

'It feels good to have drawn a line under it all, to be legally unbound by the vows that I made all those years ago. What about you? How do you feel about the whole thing? Do you ever miss Luca still, in that way?' He gazed at her intently and she wondered whether she should say something, whether she should tell him how she was really feeling.

'I did miss him, an awful lot, to begin with. But I wonder whether I missed him for himself or as a second pair of hands, a companion…someone to share my life with. The fact that he is Izzy's father made us seem like such an obvious, foregone conclusion. For us to be together and make it work would make Izzy so happy, in such a secure family unit, that we knew we had to do everything we could to give our relationship a chance. But it just wasn't enough for him. I think in hindsight I could tell that he wasn't happy, but I was so focused on Izzy and work that I didn't really stop to pay much attention.'

'I feel a bit like that about Jules,' Angus said.

'I keep coming back to what would have happened if I hadn't got pregnant.'

'What do you think would have happened?'

'I think it's more than likely that I would have come back to England as planned; that we would have had every intention of making it work, but it would have fizzled out as a long-distance relationship. Without the promise, or threat, of impending fatherhood, I'm sure Luca would never have moved away from Positano. He loves it so much. So I think maybe we were never quite meant to be.'

'When you think about him now, how does it make you feel?'

'I think I've accepted it. And actually there are so many positives. Without everything that happened, we wouldn't be here now. We wouldn't have L'Albero di Limoni. I wouldn't have Izzy…'

'Would you say you have moved on?'

'I would,' she said firmly. 'Do you think you have?' Her heart was drumming loudly in her ears and she realised she was holding her breath. The atmosphere between them seemed to have shifted up a gear. She forgot about everyone else in the restaurant; all she could see was Angus sitting in front of her, smiling at her with such fondness that a hope she hardly dared imagine swelled irrepressibly within her.

He didn't say anything. He looked as though he wanted to, but it was as if he didn't know how to find the words. He took her hand and squeezed it, stroking the side of her hand with his thumb. Taking a deep breath he said, 'Libby I feel there's something I should tell you…'

She felt riddled with tension; she didn't know what to say, so she just smiled at him and waited, hardly daring to breathe. Could he be feeling the same way?

Angus took a deep breath in. 'I've been offered the chance to host a solo exhibition in New York…' he said.

Libby felt the air force out of her lungs in a sharp exhalation. She felt sick to the bottom of her stomach. 'New York?' she repeated, dumbstruck, her voice strangely high-pitched. It was the last thing she had been expecting. She felt her eyes well with tears. She dug her nails into the palm of her left hand to stop herself from crying. 'Wow! That's amazing…' she forced herself to smile despite the wave of despair that was coursing through her.

Angus looked at her, his eyes searching, clearly desperate to see how she would react. She was determined not to let him see her vulnerability. She had completely failed in her resolve not to become dependent on him. She would not let him see how desperately she needed him, how desperately she loved him.

'My agent rang me last week. I didn't want to say anything until I had thought it through properly.'

'I assume this means you will be going to America?' Libby asked, hoping beyond hope that he would say no, that he would tell her he couldn't leave her and Izzy.

'It would be dependent on me doing a series of landscapes based in the US. I can choose anywhere I like. And yes, I would have to relocate there for a while. I think it might be good for me… a new beginning…'

Libby felt her bottom lip wobble. 'But haven't you had a new start, a new beginning here?' she asked. 'We've just got your studio ready, you were about to start painting again…'

'I know. And if you will allow me to I hope that I can keep that, as soon as this is over I will come back and pick up where I left off. This is a once in a lifetime opportunity, it's now or never. As much as I have loved setting up L'Albero di Limoni with you, I think you will be okay now without me. At least for a while…'

'How long will you be going?' she asked.

'Probably six months or so?'

Libby nodded. She felt utterly sick at the thought. He might meet someone new in that time. He might settle in New York and that would be it. He would still be a partner to her but only on paper. She would never see him, Izzy would never see him. Her heart felt like it was breaking into a thousand pieces.

'I'm really happy for you,' she said, squeezing his hand and then withdrawing her own from his grasp. 'It's an incredible opportunity, I can see why you want to take it.'

Angus was still looking at her with intense concentration. He was trying to read her and she diverted her eyes so that he could not. She raised her hand and flagged down the waiter, asking for the bill.

'It's my treat,' she said, batting away his hand as he reached for his credit card. 'It's your birthday dinner.' She was suddenly desperate to leave.

She paid the bill and they continued to talk through his plans. His words fell on deaf ears. Her head was spinning and she felt as though she had gone onto autopilot as they called a taxi and made their way home, relieving Francesca of her babysitting duties. Desperate for an escape to retreat to her own room before her tears spilt over she told Angus that she had a headache. He kissed her goodnight. She could barely stand it. She closed the bedroom door behind her and let silent tears spill down her cheeks. She held her breath in an attempt not to let him hear her ragged breathing, should he be listening outside the door.

Chapter Thirty-Two

The next day Libby tried her best to put on a brave face, going about her daily routine as if nothing had happened. The news of Angus's imminent departure at the end of the month hung over her like a black cloud. Every time she thought of him leaving she felt sheer panic. She had already lost Luca, she couldn't bear the thought of losing him too. She tried to tell herself it was only temporary, that he would be back before she knew it, but she knew just how unlikely that was. A single, attractive, successful man in New York would be snapped up by anyone in their right mind. She had been mad to think he had feelings for her beyond friendship. It was just as she had suspected all along. He loved her in a platonic way, just as she had done. It was only her feelings that had utterly spiralled out of control. It would be better if he never found out. To think how close she had come to telling him…

As they ate their dinner that evening, Angus said 'Are you okay, Libs? You've been quite quiet today. I just want to check everything is alright. If you don't want me to leave, please tell me… I realise it might feel too much for you to cope with being here by yourself with Izzy. I'm sure I can ask for a delay. I don't want to leave you if you aren't ready…'

'No, it's fine. I'll be fine…I don't want you to feel trapped here, trapped by our business. You were only every meant to be here temporarily, I knew that all along.'

Suddenly, without warning she burst into tears. Noisy, gasping sobs escaped her and there was nothing she could do to stop them. She put her head in her hands, trying to calm her breathing down. This was awful. How could she explain her reaction to Angus without giving her feelings away?

'Libby!' Angus was out of his chair in seconds. He darted across to her and wrapped her in his arms. 'Don't cry! What's the matter?'

She pulled away and looked into his eyes. They were so full of love that for a moment she was thrown. She didn't know how she could explain herself.

'I'm sorry. It's silly really. I'm embarrassed… I'm fine, truly.'

He kept looking at her, those blue eyes searching hers. 'Really?' he said.

She nodded weakly.

There was a long pause. Angus looked as though he was about to say something. She held his gaze and smiled through her tears.

'Look, Libby. The truth is, there is someone I have fallen for since Jules…' he said.

Her heart skipped several beats. She felt an icy shiver run slowly down her spine. Her eyes filled involuntarily with tears once again.

He looked really nervous. He took a steadying breath as if to calm himself. 'Libby, there's a reason why I think I should leave… I don't really know how to say this. Things have become rather complicated….'

She held her breath.

'Libby, the thing is… I think I have fallen in love with you…I know you don't feel the same way. When the offer came for a fresh start in New York I thought it would be the perfect way to get me away from you, to give me a chance to stop loving you. Being in such close proximity to you every single day is driving me mad…I am so sorry. You must think I'm crazy…I promised myself I wouldn't say anything. The last thing I want is to make you feel awkward, to ruin our friendship, I just feel I should explain why I need to go…'

Her stomach lurched as though she had just taken a step off the edge of a cliff. She couldn't believe her ears. 'Angus, I…' The words caught in her throat and she couldn't speak. Tears rolled down her cheeks as she took in what he had just told her. He was looking so worried. Her heart melted. She hardly dared believe it could be true. She felt so full of love for him, it was as if her heart was overflowing; she had never experienced anything like it.

'I love you too,' she whispered, smiling through her tears. 'I have fallen completely in love with you too. Please, don't go… I can't bear the thought of you being apart from me for even one day, let alone six months…' In a flash, Angus's expression changed from anxious worry to relief and then unbounded joy.

'I can't believe it,' he said, his breath coming out in a rush. 'I vowed to myself I wouldn't say anything. I thought you were going to think I was completely insane, that I was going to ruin our working relationship, our friendship, and that would have just destroyed me. I thought the best thing to do was put thousands of miles between us, but when I saw you crying, your reaction to my leaving gave me a shred of hope I hardly dared to believe. I just couldn't keep it to myself any longer.'

He leaned across and kissed her gently on the lips, holding both of her hands in his. At the brush of his lips a thousand electric impulses exploded inside her. She thought her heart might combust with love. She was crying with happiness and laughing at the same time. He gently wiped the tears from her cheeks with his thumbs.

'Don't go,' she whispered.

'If you want me to stay, I will,' he said.

'I want you to stay. Of course I do,' she said. 'We've been through so much together, building our business, moving to Italy… It's just been the most incredible adventure and you have made it the happiest year of my life. I can't lose you…'

'You don't have to,' he said. The way he was looking at her made her insides melt.

Angus pulled her to her feet. He moved her towards him, dwarfing her completely as he bent down to kiss her. He pushed his hips against hers as her back pressed up against the wall. His kiss was just as she had imagined all those times in her dreams. She could have kissed him for an eternity. She was bewitched by the sensations he was causing inside her. She wrapped her arms around him, moving closer to him, losing herself in the moment completely.

'God, I've wanted to do that for so long,' Angus said, smiling at her as he pulled away, leaning closer to kiss her once more on the lips. Her spine tingled with desire and her head spun. She felt desperate for him to continue. Her lips parted as she looked at him, unable to move or speak. They fell upon each other hungrily, kissing and exploring every part of each other's bodies, their clothes disappearing in a trail of discarded items up the stairs and towards Libby's bedroom door. They fell on the bed and lost themselves in each other, moving together as one, completely uninhibited, abandoning themselves in the moment. Libby had never known anything quite like it. The feelings she felt for him were so strong they overwhelmed her completely.

Later, as she lay in his arms, she felt as though she had finally found where she belonged. She couldn't believe she hadn't realised what was there, right in front of her, for all those years.

Having finally confessed their feelings, Libby and Angus's love for each other deepened quickly and passionately. He turned down the offer of an exhibition in New York. Now that they had found each other there was no way either of them were willing to let the other go. Like a young couple in their very first romance they kissed for hours and hours, unable to pass each other by without some kind of physical contact. Their appetite for each other knew no bounds; they delighted in exploring each other's bodies, spending endless hours making love. The strength of their feelings for each other had taken them both by surprise. Like a phoenix rising from the ashes of their failed relationships, they had found in each other a love that was stronger than anything they had experienced before. Over the past year Angus had become such a permanent fixture in Libby and Izzy's lives that making the transition from friend to lover had been a natural and fluid development, as unstoppable as it would have seemed unthinkable just a year before.

Libby had never known such happiness. She floated around on cloud nine, a soppy grin rarely far from her cheeks. There was something incredible about being in a relationship with your best friend. They already knew each other inside out and back to front. There were no surprises. It just felt so natural and so perfectly right.

Epilogue

A cockerel welcomed the rising sun with its cheerful call as Libby threw open the shutters to reveal yet another glorious day. She leant out the window and inhaled the sweet fragrant smell of the honeysuckle plant that curled its way around the windowsill. The hills and fields below were bathed in the golden glow of the sun. In the distance the sea lay calm and majestic, the clouds above tinged with pink. Libby's heart soared like it did every morning as she drank in her surroundings. It had been nearly a year and a half since Angus and Libby had left London and she couldn't be happier in her new life, her new home.

She looked at Angus, sprawled across the bed, and her heart swelled with love. He had surpassed her every expectation. He was the perfect friend, the most incredible lover, as well as the best father-figure to Izzy she could have hoped for. He had been her rock as they had adjusted to their new life in Italy. He had thrown himself into the adventure with verve, learning the language, networking and making friends with the locals, building his studio, helping her with the guests, and generally making every day enjoyable. He was relaxed when he saw Luca, never showing any signs of jealousy or anger, despite the upheaval, pain and suffering Luca had caused him. He was always the perfect gentleman, and Libby loved him ever more for it.

She left him sleeping peacefully in bed, and crept along the corridor to Izzy's room. She was still fast asleep, for once. Libby took advantage of the peace and quiet and went downstairs to make herself a cup of tea. She took her steaming mug outside, a canopy of fuchsia bougainvillea hung high above the patio with its large wooden table and chairs. The garden, full of flowerbeds bursting with colour, was her favourite place. Once the guests had left for their day excursions or their onward journeys, she spent hours out here with Izzy, playing and weeding.

She walked down to the bottom of the garden before turning back to wind her way through the vegetable patches and fruit cages that she and Angus had built. As she approached the house the kitchen door opened and Angus appeared. He waved and smiled at her, saying, 'Morning!' Izzy was wearing her pink pyjamas. She rubbed her eyes sleepily next to him, her tiny hand in his. Libby felt a pang of love as she looked at them both. At the same time a tiny kick pulsed deep within her swollen belly. It was as though the baby was reminding her of his presence too, not wishing to be forgotten. She rested her hand on her growing bump and smiled. 'Breakfast time!' she called as she walked back up the garden path to join them.

We hope you enjoyed this book!

Georgie Capron's next book is coming in summer 2018

More addictive fiction from Aria:

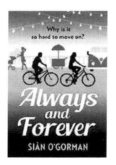

Find out more

http://headofzeus.com/books/isbn/9781784978259
http://headofzeus.com/books/isbn/9781784979577
http://headofzeus.com/books/isbn/9781786694881

Acknowledgements

This book was inspired by my lifelong love of Italy. Having studied History of Art and Italian for my degree I was lucky enough to spend four years immersed in Italian culture, including a year living in Bologna. I have travelled all over this beautiful country and adored every part of it, but my favourite place has to be Positano on the Amalfi coast. Thank you to all my lovely readers for supporting me thus far, I hope you have enjoyed visiting Italy with me.

I would like to thank my sisters, Sophie and Emma, and my mother Polly for their invaluable help shaping and editing this story as it developed. I would also like to thank my friend, Emma, for her help in answering numerous questions as I wrote the first draft, and the rest of my family for their support and guidance.

As always I would like to thank my editor, Sarah Ritherdon, for her expertise during the editing process, as well as my copy editor Penelope Isaac and the rest of the team at Head of Zeus: Nia Beynon, Yasemin Turan and Geo Willis. I would also like to thank my agent Beatrice Corlett for her help during the initial stages of writing this novel.

Finally my deepest thanks goes to my husband Tom. He has the patience of a saint and is unwavering in his support for all of my ventures. And to my daughter, Camilla, you have come into our lives and transformed them totally, for the better in every single way. We cannot imagine life without you. Thank you for arriving two weeks late enabling me to finish editing before being immersed in a world of sleepless nights and nappies!

About Georgie Capron

GEORGIE CAPRON lives in South West London with her husband. She works as a primary school teacher, and writes during the holidays. She studied Italian and History of Art at the University of Edinburgh, and loves travelling, yoga and all sorts of arts and crafts.

Find me on Twitter
https://twitter.com/GeorgieCapron

Find me on Facebook
http://www.facebook.com/GeorgieCapron

Visit my website
https://georgiecapron.com/

A Letter from the Author

Dear all my lovely readers,

First of all, thank you for reading my book. It is just amazing to be able to share the imaginary world I have created with you and to know that you are following my characters on their journeys...wherever they may lead! You are invaluable and there is nothing more exciting than hearing from you as you spread the word and leave those much-appreciated reviews online. If you can spare the time then please do so, it really is the number one best way to help a writer out!

Please follow me on social media. You can find daily updates from me on Twitter, Facebook and my website. Just click the buttons below.

I love hearing from readers so please message me on Twitter, Facebook or via the contact page on my website.

With love and thanks,

Georgie xx

Find me on Twitter
https://twitter.com/GeorgieCapron

Find me on Facebook
http://www.facebook.com/GeorgieCapron

Visit my website
https://georgiecapron.com/

Also by Georgie Capron

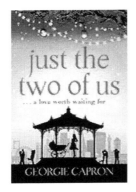 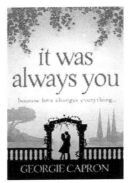

Find out more

http://headofzeus.com/books/isbn/9781786693341
http://headofzeus.com/books/isbn/9781786693358

Visit Aria now
http://www.ariafiction.com/

Become an Aria Addict

Aria is the new digital-first fiction imprint from Head of Zeus.

It's Aria's ambition to discover and publish tomorrow's superstars, targeting fiction addicts and readers keen to discover new and exciting authors.

Aria will publish a variety of genres under the commercial fiction umbrella such as women's fiction, crime, thrillers, historical fiction, saga and erotica.

So, whether you're a budding writer looking for a publisher or an avid reader looking for something to escape with – Aria will have something for you.

Get in touch: aria@headofzeus.com

Become an Aria Addict
http://www.ariafiction.com/

Sign up to our newsletter
http://ariafiction.com/newsletter/subscribe

Find us on Twitter
https://twitter.com/Aria_Fiction

Find us on Facebook
http://www.facebook.com/ariafiction

Find us on BookGrail

http://www.bookgrail.com/store/aria/

Addictive Fiction

First published in the UK in 2017 by Aria, an imprint of Head of Zeus Ltd

9 7 5 3 1 2 4 6 8

A CIP catalogue record for this book is available from the British Library.

ISBN (E) 9781786693358

Aria
c/o Head of Zeus
First Floor East
5–8 Hardwick Street
London EC1R 4RG

www.ariafiction.com

Printed in Great Britain
by Amazon